Almost Forever

**Center Point
Large Print**

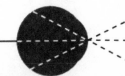

This Large Print Book carries the
Seal of Approval of N.A.V.H.

Almost Forever

a hanover falls novel

Deborah Raney

CENTER POINT PUBLISHING
THORNDIKE, MAINE

This Center Point Large Print edition
is published in the year 2010 by arrangement with
Howard Books, a division of Simon & Schuster, Inc.

The text of this Large Print edition is unabridged.
In other aspects, this book may vary
from the original edition.
Printed in the United States of America
on permanent paper.
Set in 16-point Times New Roman type.

ISBN: 978-1-60285-839-8

Library of Congress Cataloging-in-Publication Data

Raney, Deborah.
   Almost forever : a Hanover Falls novel / Deborah Raney.
      p. cm.
   ISBN 978-1-60285-839-8 (library bindng : alk. paper)
   1. Married people—Fiction. 2. Domestic fiction. 3. Large type books. I. Title.
   PS3568.A562A79 2010b
   813′.54—dc22
                                                      2010012848

To my "Club Deb" friends:

Debbie, Deb, Debbie
Elaine
Bev

When I count my blessings,
you guys are high on the list!

Acknowledgments

Many, many thanks to the following people for their part in bringing this story to life:

For help with research, ideas, proofreading, and "author support," I am deeply grateful to Rick Acker, Kenny and Courtney Ast, Ron Benrey, Tim Larson, Ryan and Tobi Layton, Mark Mynheir, Cara Putman, Terry Stucky, Max and Winifred Teeter, Courtney Walsh, the writers of ACFW, and especially the Kansas 8, who gave wings to my idea.

So many of you prayed for me as I wrote this book. You'll never know how much that means to me. And special thanks to Kim Peterson for praying me home—in writing—on the final week of finishing this book. What a blessing that was!

To my critique partner and dear friend, Tamera Alexander, thank you for everything you add to my life. You are truly a gem.

Thanks to the selfless directors and volunteers who keep homeless shelters all across our nation up and running, providing a much-needed service—and often a first introduction to Jesus—to those going through trying times.

To my agent, Steve Laube: you're the best! Deep appreciation to my wonderful editor, Dave Lambert, at Howard/Simon & Schuster, and to Ramona Cramer Tucker, who is always a delight to work with.

To our precious children and grandchildren, and the amazing extended family God has given us: you all are the joy of my life.

To my husband, Ken: it's been a rough year, but I can't think of anyone on earth I'd rather tough it out with than you, babe. May our next thirty-five years together be as blessed as the first thirty-five.

"Fear not, for I have redeemed you;
I have summoned you by name; you are mine.
When you pass through the waters,
I will be with you;
and when you pass through the rivers,
they will not sweep over you.
When you walk through the fire,
you will not be burned;
the flames will not set you ablaze.
For I am the LORD, your God,
the Holy One of Israel, your Savior."

ISAIAH 43:1–3

1

$\mathcal{B}$ryn drew the queen of diamonds from the stack of playing cards on the wobbly table between her and Charlie Branson. The grizzled Vietnam vet eyed her from his wheelchair as she discarded an ace. She put on her best poker face and pretended to rearrange her hand. From somewhere behind the peeling paint on the west wall, the pipes clanked in the bowels of the old hospital-turned-homeless-shelter, and the furnace kicked on. Not that it would raise the temperature in this mammoth icebox by one degree, but something about the hiss of radiators was comforting.

Charlie drew a card from the tattered deck and flung it away too quickly. He must be close to going out. Good. It was two in the morning, and Bryn was hoping to catch a few hours of sleep before it was time to get breakfast going for the shelter's residents.

Her husband's twenty-four-hour shift at the fire station ended tomorrow. Adam had said something about taking her to a matinee, and he'd be suspicious if she fell asleep during the movie. Of course, his invitation had come before their big fight. Knowing him, he'd still be brooding

11

and they would stay home and sulk—or argue.

Bryn shifted in the chair and rubbed the small of her back. She'd foregone sleep to stay up and play cards with Charlie in an effort to settle him down. He and the new guy had gotten into it again, and Charlie had been too worked up to sleep. He'd balked at her suggestion to read, but she knew the real truth—he was lonely. Just needed someone to sit with him.

Bryn had met Charlie at the library where she worked part-time. He was the most well-read man she knew, a fact that endeared him to Myrna Eckland, the library director at Hanover Falls' public library. Myrna had given Charlie a few odd jobs in exchange for the right to spend his days reading in a quiet corner of the stacks before wheeling to the shelter each evening—after securing his word that he wouldn't miss his daily shower, of course.

Bryn slid the jack of diamonds from the draw pile and discarded it, but something made her stop and listen. Somewhere above them she heard an out-of-the-ordinary noise. She looked at Charlie. "Did you hear that? Shhh . . ."

He put his free hand to his ear but shook his head. "I don't hear anything, sis, but that don't mean nothin'. My ears are no good." He craned his neck toward the hallway, listening again. "It's not the dogs, is it?"

Zeke Downing, a new client at the shelter, had

brought a bulldog pup named Boss with him when he checked in two weeks ago. The pup had nipped at Charlie's dog, Sparky, the first day Zeke was here, and Charlie had gone ballistic.

Sparky was a stray that Susan Marlowe, the shelter's director, let the old vet claim. Susan made Charlie keep the dog chained outside and buy its food out of his VA disability pension. But Charlie loved the mutt, a Labrador mix. Any friend of Sparky's was a friend of Charlie's, and any enemy of Sparky better watch out.

More than once, Zeke and Charlie had almost come to blows over the dogs. Bryn thought Sparky could take Boss without much effort, but Zeke was able-bodied and twice the size of Charlie. It would not be a pretty picture if the two men ever actually duked it out.

Charlie's eyes narrowed. "So help me, if that SOB let that mutt loose again . . ."

"Charlie . . ." She shook her head and feigned a stern look. "You'd better not let Susan hear you use that kind of language."

"What? *Mutt*'s not a bad word."

"You know what I mean." His smirk made it hard not to laugh. Bryn was mostly teasing, but Susan did have a zero-tolerance policy when it came to cursing.

"I didn't actually say anything."

"Yeah, but you know Susan . . . even initials are pushing it with her."

He rolled his eyes and fanned out his cards.

"I don't think Zeke's even here tonight." She held up a hand, listening for the sound again. "Besides, it doesn't sound like dogs. Maybe it's just a siren, but it sounds different . . . more like a squeal. You don't have a battery going out in your hearing aid, do you?"

Charlie laid down his cards, put his thick pinky finger to his ear, and twisted. "That better?"

She shook her head. "I still hear it."

"This old building has so many creaks and groans I'm surprised anybody can sleep here. That's the only good thing about these blame things"—he adjusted the other hearing aid—"I can just turn 'em off."

The noise didn't sound quite like distant sirens, but nevertheless, she shot up a quick prayer for her husband the way she always did when she knew he might be out on a run. Guilt pinched her. Adam wasn't even supposed to be on duty tonight. He was only there because she'd talked him into pulling an extra shift. Ironic, given all the grief she'd thrown at him about the long hours he worked.

With Adam being low man on the totem pole, he always had to work holidays, and too many weekends. Sometimes Bryn wondered why they'd even bothered to get married if they were never going to be together. She thought she would go crazy if she had to spend one more long night alone in their little cracker box of a townhome. That was the whole reason she'd started volunteering here, taken the night shift. And how much worse would it be when they had kids?

The faint noise droned on. She looked at the stained ceiling. "It almost sounds like it's coming from upstairs."

Charlie shook his head and a glint of mischief came to his eyes. "Listen, girlie, if you're just trying to weasel your way out of this game, you can forget it." He drew another card and wriggled bushy eyebrows at her. "I'm about to clean your clock."

They took turns drawing and discarding cards in silence, but Bryn kept one ear tuned to the sound. Charlie was right: the noises in this old building had scared her to death the first time she'd worked the late shift. It was probably just the pipes creaking again, but it sounded different somehow tonight.

Susan was in the dining room, sleeping. She'd told Bryn she would take the middle-of-the-night rounds, but Bryn decided she'd do a walkthrough as soon as they finished this hand, just to be sure nothing was amiss.

She'd almost forgotten about the noise when a dog started howling outside the building. Charlie's head shot up. "Now, *that* I heard. That's Sparky." Pressing his forearms to the wheelchair's armrests and lifting his rear off the seat, he repositioned himself. He picked up his cards, fanned them out in gnarled fingers, then laid them facedown on the cluttered table before maneuvering his chair backward. "I need to go check on him."

Bryn gave a little growl and jumped up. "Charlie Branson, if I didn't know better, I'd think you put Sparky up to this. I am *one* card away from gin!"

He gave a snort. "Don't you worry, sis. I'll be right back."

"Stay here. I'll go see what's up." She scooted around Charlie's chair and went to peek down the hallway. Nothing appeared out of the ordinary, but she jogged to the end of the hall, fumbling with the key on the lanyard around her neck as she ran. The doors to the shelter—housed in the building's basement—were locked at eleven each night unless the smokers could talk the volunteers into letting them have one last cigarette before they turned in.

Bryn punched in the code to disable the alarm, unlocked the door, and hurried up the short flight of stairs that led to the street-level parking behind the building. The November air hit her face, and her breath hung in a fog.

Sparky was tied in his usual spot. He yanked at his chain, alternately yipping and howling. Sparky looked like a black Labrador in color and build, but Charlie was proud of the dog's lack of a pedigree. "He's a mutt like me . . . Heinz 57," Charlie told anyone who asked.

Bryn knelt and framed the silky black head in her hands. His ears were on alert and his hackles stood stiff. "Hey, boy," she crooned. "What's wrong? Is that mean doggie giving you trouble again? Huh? Is he?"

But Zeke wasn't on tonight's sign-in list, and Boss wasn't tied up out here.

Bryn looked around to see if something else was causing Sparky's excitement—maybe another animal—but the parking lot was empty except for her car and Susan's, and the dilapidated old station wagon Tony Xavier lived in during the daylight hours when the shelter was closed.

She shushed Sparky again and stroked his head as he pushed his muzzle into the cup of her hands. But the minute she turned toward the door, he started in yapping again.

She went back and took him by the collar, unclipping the chain. "What's wrong, fella? You want to go for a little walk?" She scratched his head and panned the parking lot.

Dim light from the lone streetlight at the end of the lot caused the building to cast deep shadows. "You're okay, boy. Let's walk a little bit."

Sparky stood at her side, on alert, his breaths coming short, like he was on the trail of a rabbit.

She tightened her grip on his collar and clicked

17

her tongue like she'd heard Charlie do before he wheeled his chair around the bumpy parking lot, Sparky in tow. She started away from the building, not liking how dark it was out here, and already hearing Adam's lecture if he found out she was here by herself at two in the morning—if he found out she was here at all. Sparky angled back toward the building.

"What's wrong, boy? I thought you wanted to go for a walk."

He kept tugging, so Bryn let him lead her back to the building. Making an odd whimpering noise, he angled toward the door.

"Uh-uh, boy. Sorry. You know you're not allowed. Come on, now. You go to sleep. Charlie'll be out in the morning."

She leaned down to reattach his chain, but at the sudden *bleep! bleep! bleep!* of an alarm blasting, Sparky shook loose of her and took off around the side of the building. Stupid dog.

But what was going on? She was certain she'd disabled the alarm before she came out.

Leaving the dog, she ran back into the building. "Where's Susan?" she shouted. Surely all the racket had awakened the director.

"Haven't seen her. What's going on?" Charlie wheeled toward her, confusion clouding his face.

"I don't know. Could it be a fire drill? Do you have those here?" She'd only been volunteering at the shelter for three months, but they'd never had a fire drill while she was on call. Charlie would know, though. He was a fixture here.

He waggled his chin at her. "Drills, yes, but never known 'em to do one at two o'clock in the morning."

According to Susan, Charlie was the first person they'd taken in when the shelter opened two years ago, and he'd been here ever since, in spite of a policy that discouraged long-term residency.

Charlie made a three-point turn with his chair. "Sparky's okay?"

"He's fine, but I took him off his chain, and he got away from me." She had to shout over the blare of the fire alarms. She didn't even know where the alarms were . . . where to shut them off. She fought to remember what she'd learned at the training sessions about the procedure in case of fire—and came up blank.

She cast around the hallway, trying to think what to do next. Sixteen clients had signed in tonight, not counting the guys who worked night shift but had called to reserve beds for the night. Why wasn't anybody awake? This shrieking was enough to wake the dead. But the hallway was empty except for her and Charlie.

She hurried toward the dining room to find Susan. Even if it turned out to be a false alarm, the director would no doubt call the fire in. Susan's husband was a lieutenant at Station 2—

Adam's boss. If they called it in, Adam would make the run, and he didn't know Bryn was here.

If he found out . . . She blew out a breath and with it pushed away the memory of the argument they'd had before Adam left for his shift Wednesday. He hadn't called her once since then. But then, she hadn't called him either. She sniffed the air and thought she detected a hint of smoke. Bobby. Sneaking another cigarette.

Where was Susan anyway?

"Hang on, Charlie. I'll be right back." She headed for the service elevator, breaking into a jog. But a shout brought her up short.

Susan appeared around the corner at the end of the T-shaped hall, racing toward them. "Get everybody out! Get out! *Now!*" She swept past Bryn and pounded on the door of the shelter's family quarters, where Linda Gomez and her children slept.

Bryn stared, and for a moment dared to hope Susan was just adding a little urgency to a routine fire drill. But when the director turned to her, Bryn saw panic in her eyes. This was no act.

"What's going on?" Bryn felt like she was moving through wet concrete.

"The hallway on the second floor is full of smoke," Susan yelled over her shoulder, running toward the dining room. "Get everybody out. There's fire somewhere!"

"Fire? Where?" Charlie wheeled down the hallway toward them, cradling a canvas bag.

"Upstairs. Second floor." Susan pointed down the hallway to where the elevator led up to the shelter's office space. "I got off the elevator up there and I couldn't even see."

"I hope you didn't ride the elevator back down," Charlie scolded.

"I didn't have a choice. I couldn't see my way down the hall to the stairs."

Susan was a firefighter's wife. She knew the fire safety codes. She wouldn't have used the elevator unless she had no choice.

Panting and coughing, the director pounded on the door to the family quarters again. "Bryn, go check the men's quarters and make sure everybody is out. I'll get Linda and the kids up and get the other women out."

"Charlie, *get out* of here! Now! You know the plan. We'll meet outside in the parking lot."

Bryn looked past Susan. "I was just up there . . . not forty minutes ago. Everything was fine." She retraced her steps in her mind. She'd just finished charting and filing the new intake forms when Charlie had appeared in the doorway and challenged her to a game of gin rummy. Clients weren't supposed to be in the office area except for the intake interview or to make a phone call or get their prescription meds out of the locker, but Charlie was almost like an employee and had special privileges.

She searched her brain, trying to remember

those last minutes in the office, then riding down in the elevator with Charlie. A hazy image formed and her pulse lurched. Surely she hadn't forgotten to—

"You didn't smell smoke when you were up there?" Susan's voice sounded accusing.

"No. Nothing. Did you, Charlie?" The flood of dread rising inside her took firmer hold.

The veteran shook his head. "No, but my sniffer don't work too well."

Susan grabbed the receiver from the phone hanging in the hallway. "I called 9-1-1. Why aren't they answering that alarm?"

Bryn froze. "You already called it in?" If he wasn't out on another call, Adam would make the run. And if he discovered her here, she would never hear the end of it.

At the end of the hall, Linda Gomez and her children, all still in their pajamas, scurried toward the shelter's main entrance.

Susan took charge. "I'll call again and then get the women out. Bryn, go! You take the men's wing. Hurry!"

Bryn nodded and crossed the hallway to the men's section with a new sense of urgency. The musty locker-room odor this wing always seemed to hold deluged her. Half a dozen shapes sat hunkered on cots against the far wall.

"What's going on?" Tony X alternately clapped his hands over his ears and rubbed his eyes.

"We've got a fire in the building. We need to evacuate." She had to shout over the blare of the alarms.

Bobby, a twenty-something addict whose parents had finally kicked him out of their house, crawled back under the thin blanket and yanked it over his head. "Wake me up when it's over," he moaned.

"No, Bobby. This is serious. Get up. Everybody out. Where are the rest of the guys?"

A heavily tattooed man—Bryn couldn't remember his name—pointed toward the dining room. "Some of them headed for the back exit."

"Okay . . . okay. Come on guys, move it. Bobby, come on!"

He didn't argue and trudged after the other men into the hall. Bryn peered into the darkened room. All the beds were empty. A couple of the new guys had gotten on night shift at the plastics plant and, according to the log, they didn't get off work until three a.m. She glanced at the clock. *2:27.* They wouldn't be coming in for a while.

Out in the hall, Charlie rolled his chair ahead of them, the canvas bag holding all his earthly goods balanced on his lap. The air was still clear, but now another set of smoke alarms kicked in. This time when Bryn inhaled, she clearly smelled smoke.

The crescendo of distant sirens rose from the west—Station 2.

Bryn darted into the game room across the hall and grabbed her purse from the back of the sofa. She looped the narrow strap over her head and slipped an arm through, crossing the strap over her chest. Thank goodness she'd brought it down with her. She usually kept it locked in the office, but tonight she'd brought it downstairs so she'd have her cell phone and change for the vending machine.

She traced her steps back through the doorway only to see Sparky barreling through the back door. The dog skidded to a stop three feet in front of her and gave a high-pitched yelp, then ran back outside, nearly tripping Susan.

Bryn heard Charlie hollering Sparky's name from outside the door. Good—at least Charlie was safely out. Someone must have helped him maneuver his chair up the rickety makeshift ramp.

Susan scowled. "Why is that dog loose? What are you doing, Bryn? *Get out!* Is anybody still in the men's quarters?"

"No. The beds are all empty."

"You're sure?"

"Yes. Everybody's out."

"Let's go, then! We'll do a head count in the parking lot." Susan motioned for her to follow and ran back toward the entrance.

"I'm right behind you."

She jogged behind Susan, but a nagging image

wouldn't let her leave the building yet. She had to check . . . had to make sure she was wrong. The minute the director disappeared through the outside door, Bryn wheeled and ran in the other direction down the hallway to the door that opened onto the stairwell.

2

Bryn reached for the heavy steel door. She was positive—*almost* positive—she'd blown out the candle before she came down, but she had to make sure.

Susan's panicked voice echoed in her mind, talking about the second story being filled with smoke, but she pushed the voice away. Surely Susan was exaggerating. She placed a palm flat on the door. It was cool to the touch. The handle too. If it was only the candle smoking, setting off the alarms, she could take care of it before the fire department got involved. Adam would be furious with her if she'd brought the trucks out on a false alarm.

She yanked the door open, but quickly shut it again. The stairwell beyond was a haze of smoke. No wonder the fire alarms were going crazy. Oddly disoriented, she leaned against the closed door, her breath coming in short gasps. Her throat burned and expanded, making her cough the way

she had the one time she'd tried smoking a cigarette in junior high.

Susan said she'd come down the elevator. Bryn
looked back toward the bank of doors. Maybe she
could still get to the second floor that way. There
were fire extinguishers just inside each entrance
to the stairwell. But one look down the smoke-
filled hall told her it was too late for that.

She ran toward the main entrance where
everyone had exited, but a flash of lights beyond
the door stopped her in her tracks. She had to
stand on tiptoe to peer out the square of glass in
the top of the door. In the parking lot a ladder
truck braked, and four firefighters in full gear
jumped off as it rolled to a stop. They ran toward
the building, two by two. Even dressed out,
Adam's gait was distinctive. The firefighter
beside him was obviously feminine in spite of the
heavy gear she wore. Molly Edmonds. Bryn dismissed a twinge of jealousy. Adam had never
given her one reason to mistrust him.

She turned and pressed her back against the
door. If she went out there now, Adam would see
her for sure.

Holding her breath against the encroaching
smoke, she sprinted for the tiny kitchen across
from the game room and used the master key on
the lanyard around her neck to let herself out that
door. She dashed around the side of the building,
gasping for fresh air. Leaning over, hands on

knees, she coughed hard and tried to seine oxygen through the ash and smoke. She pushed her hair off her face. Her skin felt gritty.

She spotted Susan near the ladder truck, talking to the station captain, Manny Vermontez. Susan pointed as the two shouted over the roar of the truck's engine, but Bryn could barely make out what they were saying.

The shelter's residents huddled in a half circle about twenty feet from the building. They stomped and blew on their hands, looking dazed. Charlie had one of Linda Gomez's kids wrapped up in his lap robe and sitting with him in the wheelchair. The other two stood shivering, wearing only footed pajamas, clinging to their mother's knees.

Susan's gaze flitted over the group, and she stabbed at the air with her index finger, reading names off the sign-in sheet over the raucous chorus of sirens and smoke alarms. She must have grabbed the list off the bulletin board as they evacuated. Sparky circled the huddled group yipping, as if he was herding cattle.

Bryn jogged in a wide arc behind the cluster of emergency vehicles parked on the grounds and eased into the huddle. Charlie spotted her and gave a shout. "There's Bryn!"

Susan whirled and her shoulders sagged. "Thank God! Where were you? We thought you were still in there."

"I came out through the kitchen."

"Why?" Susan's nostrils flared. "I thought you were right behind me."

"I had to check . . . one more time."

Susan glared at her, but only said, "Help me count. We've got to make sure everybody got out. The night shift guys weren't back yet, were they?"

"No, they hadn't checked in . . . unless they came in while I was upstairs. Charlie said they don't usually get in until around three-thirty. All the beds in the men's quarters were empty when I left."

"Okay, good." Susan looked past Bryn and hollered, "Bobby!"

Bobby shuffled over and the director grabbed his shoulder and pointed at the cluster of emergency workers skittering around the building. "Go tell them we found Bryn. Be sure they know."

He ran off across the lot and Susan inhaled deeply and went back to counting heads, but when she came to Charlie, she whirled, eyes wild. "What about Zeke Downing? Has anybody seen him?"

Charlie shrugged. Zeke had mostly kept to himself after the dog fight.

Bryn shook her head. "I didn't think he was here tonight. I never checked him in. I don't remember seeing him on the sign-in sheet."

Susan scanned the paper frantically. "No. But he was here!" she shouted. "I saw him. He came up to the office to make a phone call. I chased him out of the stairwell right after you came on duty."

Bryn lifted her shoulders and kept shaking her head. "I didn't see him at dinner . . . or all night for that matter. Boss wasn't tied up outside either, and—"

"Bobby!" Susan cupped her hands and yelled across the lot.

The young man waved over his shoulder at the firefighter he was in animated conversation with and loped back toward Susan.

Susan met him halfway, shouting as she ran. "Did you see Zeke? Did he get out?"

Charlie turned to Bryn and shrugged. "I never saw him tonight either." The veteran grabbed the wheels of his chair, his arms making rowing motions as he bumped across the overgrown parking lot toward Susan and Bobby. Sparky bounded behind the wheelchair. Bryn heard Charlie repeat to Susan what he'd told her.

Susan's eyes held a frantic sheen. "You never saw him get out, or you didn't see him at all tonight?"

"I ain't seen him tonight. But then he steers clear of me. You know that."

An odd noise made Bryn turn back to face the shelter. At that instant, something popped above them, near the roof of the building. Glass exploded from the second-story windows, and flames shot out the gaping craters.

Bryn gasped and covered her mouth with her hands. Not more than ten minutes ago they'd been playing gin rummy and sniffing the air for invisible smoke. Now tongues of bright red and orange flames licked at the windows on the upper story. Thick smoke billowed into the night sky, silhouetted against the faint neon glow from downtown Hanover Falls, six blocks to the west.

Susan ran toward the truck, and Captain Manny Vermontez met her halfway, shouting over the noise of the engine and a low rumble that Bryn now realized was caused by the fire itself.

"All your people are out now? You're sure?" Manny motioned toward the building, his fingers hovering nervously on the radio he carried.

Susan pressed her hands to her temples. "There's one possible client unaccounted for. Zeke Downing. Two others haven't checked in yet tonight . . . we're pretty sure."

"Pretty sure?" Captain Vermontez shook his head. "You gotta be positive, Susan." He nodded at the list crumpled in her fist. "You've checked everyone off?"

Bryn heard Susan explain to the captain about Zeke, and about the shift workers at the plastics plant.

"Okay, we'll make one more sweep,"

Vermontez said. "But then I've got to get my men out. You clear everybody away from the building." He motioned across the lot to where they were huddled, then turned and ran toward the building, shouting into his radio.

Susan nodded and sprinted across the parking lot, motioning in broad strokes. "They want us out of the way. Everybody move to the other side of the street. We need to get away from here."

Bryn scooped the baby, Miguel, from Charlie's lap. The littlest Gomez girl whimpered and her mother picked her up. Bryn bent with the baby heavy on her right arm and wrestled the older girl into her other arm. She followed the ragtag group as they made their way across the pavement. They huddled together on the steps of an empty office building, mesmerized by the fire. They'd been shivering before, but now—even from across the street, Bryn could feel the heat from the blaze.

Bobby, Tony X, and the two other young men from the shelter hadn't crossed with them, but stood in the parking lot, hands on hips, staring up at the flames. Sparky had left Charlie's side and trotted between the four men, alternately nuzzling their hands and barking at the fire.

A second engine from Station 2 arrived and joined the battle. When the first truck from Station 1 showed up, Bryn knew it must be bad. She hoped Manny got his men out of there before it was too late. She watched the entrances, looking for Adam . . . praying he was safe, willing him to come out of that building.

The Station 1 crew set up floodlights, but by now the fire itself illuminated the night sky. Bryn had seen Adam and three other firefighters head inside, dragging the hoses. Manny had gone in, too, after he talked to Susan. Bryn hadn't seen any of them come out yet. What were they waiting for? Zach Morgan, and another firefighter—maybe Manny's son, Lucas Vermontez?—were talking on the radio. She recognized Zach's bass voice, but his words were gobbled up in the roar of the inferno.

She watched as Zach motioned to the engineer, then ran toward the building. Manny's son—if that's who it was—followed. Bryn put a hand over her mouth. They surely weren't going inside? Not now. They should be ordering men out, not sending more in!

Adam always reassured her that he knew what he was doing, that he'd been well-trained, that his buddies watched his back. "I'm safer on the job than you are driving to your dad's on the Interstate," he was fond of saying. But she knew he only told her that so she wouldn't worry. Judging by the fire that blazed behind every window on the second floor, she couldn't imagine where anyone could be inside the building that wasn't consumed with—

"Get out! Get out!" A shout went up from the firefighters working outside the building. The earth rumbled beneath Bryn's feet, and a deafening explosion made her clap her hands over her ears. When the earth finally stilled, Bryn looked up at the shelter, her blood like ice.

The few windows that remained after the first blast now burst out of their casings. A spray of glass and ash rained down on them, and Bryn turned away from the terrific onslaught of debris, trying to make herself a shield for the babies.

Susan shouted something she couldn't decipher. Bryn dropped to the ground, pushing the children onto the brown grass between the sidewalk and the curb. Linda Gomez screamed, and her kids wailed in unison.

Bryn scrambled to her knees and spread her arms wide, as if she could gather the kids beneath protective wings. She craned her neck to peer over her shoulder. It was chaos across Grove Street, but she buried her face in her shoulder and strained to peer through the gray smoke and debris that swirled in the air around them.

Oh, dear God. There were men still in there. Had Adam made it out? Surely he had? But where was he? She needed to see him. Her gaze scoured the lot, and she counted firemen, desperately trying to locate him among the firefighters scurrying around the building. It was chaotic and impossible to see through the dense smoke, but there were too many unaccounted for. Where were all the firefighters who'd gone into the building?

Zach and Lucas had gone in only seconds ago. She hadn't seen them come out. Manny was nowhere to be seen. She couldn't remember *anyone* coming out, but things were so crazy, maybe she just missed it. Maybe they'd left through the back door like she had earlier.

Most of the crew were working the fire from the outside. Surely Manny had ordered them all to evacuate the building by now. Adam had a lot of respect for the captain. All the firefighters did. He wouldn't have let them stay if they were in danger. Adam always said Manny's motto was "Risk a lot to save a lot; risk nothing to save nothing." So why weren't they coming out?

Three fire engines were parked beneath the building now, one of them blocking her view of the main entrance. A ladder truck from Station 2 backed slowly around behind the building, ladder extended high into the night. Bryn held her breath as two firefighters scaled the rungs and disappeared over the ledge of the roof. She didn't think Adam was one of them, but from such a distance she couldn't be sure. What were they doing?

The fire roared, spilling from identical rows of arched windows on the northern and eastern sides of the building. There was an eerie hissing as the water from the fire hoses hit its mark.

The battle seemed to go on forever, yet it seemed the more the hoses doused the fire, the larger it grew. Droplets of water pelted her head. Bryn glanced up, thinking it must be raining. Then she realized the gutters were flowing with runoff from the fire hoses. The gutter across the street started to fill with water, whirls of steam lifting off the surface of the black brine.

Someone shouted, and suddenly the whole world seemed to tilt. If she didn't know better, she would have thought they were having an earthquake.

Across the street, a groan like something from the throat of a living beast split the air. Wood against metal, creaking, splintering. And then another explosion. Like seeing a train wreck in slow motion, she watched her world tumble around her.

As if they shared one voice, a shout went up from the crews below. And before all their eyes, the building buckled and caved. Beams fell away, piercing what was left of the roof, angling against girders and rafters, and piling up on each other in slow motion, like the pickup sticks game she used to play when she was a kid.

The sounds that tormented her ears morphed into something otherworldly. The structure screamed and moaned as it collapsed, as if it had a life of its own.

If anyone was still inside—

Bryn couldn't let herself finish the thought. No one could have survived that inferno, let alone the weight of the old building crashing in on itself.

On her knees in the tough grass, she stared into the flames, her thoughts as lucid as they'd ever been, and yet somehow, at the same time, completely chaotic. Someone was screaming. It took her a minute to realize the sound was coming from her own throat.

The Gomez children huddled in front of her, and she spread her arms and leaned over them, trying to protect them from the debris. Someone pressed heavily against her back. Linda? She couldn't hold steady any longer. She went down on her side, rolling to the left so she wouldn't crush the children.

She struggled to her knees again and gathered the youngest girls close. Shivering, panting for oxygen, she watched the thick, ash-pocked smoke billow up into a black November sky.

They had to get the kids to safety, had to get the clients farther away from the building before another explosion rocked them.

She passed Miguel off to someone, and held the little Gomez girl on her hip as she helped Susan herd people around the east side of the office building.

But she worked with a numb certainty. Somehow she knew: Adam was dead.

And she was to blame.

3

The sun sketched a thin line of scarlet on the eastern horizon between the office park and the Co-op's grain elevators. The charred skeleton that had been the Grove Street Homeless Shelter stretched its bones against the dim glow, puffs of smoke still rising from the debris. Bryn viewed the scene through slits of eyes swollen with smoke. She felt numb, unwilling to let her mind function, for fear it would reveal a truth she could not bear.

Less than three hours ago, she'd been playing gin rummy with Charlie, oblivious to the horror this sunrise would lay bare. Now she was as empty as the smoldering ruins across the street.

Moments ago two pastors from one of the Hanover Falls churches had taken Linda Gomez and her children away in a van. Said they'd put them up in a hotel for a few days until something could be worked out.

Somehow Bryn managed to stand of her own volition and answer the queries of the police officers and investigators who questioned her and Susan and the others at the scene. No, she hadn't seen Zeke since she came on duty at eleven tonight. No, she hadn't smelled smoke . . . not until the alarms were already going off and the first

37

floor hallway was rolling with it. Yes, she'd seen several firefighters go into the building. Molly Edmonds was among them. And she thought she'd recognized Zach Morgan. But she could identify only one of them with absolute certainty.

Adam Hennesey. Her husband.

Inexplicably a hush fell over the crowd milling at the edge of the parking lot.

And then Bryn saw why. A stretcher was being carried from the ruins of the shelter. And then another. And a third. Even from across the street where she stood, there was no doubt that it was bodies—dead bodies—that weighted the canvas. Not survivors.

Where was Adam? Oh, dear God, where *was* he? Maybe he had gotten out after all. Maybe he was inside, helping them bring out the survivors. *Please, God.*

Even the wind ceased as the stretchers were carried from the building and lined up in the parking lot like so many funeral biers.

Dozens of firefighters and emergency crews clustered at the site. And as the stretchers lined up, one by one, the men and women lifted hands to soot-blackened, tear-stained faces and saluted.

Bryn couldn't look at that row of bodies any longer, but her eyes darted from one uniformed firefighter to the next. They stood at attention, horror and overwhelming grief turning their expressions to stone. She watched two of the men sink back onto the bumper of a ladder truck and bury their faces in their hands.

A wave of horror surged through her, shoved her to her knees. How many men had died today? How could it all have happened so fast?

As if in a vision, she saw herself in the office early in her shift, filling out admission papers for a homeless man who smelled like a garbage truck. Disgusted, she had leaned away from him, attempted to breathe through her mouth. The stench was so bad she'd started to feel queasy. In her mind's eye, she watched herself open a book of matches, tear one off, and strike it on the cover. The man—she couldn't even remember his name now—had watched her light the cinnamon-scented candle and extinguish the match. She hadn't even thought about whether he knew she'd lit it because of his body odor.

A cloak of dread hovered over her, and she racked her brain to remember if she'd blown that candle out before she and Charlie rode the service elevator down together. Her heart stuttered. *Surely* she had. You couldn't be married to a fire-fighter for two years without getting the candle lectures. The one she'd lit was a cheap pillar candle, but it sat on an acrylic coaster on a clear surface of the desk. It should have been safe even . if she *had* left it burning. But sometimes those cheap candles smoked like crazy—especially in that drafty office.

Susan kept a couple of candles in the office to help with the odors. Technically, the candles weren't supposed to be lit, but Bryn wasn't the only one who sometimes put a match to the wick when the person sitting across the desk smelled like they hadn't bathed in weeks.

They were always careful, but Adam would have a fit if he knew a candle had even been allowed in the building, let alone lit.

A chilling thought sliced through her. The fire alarm system in the hospital hadn't worked properly when Susan bought the building, and she'd replaced it with a series of individual units, but they were touchy and triggered by the least bit of smoke or dust. A couple of weeks ago the alarm in the office had gone off at one o'clock in the morning when one of the volunteers burned a bag of popcorn in the microwave. Bryn reset it, but it started blaring again. She must have climbed up on the desk half a dozen times, resetting the detector and trying different batteries. But every time she thought she'd fixed it, it would start shrieking again. She'd finally popped out the batteries just to shut the thing up.

The office was small, and there were smoke detectors just outside in the hallway. Susan hadn't been on duty that night, and she hated to wake her up at home in the middle of the night over a stupid faulty smoke detector. She'd scribbled a note to herself to leave a message for one of the trustees to take a look at the smoke detector, but she couldn't remember if she'd ever actually delivered that message.

A reporter thrust a microphone in Bryn's face, yanking her back to the present. Another young man stood by with a TV camera. But Bryn turned her back on them. She couldn't have formed a coherent sentence if she'd wanted to.

Her breath hitched. *Had* she left that candle burning? *Oh, dear God. Please. No.* But . . . she couldn't have. She rubbed her temples as if she could somehow magically make her brain call forth the memory of blowing that candle out. She *needed* that memory. Needed it the way she needed oxygen.

But even if that memory crystallized in her mind, she wasn't entirely innocent. The thought almost sent her to her knees. Adam had only been on duty tonight because she'd talked him into working overtime, told him they needed the money with Christmas coming. Which was true. But it wasn't the real reason. She'd convinced him because Susan had asked her to fill in for another volunteer. And the only way she could be at the shelter was if Adam didn't know.

Even though it had been Adam's boss, David Marlowe—Susan's husband—who had suggested Bryn volunteer at the shelter in the first place, after the first time Adam picked her up at the shelter and saw the motley group of men smoking and leering

41

outside the entrance, he had been on a campaign to get her to resign. Then last month, after one of the shelter's teenage resident-volunteers was assaulted and nearly raped by another resident, Adam forbade Bryn to come back.

"It's too dangerous," he declared. "If you think you have to have more hours, tell them at the library. At least there you'd be getting paid for your time."

Adam just didn't get it. Even if the city library had the extra hours to give her, they closed at eight every night. Filling those lonely nights at home was the reason she'd been attracted to the volunteer shifts at the shelter in the first place. She'd grown to love the work for so many other reasons.

But since the day they'd started thinking seriously about having a baby, Adam had gone overboard worrying about her. If the sidewalks were slick, he walked her to the car. If she got out a ladder to change a lightbulb, he jumped in and did it for her. He'd about come unhinged when she got a speeding ticket a couple of months ago. And this time it wasn't about the money. "If you're going to be a mom, you've got to start taking care of yourself, babe." His expression had been so serious when he said it. It was kind of sweet, really.

This thing with the shelter, though, wasn't negotiable for her. They were desperate for volunteers.

They needed her. And she needed them. From the first day she'd started working with the clients at the Grove Street Homeless Shelter, she'd felt like she had something to offer, that her life counted for something for the first time in a long time. And so, for the last few weeks, she'd secretly continued to come, arranging her shifts around Adam's so he wouldn't know. She hated having to be secretive. But what was she supposed to do when he was so pig-headed about this?

The wail of sirens started again, and Bryn looked up to see Chief Brennan crossing the street to where they were. His head was bowed, and his broad shoulders looked like they bore the weight of a thousand worlds.

"Mrs. Marlowe? Susan . . . ?"

Susan looked up, and Bryn didn't think she had ever seen such dread, such *knowing* dread, in a pair of eyes before. *Oh, dear God.* David Marlowe must have been inside the building.

Peter Brennan lifted his head, removed his fireman's helmet, and clutched it in front of him like a shield. He held Susan's gaze. "I'm sorry."

Bryn's breath lodged in her lungs.

Susan started shaking her head, a low moan seeping from her throat. Her knees buckled, and before Bryn could reach her, she slumped to the ground. Brennan went to her, and with Bryn on one side and the fire chief on the other, they helped Susan to her feet.

"Maybe he got out," Susan keened. "Maybe . . ." She sagged against Bryn, making her stagger to keep from losing her own footing.

"We . . ." Peter Brennan cleared his throat. "We've identified him, Susan. I'm so sorry."

"No . . ." Susan shook her head again.

"Do you want to see him?" He motioned to the makeshift morgue across the parking lot.

Susan nodded and squared her shoulders.

Peter offered his arm. "Come with me."

Susan let go of Bryn. Putting her arm through the crook of Peter's elbow, the shelter director took a step into the street.

Bryn watched, numb, a sure knowledge rising inside her. One of the ambulance attendants strode into the street, stopping to speak with Peter. She saw the chief motion behind him—toward her—and her breath caught.

"No!" The word caught in her throat, strangling her. She sank to her knees in the dead grass, willing the man to walk on past her, pleading with heaven for this to all be a terrible mistake.

She watched the street through a haze. When the man drew close enough for her to see the dread and regret in his eyes, she knew the truth.

4

*T*he procession of caskets was almost more than Garrett Edmonds could stomach. Worse was the fact that his wife's white coffin stood at the end of the row, in contrast to the sleek, dark mahogany and oak boxes lined up at the front of the auditorium. *Molly's coffin.* Those were words he'd never dreamed of uttering. She was twenty-eight. And twenty years from now, when he was fifty-two, Molly would still be twenty-eight. Forever young, forever beautiful.

Forever dead.

The velvet seats in the Hanover Falls City Auditorium were nappy with age and abuse. Garrett sank deeper into the chair they'd escorted him to, in the second row with other family members of the fallen. Now he wished he'd insisted on sitting in the back.

He felt vulnerable, claustrophobic, with so many people filing in behind him. It took everything he had not to stand up and walk to the back . . . keep on walking right out the door.

But he would stay. For Molly, he would stay.

The auditorium filled quickly, and within minutes, ushers were opening the banks of exit

45

doors to the east and west to let the outside crowds spill in. The cold air offered a little relief, but the outside aisles quickly overflowed with mourners and curious onlookers, and the room grew stuffy again.

It struck Garrett as a strange irony that they should be breaking fire codes left and right on an occasion like this. But no one dared suggest turning anyone away. This was history in the making, and every resident of Hanover Falls would be bragging twenty years from now, "I was there. I stood right here in this aisle at the funeral for the fallen firefighters of the Grove Street inferno."

Odd how the media had adopted that title for the event. Some of the newspapers had even taken to capitalizing the words, as if it were the title of a best-selling novel or a blockbuster movie. *The Grove Street Inferno.* Local reporters had to be in their glory with reporters and camera crews from *Good Morning America* and *Nightline* and even, reportedly, Oprah's people, descending on the Falls.

This tragedy had put Hanover Falls on the map of the nation. Garrett winced to realize that he felt a twinge of pride that Molly was a part of it all. He'd glued himself to the TV over the weekend of interminable nights, clicking through channel after channel, searching for another story with a new angle about the fire, another flash of

Molly's picture on the wide screen, until he fell into a drugged stupor.

Or maybe that was from the bottle of Ativan his friend Rick had pressed into his hand that first morning after Molly's death. It didn't really matter . . . as long as he didn't have to feel anything.

A commotion at one side of the auditorium caused him to look up. He spotted his principal, Barbara Cassman, and her husband, and Mary Brigmann, who taught with him at Hanover Falls Middle School.

Behind Mary, in dress shirts and ties, Trevor Hanes and Mark Lohan trudged. And behind them, Jillian Payne and Michaela Morrison in fancy dresses, Michaela's hair all done up in curls on top of her head. They kept coming, a dozen or more of his fifth-grade students filling the third row, sober expressions marring their youthful faces, their eyes searching the auditorium. Looking for him, he realized. Worried about him.

He swallowed hard, looked away, and bowed his head. He couldn't meet their eyes without breaking down. And they didn't need to see that. They needed to know he would be okay. That he was strong. That he was getting through this.

An overhead projector cast the names of the fallen firefighters onto a tattered scrim at the rear of the stage. The caskets—and thus the list of names projected onto the wall—were arranged by rank and seniority.

Captain Manuel Vermontez
Lieutenant David Marlowe
Engineer Zachary Morgan
Firefighter Adam Hennesey
Firefighter Molly Edmonds

A scratchy soundtrack began to play, and the names of the fallen faded to black to be replaced by a series of projected images. One by one, the official portraits of the five firefighters flashed on the wall. Manny and David Marlowe held their helmets at their sides and wore stoic expressions, as if they understood the gravity of their jobs. Even filtered through the camera's lens, Morgan and Hennesey had a certain light in their eyes— one the uninitiated might mistake for mischief. But Garrett recognized it for what it was. It was the same spark he'd so often detected in Molly's eyes, especially when she'd first started with the department. It was the gleam of adventure, compassion, the promise of heroism, and a deep sense of purpose in what she'd signed on to do.

Molly's face appeared on the screen—life-size—and it literally took his breath away. Her pale blond hair was in its customary ponytail, and she wore a broad smile, as if she'd attempted the stony expression of her compadres, but the joy she took in her job—her calling—simply wouldn't be subdued.

He'd never supported her in her career the way

he should have. Though he was proud of her, he'd always secretly wished she could be content with a normal, nine-to-five job. He'd worried about her safety and about how being a firefighter would affect her as a mother. He'd always wanted kids more than she did, and her job was one of the things that deterred her desire for children. None of that mattered now. He wished he could tell her, just once, how proud he was to be her husband.

The music changed, a haunting tune Garrett recognized but couldn't place. Someone had put together a video montage, clips from the parade down Main Street on the first day of school, and last summer's company picnic. Molly hammed it up for the camera dressed in her favorite Hanover Falls Fire Department T-shirt and shorts that showed off her long, muscled legs. This time her hair was down, the way he liked it best, swinging around her shoulders, the sun making a halo for her. Arm-in-arm with Adam Hennesey and Zach Morgan, Molly looked straight into the camera's lens. Garrett read her lips—"Hey, baby!" He couldn't have said who'd been behind the video camera that day, but he remembered Molly's smile with crystal clarity and knew it had been only for him. Despite that knowledge, he felt oddly jealous, seeing her on the arms of her comrades, knowing they were together in eternity now, while she was lost to him.

Wordlessly the scenes played out before the mourners, the somber music an odd backdrop to the picnic's merriment. Adam and Bryn Hennesey sat shoulder-to-shoulder at a picnic table, intent over corn on the cob. Something caught their attention and they glanced up as one, then tilted their heads together to mouth "cheese" for the photographer. They seemed unaware that the camera lingered on them, and he brushed a kernel of corn from the corner of her mouth, laughing as she wiped at the rest of her face, suddenly self-conscious. It was an oddly intimate moment, and Garrett froze, feeling he should look away, yet wondering if there might be a similar scene with him and Molly. He felt divided—longing for a glimpse of them together, but praying he wouldn't have to watch it in front of this crowd.

The camera panned the crowd before focusing on David and Susan Marlowe. Marlowe waved the camera off, but when the lens held steady on them, he looked resigned and hugged his wife close, holding a pose.

A crescendo of flutes and piano as the camera jerked and faded in and out of focus. But when the scene finally sharpened, it took away the breaths of the mourners as one. Zooming back from a close-up shot of Manny Vermontez, the camera captured a tug-of-war between Station 1 and Station 2. Manny was at the front of the rope with Lucas, his son. And lined up behind them, in order of rank, were David Marlowe, Zach Morgan, Adam Hennesey, and Molly.

What fluke of fate had put this particular team at the front of the rope that day? Garrett could only imagine how it would make Lucas Vermontez feel to see himself with this team of fallen heroes.

The camera focused again, sharpened, and morphed to a black-and-white image of the tug-of-war. Garrett closed his eyes, unable to look at Molly's jubilant face for another minute.

When he dared to open his eyes a minute later, the screen had gone black. The music faded, but the silence was taken up with sniffles and open weeping. Someone Garrett didn't know stood and read a cheesy poem in a voice that quavered with emotion. It made him grateful this would be the only service for Molly.

He'd heard last night that some of the men's families also planned to hold private memorial services in their own churches. He had considered a church funeral for Molly, but they didn't really have a church home yet, and he knew she would have been most honored to be remembered here with her fellow firefighters. Besides, he could not bear the thought of "burying" Molly twice.

He wouldn't do it. The engines of Station 2, shrouded in black bunting, sat on the closed-off street outside the auditorium. They would transport the flag-draped caskets to the cemetery on the edge of town, and Molly would be buried there under the same patch of sky as her fallen comrades.

That would be the end of it. And he would just have to find some way to go on without the woman he'd loved for as long as he could remember.

*L*ike neatly embroidered threads, fire engines of every color and size stitched a full mile of the road that led to the Hanover Falls Cemetery. Every fire department in the neighboring counties had sent a delegation of firefighters to pay their respects.

Even the drone of forty idling engines couldn't drown out the wail of bagpipes. Bryn fought the urge to cover her ears. But with Susan on one side of her and her friend Jenna Morgan, Zach's wife—Zach's *widow*—on the other, Bryn's hands were otherwise occupied as they stood arm-in-arm at the entrance to the cemetery where Adam and three of the other four fallen firefighters would be laid to rest.

Finally the engines were shut down, and the bagpipers ceased playing for a few minutes as dozens upon dozens of men and women in dress blues spilled from the trucks' cabs and filed across the cemetery lawn.

A flash of memory pierced her. A Friday night

last summer. She and Adam sat across from Zach and Jenna at Applebee's, roaring at Zach's spot-on impersonation of a local politician. They'd gone back to their townhouse after dinner for ice cream.

She and Jenna's friendship had blossomed after that night. They'd become shopping buddies, mostly, lingering at the mall for coffee or lunch after they'd blown their budgets. Jenna's budget was always considerably bigger than Bryn's, but it was nice to have a friend who understood the challenges of being married to a firefighter. Being the new kids on the block, Adam and Zach got stuck working holidays more often than not. It was nice to have Jenna to commiserate with her.

Garrett and Molly Edmonds had stopped by later that night, and the six of them played a new board game Adam had picked up at a little game shop in Springfield. They'd joked about what geeks they'd become in their old age.

But when they closed the door behind their guests long after midnight, Adam had turned to Bryn, still standing in the foyer. "Those guys are like the brothers I never had, you know?" he said, his voice husky.

She'd cracked up at that because she knew he wasn't talking about Garrett. He meant Zach and Molly, the two firefighters in the group.

Molly Edmonds was a gorgeous woman when you got past the messy ponytail, and station-issued T-shirts and fatigues. A twinge of jealousy had pinched Bryn, and she was only half teasing when she told Adam, "I guess I should be thankful you see Molly as a brother."

He brushed her off. "You know what I mean."

She'd been touched to hear the catch in his voice. His only sibling, his sister, Donna, was eleven years older, and since the deaths of their parents, he'd lost touch with her. Thursday, the morning of the fire, it had taken Bryn two hours to track Donna down at a new address in California to tell her about Adam. Bryn didn't expect to see Donna at this funeral, and she wasn't sure she would recognize the woman if she did show up.

Bryn forced her head up and stared at the row of fire engines swimming in front of her. While a uniformed firefighter rolled a portable staircase from the back of one engine to the next, she worked hard to not think about anything at all. Truck by truck, a color guard mounted the steps and bore four red-white-and-blue-draped coffins down and through the cemetery's iron gates.

The engine bearing the casket of Susan's husband, David Marlowe—a truck on loan from the neighboring Major County Fire Department—pulled away with its cargo still onboard. Susan's gaze followed the casket, and she gripped Bryn's hand so hard Bryn thought she might faint from the pain.

Tomorrow morning a hearse would carry Lieutenant Marlowe's casket up the Interstate to Springfield, where he would be buried beside his parents' graves. But today Susan stood in solidarity with the other widows, and with Garrett Edmonds, Molly's husband.

At Susan's suggestion, the five of them had walked in the cortège from the auditorium rather than riding in the hearses that tagged behind the fire trucks. David and Susan's two sons—both called home from college by the tragedy—walked behind their mother in the parade, somber-faced. Ten city blocks they'd all marched, in front of the slow procession of fire engines bearing the caskets.

On the other side of her, Jenna Morgan scanned the gathering crowd, weeping softly. "Oh, there. I see Zach's parents. I need to go be with them."

Bryn nodded and squeezed Jenna's hand, then watched her cross the leaf-strewn lawn and fall, weeping, into her mother-in-law's embrace. Bryn envied her friend's ability to let loose of her tears, even though it surprised her to see Jenna so close with Clarissa Morgan.

She wiggled her toes in too-tight pumps that had rubbed twin blisters on her heels. But the blisters were nothing. Every ounce of energy not taken up with gathering her next breath was expended on simply remaining upright.

The last three-and-a-half days had been a blur

of funeral-home visits and phone calls, and interrogation by television and newspaper reporters. Since talking to the police in the chaos of that night, Bryn had managed to dodge the formal police interviews Susan and fire personnel were subjected to, but a reporter from the *Hanover Falls Courier* had called her house half a dozen times, and twice she'd seen a van with the paper's logo on the side sitting outside her house.

And then there'd been the mortuary. The caskets were all closed, of course, but Bryn's imagination could conjure all too well what those satin-lined boxes contained. Only a steel skeleton and a pile of ash remained where the Grove Street Shelter once stood.

The mortuary hadn't had need of Adam's clothes. His uniform, with his boots, sat folded on the front of Engine 1. Bryn wondered if they were the boots he'd been wearing when he died. Surely those hadn't survived the fire. She shuddered. Morbid thoughts. But they kept coming.

After the first explosion, almost twelve hours had passed before they'd recovered Manny Vermontez's body, trapped beneath layers of rubble. By that time, a crowd had gathered, keeping quiet vigil on a day that had dawned bright and sunny.

Bryn had kept watch with them, in spite of the fact that Adam—Adam's body—had been carried away in an ambulance hours before. As long as she lived, she would never forget Emily Vermontez's keening wail when her husband's body was carried out. Manny's was the fifth and final body to be removed from the carnage.

Manny and Emily's son, Lucas, a handsome rookie firefighter, was still in the hospital in serious condition. Lucas Vermontez would live. His mother would not have to bury two men she loved.

Bryn had heard someone tell Susan, as the families of the fallen were being seated, that Lucas had not yet regained consciousness. Which meant he probably didn't know yet that his father was dead. And that, against Chief Brennan's orders, Manny had run into the burning building just before it collapsed, searching for his son.

Lucas had his life, but he was not here to bid his father—the man he revered above all others—farewell.

Bryn searched the crowd for her own father. She knew Dad was here somewhere, but in the mash of people streaming onto the cemetery grounds, she couldn't find him. He'd volunteered to walk with her in the cortège, but she had made excuses, worried he wasn't strong enough. Now, thinking about him alone in the crowd, she wished she'd accepted his offer. Dad had barely had time to grieve her mother's death three years ago, and now they were burying Adam.

Again she pushed aside a terrible truth that kept

trying to get her attention as the wind whipped her hair about her face and drove spears of cold into her bones.

The rest of the short graveside service was torture, and when the bagpipes began to play again—a mournful rendition of "Amazing Grace"—Bryn thought she might be going mad.

For if the hellish nudgings of her imagination were true, surely there was no grace on earth or in heaven that could save a wretch like her.

5

Monday, November 12

Bryn gazed into the mirror above the bathroom sink. Her reflection stared back, pale and devoid of makeup, purple circles rimming her eyes, the irises a muddier shade of brown than usual. Her hair hung in shapeless hanks to her shoulders. She couldn't remember the last time she'd washed it. Adam had always loved her auburn hair, but now it looked dull and brittle. Almost lunchtime and she'd just changed out of her pajamas. How had she aged ten years in the week that had passed since the funerals? Those seven days seemed like an hour. Or a year. Time had ceased to have meaning.

She'd requested two weeks off from her part-time job at the library, and for a week she'd holed up in their house—*her* house. Adam had the foresight to insure their mortgage so that she now owned their townhome free and clear. Whether she could afford the taxes and the monthly maintenance fees, though, remained to be seen.

The little two-bedroom townhome had always been a cozy haven for the two of them. But when Adam was working too many shifts and she stayed here by herself, even the mellow shades of gold and burgundy in the paint and rich fabrics she'd chosen seemed cold. But it was a very different kind of alone, knowing Adam would never walk through that door again. Without his presence, the space had been rendered cold and sterile.

In seven days, she hadn't left the building except to get the mail in the entryway. And she'd stopped even that when the sympathy cards started pouring in.

She didn't dare turn on the radio or TV for fear of hearing another story about the heroic fallen firefighters from the Grove Street Inferno, and except for a couple of calls from Susan Marlowe, unless caller ID showed her father's number, she ignored the phone the dozen times a day it rang, knowing it would be a reporter. Or a fire investigator. Or the police.

She opened the medicine cabinet, and reaching for the mouthwash, her hand rested on Adam's bottle of aftershave. Before she could think through the consequences, she unscrewed the lid and brought the bottle to her nose. It was like letting a genie out of a bottle. If she closed her eyes, she could almost imagine Adam standing at the counter beside her, fresh from the shower and wrapped in a towel, his hair spiky and smelling like a little bit of heaven. *Dear God, I miss him.*

She capped the bottle and replaced it on the shelf. She turned on the faucet and held a hand under the stream, waiting for the water to warm, but turned it off again, thinking she'd heard something. Eyeing her reflection, she froze, listening. Down the hall, the doorbell chimed. She was in no mood for company.

She dried her hands and crept down the hall to the front door. Peering through the peephole, she let out her breath. *Dad.* Her father tried to talk her into moving in with him after the funeral. Hugh Terrigan could be stubborn, but he hadn't pushed her on this. Instead, when she declined, he'd taken to stopping by every couple of days just to check on her, or bring by fast food—most of which got tossed in the garbage as soon as he left. If she didn't answer the door now, Dad would worry himself sick. Sighing, she pushed her hair off her face, turned the lock, and opened the door.

"I was starting to think you weren't home." He looked her up and down. "You okay, honey? You don't look like you feel very well."

"I'm okay, Daddy." She forced a laugh, and the tug at the corners of her mouth felt foreign. "I just don't have my makeup on yet."

"Well, go do something about that. You look terrible."

"Gee, thanks."

He grinned and patted her cheek, but deep furrows carved his forehead. She wasn't going to get off that easily. "I thought I'd take you out to lunch."

"Dad—I'm really not hungry."

"You're too skinny. You're not eating, are you?"

"I'm eating. It wouldn't kill me to lose a pound or two."

He shook his head. "You're too skinny."

"I'll make us something here. I'm just—I don't feel like going out, Dad. Please."

"Bryn, you can't hide out here forever. I know it's hard. Believe me, I remember how it was when your mother—" Even after three years, he still couldn't talk about Mom without choking up.

He held out his arms, inviting her to cry on his shoulder. But she bent and picked at an imaginary thread in the carpeting. Anything to keep from having to pretend she could cry. The ashes stinging her eyes the night of the fire had elicited more tears than she'd shed this week. She could not cry. And she couldn't tell her father why.

When she'd composed herself, she straightened and reached to touch his arm. "I'm okay—"

"Honey, you've got to get out of here. Come stay with me. I've got the extra bedroom just sitting empty. It's not good for you to be alone all the time."

"Thanks, Dad. I appreciate it . . . I really do. But I can't be that far out of town." She forced her voice to sound upbeat. "I start back to work soon—at the library. And I've got leads on a couple of jobs. Full-time, I mean."

"Do you need some money?" He fished in his back pocket.

She reached out and put a hand on his arm. "I'm fine. I promise I'll let you know if I'm starving."

He narrowed his eyes and gave her a look that said he thought she was already there.

"I'm fine," she said again. She was the one who should be taking care of him. Dad was two years from retirement and already worried about how he would make it on a fixed income. His health had deteriorated drastically since Mom's death three Christmases ago. It would be a miracle if he made it another two years at Eberfield & Sons, where he worked as a production manager.

She hadn't been lying about the jobs. She'd seen a couple of things in the paper, and she did have to find something with full-time hours and benefits. Or she'd be *living* in a homeless shelter, not volunteering in one.

Dad was right. She couldn't stay locked up here forever. There were things she had to take care of, like figure out how she would make a living. Adam's pension benefits didn't amount to much since he'd only been with the station two-and-a-half years. He'd had a separate life insurance policy worth twenty-five thousand dollars, but she hadn't gotten the check yet, and that would barely keep her going a year—if she cut way back.

But she couldn't let herself think about all that now. "Come sit down, Dad. I'll make you something to eat."

He waved her off. "No, no. If you won't go out to eat with me, I'll just go home and eat leftovers by myself." He pouted a little, but Bryn caught the good-natured twinkle in his eyes. "Besides, there's a game I want to see on TV tonight."

Behind him, the doorbell rang. Dad looked at her with a question in his eyes, but she shrugged. She wasn't expecting anyone.

She opened the door a crack. Jenna stood on the stoop, her head bowed. "Jenna? Is everything okay? Come in." She backed up so her friend could enter. "Dad, this is Jenna Morgan. Zach's wife."

Her father's eyes lit with recognition at Zach's name. "Of course, of course. Nice to meet you, Jenny."

Bryn didn't correct him.

He dipped his head. "I'm so sorry for your loss." He touched Jenna's arm lightly, reaching for Bryn with his other hand. "You girls have had more to bear than any young wife ever should." His voice broke, and Jenna teared up.

But then Dad brightened. "Well, I'll leave you two to talk. I was just leaving." He winked at Bryn.

She walked him to the door. "Thanks for coming by, Daddy. I'll be fine. Don't worry about me."

"I know you will. You give your old man a call now and then, okay?"

"I will." She closed the door behind her, and when her eyes had adjusted to the dim room again, she met Jenna's gaze.

"So how's it going?"

Jenna slumped into the overstuffed chair by the window. She gave a little moan, tears clogging her voice. Even with her makeup smudged and her hair disheveled, she looked beautiful. Bryn had always envied Jenna's fair complexion and blond hair. It didn't help that Adam had always referred to her as "drop-dead gorgeous."

"I'm going crazy, Bryn. I can't eat, I can't sleep . . ." She bit her lower lip. "I think . . . I think I'm going to lose the house."

"Oh, Jen. I'm so sorry. But . . . are you sure? Can't you refinance or . . ."

"Zach's parents want me to move in with them."

Bryn nodded. "I just had the same conversation with my dad. Are you considering it?"

"I'm not sure I have a choice."

Jenna's relationship with Zach's mother was tenuous at best. Zach's father had some upper-six-figure banking job in Springfield, but according to Jen, the Morgans chose to live in the Falls so Zach's mother could preside as queen bee over Hanover Falls' social circles. And so she could keep an eye on "Zachy."

Bryn shuddered, remembering some of Jenna's horror stories about her mother-in-law. She could be thankful she hadn't had to deal with Adam's family grieving. "Surely you can work something out."

Jenna broke down. "We're dying financially, Bryn. Our credit cards were already maxed out, and I'm not even sure how we—how *I* am going to make the next mortgage payment."

"I'm sorry. I didn't know . . ."

Jenna hung her head. "The money seems minor compared to everything else. I just can't make this whole thing seem real, you know?"

Bryn nodded and touched her hand. "My dad always says God won't ever give us more than we can bear." The words turned to ash in her mouth, but she plastered on a brave face and made the same speeches her dad had given her when Mom died. "We just have to trust God even when we can't understand why things happen the way they do. God loves us and is with us, even—maybe especially—in the hardest times."

Somehow she'd believed it when Dad said it to her. Now, parroting the words to Jenna, she wasn't sure at all. And since the night of the fire, she wasn't on speaking terms with God that she could ask Him.

A shadow crossed Jenna's face. "I don't know how you can say that, Bryn. After everything that happened. You say God's with us, but where was He when Zach and Adam were trapped in that building? If He's so all-powerful, why didn't He stop that fire from starting in the first place? Why did He let that homeless guy get away? You can't have it both ways. Can you?"

"I . . . I don't know, Jen." She didn't have an answer for her friend. And Jenna's words brought a new thought. Jenna apparently believed the theory the fire inspectors were working with— that Zeke Downing had started the fire.

How long before they would find Zeke—or at least somehow prove that he did it? Her heart revved, and she worked to keep her breathing steady. She had somehow mustered up a fragile certainty that allowed her to live with herself: it must have been Zeke. Everyone seemed so sure that he was responsible. She simply could not have left that candle burning. Surely she had blown it out before she left the office. She *must* have. But the solid, visual memory she desperately needed—the memory that would absolve her of guilt—eluded her.

She took comfort in the preliminary reports that cited dozens of old hospital mattresses stored on the second floor as the reason for the intensity of the fire and subsequent explosion. But the initial cause of the fire remained "as yet undetermined due to the extensive damage to the building," according to the fire inspector the media quoted most recently.

She'd lived in equal anticipation and dread of the day the fire inspectors would turn in their final report.

"Bryn? Hey, are you okay?" Jenna's voice pierced through the fog of dread.

Bryn shook her head, trying to focus her thoughts. "Sorry. What did you say?"

Jenna shrugged. "It doesn't matter. I'm tired of thinking about it."

The phone rang, and Bryn shot her an apologetic frown. But Jenna waved her off. "It's okay. I need to be going anyway." She rose and started for the door. "I'll stop by later this week."

The phone trilled again, and Jenna waved and slipped out the door, closing it silently behind her.

Bryn went into the kitchen and checked the display. No name showed up, but she recognized Susan Marlowe's number and picked up the cordless handset. "Hello?"

"Bryn, it's Susan. How are you doing?"

"I'm okay. How are you?"

Susan's sigh filled the line. "One day at a time."

"Yeah . . . same here."

"Listen . . ." Susan's voice brightened, and Bryn recognized the same tone she affected herself whenever Dad called. Don't let anyone know how it really is. Because if they knew, they couldn't take it. Odd that she and Susan played the game even with each other.

"I have a huge favor to ask of you," Susan said.

Bryn hesitated, her defenses on alert. "What's that?"

"The Humane Society picked up Sparky yesterday—you remember Charlie's dog?"

"Of course."

"He was hanging around the shelter . . . the site, I mean . . . and the pound picked him up. I talked to Charlie last night and he's really hurting. They won't let him keep a dog at the Springfield shelter, and he's afraid the pound will adopt him out—or worse—before he can get back to the Falls."

Bryn brushed her hair off her forehead. What did this have to do with her?

"I'd take him in myself, but I'm allergic like crazy," Susan said. "Would you . . . consider keeping him? Just until we get the shelter up and running?" she added quickly.

"Susan—"

"I've promised Charlie his job back the minute we have a place. And I've got a couple of strong prospects." Susan's voice lifted on a hopeful note. "It might only be for a few weeks. A couple of months at the outside . . ."

"Susan, we're not supposed to . . ." She'd started to say that the townhome association didn't allow dogs in the complex, but that wasn't true. In fact, she and Adam had talked about getting a dog. A pet to keep Bryn company while Adam worked long shifts. There was a fee for keeping a pet, but it wasn't much. She owed Charlie at least that much, didn't she? "I guess I could take him. For a little while."

"Oh, thank you. You just don't know how much that will mean to Charlie."

"Do I need to go pick him up?"

"Would you mind? I'd do it, but then I'd be out of commission for two days sneezing and puffed up like a balloon."

"I'll do it. Does it cost something to get a dog out of hock?"

"I don't think so. Charlie promised his shots are up-to-date, and I know he's been neutered. Sparky . . . not Charlie," she added quickly, giggling.

Bryn envied her ability to laugh. "I'll go get him this afternoon. What time do they close?"

"Probably five, but I can check and get back to—"

"It's okay. I've got to take a shower, but I can get there by one in case they close early."

"You're a lifesaver. I'll let Charlie know. He'll love you forever."

69

"Yeah, right." Bryn clamped her mouth shut, afraid her tone would make Susan ask questions.

But she just laughed. "Thanks, Bryn. I really do appreciate it. Listen, I want to have you and Jenna and Emily Vermontez over soon. Do you think it would be too awkward if I invited Garrett Edmonds, too?"

"No," she said, not knowing what else to say. Was Susan planning some big group grief therapy session or something? The whole thing would be awkward.

"I don't know if everyone will be on board, but I'd like to put something together to honor our guys when we open the shelter again. You know . . . a memorial or something."

Susan was obviously dealing with her grief by throwing herself into this new project. Bryn admired that deeply about her. Envied her. But she wasn't sure she could pretend. "Have you heard from anybody else . . . besides Charlie?"

"Community Christian took Linda and the kids in. They're providing temporary housing in one of their member's rental homes, and providing meals and clothes for the kids until Linda can get back on her feet."

"Oh. That's good." Hanover Falls CC was the church she and Adam attended—well, on the rare occasions when they got up early enough to go to church.

"Tony X and Bobby and most of the other guys

are in Springfield," Susan continued. "But the shelters there are overflowing. There's no promise they can stay more than a few days, and, of course, they're starting all over in their job searches. That's why I want to get back up and running as soon as we can. Since we're not a residence shelter, I'm hoping some of the churches will step up to the plate. But I'm not having much luck so far."

"I can imagine. They're probably not crazy about the idea of these guys sleeping in their Sunday school rooms."

"I don't think it's that as much as them being super sensitive about code violations and liability after what hap—" Susan's voice cut out, but a second later she came back on. "Sorry, Bryn, but I've got another call coming in. It's Davy. He's . . . really struggling. I probably better take this."

Susan and Dave's elder son was spending his first year of college out of state, and Susan had confided that Davy threatened to quit school after his dad's funeral. She'd convinced him to go back, but it was apparently a daily challenge for the kid.

Bryn rested her head in her free hand under the weight of that knowledge. "Don't worry about Sparky, Susan. I'll take care of him."

In slow motion, she set the phone in its cradle. But something stirred inside her. A tiny spark of hope. For the first time since the funeral, she had an assignment—something with purpose to do.

She grabbed a clean towel out of the dryer and headed down the hall for the shower.

6

Wednesday, November 14

HANOVER FALLS, Mo. (AP)—Fire investigators have not ruled out arson as they continue to investigate a tragic fire that destroyed a homeless shelter and left five Missouri firefighters dead and one seriously wounded. The blaze, which started on the second floor of the former hospital building in this south-central Missouri town, was fueled by dozens of mattresses that had been stored in the building. The fire and resultant explosions completely destroyed the building.

Police Chief Rudy Perlson said a homeless man who had checked into the shelter around October 15 is missing after the fire. The man, known to shelter employees as Zeke Downing, is wanted for questioning. Perlson said there is a warrant for a man by that name in Coyote County, Kan. The man is wanted on several charges, including burglary and receiving stolen property. However, records from the Grove Street

Homeless Shelter in Hanover Falls were destroyed in the fire, and officials were unable to confirm if the missing man is the same Zeke Downing wanted in Kansas.

Police are also seeking another man for questioning. James Daniel Friar was evicted from the shelter last month and arrested for assaulting another shelter resident.

The shelter's director, Susan Marlowe, whose husband, Lieutenant David Marlowe, is one of the fallen firefighters, said the description of the man wanted in Kansas matches that of the man missing from the shelter, but without the shelter's records, there is no way to verify. A volunteer from the shelter remembered that Downing had been reluctant to turn over his identification and refused to be photographed in compliance with the shelter's policy until Marlowe threatened to refuse him admission.

Only two weeks after her husband's tragic death, Marlowe is working to reopen the Grove Street Shelter at a new location in Hanover Falls. Marlowe opened the original shelter two years ago, buying the former Clemens County Hospital building from the city for a token fee. The shelter—an overnight-only facility—was funded by donations from area churches that also provide meals for an estimated 15 to 20 clients daily. Marlowe receives no salary, and the shelter was staffed solely by volunteers.

• • •

Garrett drained his coffee mug, folded the newspaper, and tossed it into the trash along with his uneaten bagel. Molly's name had ceased being listed in stories about the fire. At first she'd been singled out because she was the only female firefighter who died in the tragedy. Now his wife was one of five nameless people who'd lost their lives. Five nameless heroes who would be forgotten by the time spring came to the Falls.

He rinsed his mug and added it to the overflowing stack in the sink. He hadn't done dishes in a week. But then, there weren't many dishes to do. He hadn't eaten more than a few bites since the fire. His appetite was gone.

At least he was off the pills. The prescription—Rick's prescription—had helped him get through the first few days while he was in shock, almost out of his mind with grief and fear. But he had to get back to living at some point.

Next week, to be precise.

He'd told his principal he'd be back to work on Monday. How he could ever stand in front of his fifth graders and talk to them about what had happened, he didn't know.

He still choked up every time he thought about seeing those kids file in to the auditorium the day of the funeral. They'd looked so grown up. So somber. He'd been too out of it to appreciate their presence that day, but he was touched that Mrs.

Cassman and Mary had made arrangements to get the kids there. He'd organized enough field trips over the years to know what a feat it must have been.

Somehow, thinking about his fifth graders spurred him to action. He flipped off the kitchen light, grabbed his jacket off the back of a chair, and headed out to his truck.

Five minutes later, he parked at the curb in front of Station 2, Clemens County Fire District. He leaned over the steering wheel and rubbed at the three-day stubble on his face, trying to erase the barrage of memories assaulting him. He could almost imagine that Molly would come walking through those bay doors, hair bouncing in her workday ponytail, face dewy with perspiration, still wearing her warm-ups and T-shirt with the fire station logo.

He inhaled and put a fist to his chest, trying to stave off the physical pain her memory still provoked.

He climbed out of the truck and strode up the walk, following the spicy aroma of spaghetti sauce past the bunk room, to the break room. When the firemen spotted him, he was besieged.

"Hey, man, how's it going?" Jake Young, who'd been on Molly's team that night, shook Garrett's hand, and the others lined up for a turn to offer sympathy, including a couple of the rookies he didn't know. They must have come on since the fire. But he was Molly's family, and that made him family to these guys.

The pain ratcheted up a notch. But he thanked these men who'd loved Molly like a sister, and he lied through his teeth about how he was doing without her.

"Is Brennan around?" he asked, after he'd made as much small talk as he could stomach.

"He was out in the south bay a few minutes ago." A young guy—a rookie Garrett didn't know—pointed toward the station's three-bay garage.

Garrett found Peter Brennan with his head under the hood of the station's ambulance. The fire chief wiped his hands on an oily rag, tucked it in his pocket, and shook Garrett's hand.

More sympathy, more stab wounds, but thankfully Chief Brennan didn't linger on the subject for long. "What can I do for you, Garrett?"

Garrett sucked in a breath and blew it out. "What are they doing about finding this Downing guy?"

Brennan narrowed his eyes and frowned. "Downing's just a theory, Garrett. For now, all their energy is going into finding out what caused the fire."

"And what do they think did start it?"

The chief lifted his shoulders and shook his head. "They haven't finished their report."

"What's taking so long?"

"Have you seen the burn site?"

"Yeah, well, it's been two weeks. If they haven't found anything by now, what makes them think they ever will?" He fought to keep his voice down.

"They're working on some leads. They know the fire started on the second floor and—"

"The *Courier* reported that the morning after the fire. They've surely got more than that by now."

"They're doing everything they can. We've got one of the best inspectors in the Midwest working on this. They don't always release everything they know to the public."

"So you know something you're not telling?"

"I didn't say that." Brennan yanked the rag out of his pocket and twisted it between his hands. "Listen, I can assure you we are doing everything humanly possible to find out what—or who—started that fire."

Garrett nodded, forcing himself to calm down. "I know . . . I know. Sorry. I just . . . It's eating at me, you know?"

"I know." Brennan clapped him on the shoulder, started to say something, then seemed to change his mind. But after looking around the bay, he lowered his voice. "Between you and me, I know they've been talking to some other shelters—homeless shelters—from here to Minnesota. Places that guy—Downing—stayed. But apparently he never stayed in one place too long. It was his MO to up and disappear without notice, without checking out of a place. Supposedly he was crazy"—he spiraled his index finger at his temple—"like most of 'em."

"Thanks, Chief. I appreciate it. You'll let me know if anything else comes up?"

"If I can, I will. You have my word."

It was all Garrett could ask of the man.

The November air was crisp, so Garrett pulled up the hood on his sweatshirt. He might soon wish he'd worn a heavier jacket, but the sun was bright and it felt good to be outside. He leaned to one side, stretching, unable to quit thinking about his conversation with Chief Brennan that morning. The red tape was going to drive him straight up a wall. At the rate this investigation was going, that loser—Downing—would be in Canada by the time they finally caught up with him.

He set out at a jog, but it didn't take him long to realize he was sadly out of shape. He'd missed several weeks of the pickup basketball games he and some of the other male teachers played in the gym after school three days a week.

He slowed to a walk, no destination in mind. Anything to keep from sitting at home like a zombie. The apartment he and Molly had rented for the past two years was only a block from the river—a tributary of the Gasconade—and the spot where the "falls" of Hanover Falls were purported to be. According to the city's website, the bluff where the water descended was blasted when the railroad went through and thus ended the namesake of Hanover Falls. A few years ago the city had built a riverwalk on the tributary to serve as a walking/jogging path. He and Molly had walked there almost every evening when she was off duty.

Habit led him in the direction of the river now, and he fought off a swell of intense loneliness. He still couldn't wrap his mind around the idea that Molly was gone. That he'd never see her again this side of heaven. He did believe in heaven, and that offered him the only comfort he'd found these past days. But now he shook off the thought. He didn't want to think about that today . . . any of it. Not even Molly. He was drowning in memories of her, and if he didn't break the surface and think about something else, he wouldn't make it.

He took off jogging again. That was something different. Molly always insisted their walks together should be leisurely strolls. "Walkie-talkies," she called them. Garrett smiled at the remembrance. She could have jogged the distance without breaking a sweat, though. Molly had worked out with the guys at the station and was in better shape than Garrett ever hoped to be—basketball or no.

He lengthened his stride. There he went again, thinking about her. How would he ever cure that?

A shout from behind him left the question unanswered. He turned to see a woman some distance away rounding the corner, arms stretched out in front of her as she tried to keep up with the muscular black Labrador on the end of the leash she clutched in her fist.

"Heel! Heel!" she yelled. If anything, the dog sped up at the command.

Molly would have nudged him and winked, saying, "Oh, look. A dog walking a woman." Garrett laughed out loud, the sound of his own voice causing him to start. How long had it been since he'd laughed? But he knew the answer to that question immediately. Two weeks tomorrow. Since the day Molly died. The memories had started to come like a flood the past couple of days—simple everyday memories of the short life they'd shared together. Mostly he welcomed the reliving. At least until the inevitable moment when he'd be startled again by the realization that Molly was gone. Forever.

The runaway dog came closer, and Garrett shut his mouth, hoping the woman hadn't heard him laughing at her expense. *Wait a minute.* He took a closer look. Wasn't that Bryn Hennesey? Adam's wife?

When the dog came closer, Garrett bent and coaxed the animal to come to him. "Here, boy.

Come here . . ." Thankfully, the dog obeyed, yapping and yanking at the leash, then putting its paws on his shoulders and trying to dance with him. He drew the line when the brute tried to lick his face. Molly would have been delighted. She'd been begging him for a dog since before they were married.

"Who's walking who here?" Garrett looked up at Bryn and smiled. "Ah. It *is* you. I thought I recognized you."

Bryn Hennesey stood in front of him, shoulders heaving, drawing in hard breaths.

"You've got a frisky one here."

She looked up at him from under the fluffy stocking cap she wore. "Thank you for rescuing me." Her shoulders hunched in relief. "I was beginning to think I was going to have to let go of him."

Garrett patted the dog's head. "Settle down, boy." He turned to Bryn again. "What's his name?"

"Sparky. But I'm thinking of changing it to Killer," she deadpanned. She turned to shake an index finger at the animal. "Bad dog, Sparky."

"I noticed he wasn't paying much attention to the 'heel' command. Obedience school dropout?"

"Apparently." She rolled her eyes, but a hint of a smile hid behind them.

His mind raced. He should say something about Adam. How sorry he was. How terrible it all was.

But then she'd feel obligated to say something about Molly, and he'd be right back to where he was when he left the house to escape all that. So he said instead, "How old is Sparkles?"

"Sparky," she corrected, a wry smile tilting her mouth. She shrugged. "I really don't know. He belonged to one of the guys at the shelter. You probably heard they relocated everybody to Springfield? Anyway, Charlie couldn't keep Sparky, so I volunteered. Temporarily."

Garrett knelt in the grass beside the sidewalk and stroked the Lab's thick black coat, surprised at the calming effect his affection seemed to have on the dog. "I'd guess he's still got some puppy in him."

"Well, he'd better grow out of it in a hurry because I can't take these so-called 'walks' much longer."

Garrett laughed, then turned serious. "So . . . how are you doing?"

She looked at him, and he felt something pass between them. They were members of a survivors club. He had a pretty good idea what her life had been like these last two weeks.

"I'm hanging in there," she said. "How about you?"

"The same." He looked out over the water, fighting off a new swell of grief. "It . . . feels good to get out of the house."

"Yeah, it does."

He glanced up at her, methodically stroking the dog. "This your first time out?"

"Monday. That's when I got Sparky."

"Ah . . . you're a couple days ahead of me, then."

"Today's your first day to get out?"

He nodded and rose, brushing shreds of brown grass off the knees of his warm-ups. He reached for the leash. "Can I help you handle this beast?"

"That would be wonderful." She turned the leash over to him, her smile making him glad he'd offered.

Sparky pranced around the two of them until Garrett started walking. Bryn fell in step beside them. They continued along the riverwalk just a hair above walkie-talkie pace. He had to keep a tight rein on the leash to keep Sparky from racing ahead, but when the dog figured out that Garrett wasn't going to give an inch, it seemed to accept that and trotted happily ahead of them.

The smooth surface of the water reflected blue-gray sky and against it, the tracery of naked tree branches that hung over the banks of the river. A skein of geese trailed overhead, their distant *honk honk honk* taking up the silence.

He and Molly had hung out with Adam and Bryn a couple of times last summer—and sometimes with the Morgans, Jenna and Zach. Now Zach was gone, too. It was surreal.

He had a feeling Bryn was having some of the

same thoughts beside him, and he scuffled to land on a lighter topic.

She saved him the trouble, looking up at him with affected exasperation on her pretty face. "Why is it this stupid dog is being an absolute angel for you, but he's Satan incarnate when I'm holding the leash?"

Garrett smiled. "I think he knows he can push you around."

"Well, he's got that right." She shrugged. "Thanks again."

Two joggers came toward them, and Bryn slipped behind Garrett while they passed on the narrow sidewalk. He slowed his pace until she caught up again. They were approaching one of the entrances to the riverwalk, and from the corner of his eye, Garrett noticed a van in the small parking lot across from the riverwalk. There was a logo on the side door he couldn't quite make out, but he'd seen enough similar trucks in the days following the fire—on television and outside his apartment—to make an educated guess about the passengers' intentions.

He lowered his voice and touched Bryn's arm. "Don't be too obvious, but does that van look familiar?"

She snuck a glance and gave a low growl. "It's that reporter from the *Courier*," she whispered. "The guy has been trying to get an interview since the funeral. Do you think he saw us?"

"I don't know, but how about if we do a quick about-face and jog for a few minutes?"

She took his arm lightly, whirled in her tracks, and took off at a graceful lope. The dog was delighted with the change of pace and shot off like he was after a rabbit.

Garrett risked a glance over his shoulder. "Oh, brother . . ." The van was turning around in the lot.

Bryn followed his line of vision. "It looks like they're trying to follow us."

Garrett panned the horizon, scrambling to think where they could go to get away from the invasion that was sure to follow if the occupants of that van had figured out who they were.

There was a little shopping center with a coffee shop and some office buildings a block or two back toward downtown, but they risked crossing paths with the van before they could get there. Besides, they'd be sitting ducks if the reporters followed them to the coffee shop.

Then he remembered a wooded path that ran behind an apartment complex on the other side of the river. He made a visor of his hand and scanned the road. The van had disappeared behind a hedgerow.

"Come on!" He motioned for Bryn to follow him in the direction they'd come from.

7

*B*ryn let Garrett pull her along until they rounded a curve in the sidewalk. She stopped to catch her breath and pan the area, looking for the van that had appeared to be pursuing them.

There it was, back in the parking lot where Garrett first noticed it. "Look!"

Garrett followed her line of site. Just then the passenger side door of the van opened and a long-haired man jumped out and jogged to the edge of the parking lot. He had a camera with a monster lens strapped around his neck, and he cradled it in one hand as he ran.

Bryn turned her face away from the camera.

Garrett pointed to the footbridge that spanned a narrow segment of the river. "Follow me." Yanking on Sparky's leash, he jogged across the bridge, glancing back over his shoulder.

"I'm right here," Bryn assured him.

She stuck close behind as Garrett ran up the sidewalk on the opposite side. He darted between two apartment buildings, yelling over his shoulder. "I know where we can go." Panting, he led the way behind the easternmost building in the complex and into a wooded area.

"There used to be a walking path back here— before they built the riverwalk. It's probably pretty overgrown, but they can't get back here in the van, and I'm betting they won't try to follow us on foot."

Bryn rolled her eyes. "Don't count on it."

"Well, then maybe we need to keep walking."

She nodded her agreement and trudged after him, grateful she wasn't trying to handle Sparky in the dense undergrowth. A carpet of old leaves squished under their feet, and the pungent scent of moss and decay rose up from the mash.

When they'd gone about fifty feet into the woods, Garrett stopped and did a slow 360. "I know there's a better trail here somewhere. At least they won't be able to see us from the road now. You want to just hang out here for a while . . . until we're sure we've ditched them?"

"Sure."

He slowed the pace, letting Sparky stop to sniff every tree and explore the undergrowth. Without the sun to warm them, it was chilly in the shadows of the towering trees. Bryn rubbed her arms briskly.

"You cold?" He unwound the black wool scarf from around his neck and held it out to her.

"You don't need to do that."

"No. Take it. I'm fine."

She did so, just to save an argument. The fabric felt warm and soft against her skin and smelled of wood smoke and something masculine and piney. It smelled like Adam. She gulped in a breath and tried to push the thought aside. "So, have reporters been hounding you, too?"

"At first. I finally just quit answering the phone."

"Me too. I don't know what they want us to say."

He shrugged. "They're just after something that will keep this story going. It's the biggest thing to happen in Hanover Falls since the tornado of 2003."

"Have you heard anything new? About the fire?"

He stuffed his free hand into the pocket of his warm-ups and watched Sparky sniff at a clump of mushrooms. "You mean if they figured out what caused it?"

She held her breath. She'd broached the subject without thinking.

"I doubt they ever find anything conclusive. With that kind of damage, they don't have a lot to go on. They'd be lucky to get a conviction even if they were pretty sure the guy did it. Did you know him?"

"Zeke?" She shook her head. "I was there a few times after he started coming to the center, but I wouldn't say I knew him. I'm not even sure I could pick him out of a police lineup. He had a scruffy beard, and he wore a stocking cap all the time."

Garrett gave a little snort. "Sounds like me . . .

well, until this morning anyway." He ran a hand over his clean-shaven face.

She grinned, remembering how awful she'd looked when Dad dropped by the other day. But her mind was chewing on what Garrett had said. *They don't have a lot to go on . . . doubt they'd get a conviction . . .* His words added a layer to the veneer of consolation she'd built up. There really wasn't any reason to think she had been responsible for that fire. No one—from the media to fire officials to those who were actually there that night—had suggested the possibility that the fire had been started by a candle. Surely they would have known if that were the case.

Maybe she could finally stop racking her brain for that elusive memory. Blowing out a candle was like turning out a light or unplugging the curling iron before you left for work. You did those kinds of things without even thinking. Especially if you were married to a firefighter. That had to be why she couldn't seem to come up with a lucid memory.

"Are you warming up a little?"

Garrett's voice turned her thoughts back to the moment.

"I'm fine. Thanks again." She touched his scarf at her throat.

"I'd suggest we go get a cup of coffee if I wasn't afraid we'd run into our reporter friends again."

She gave a little shake of her head. "No. I don't want to risk that either." She opened her mouth to invite him back to her place for coffee, but the image of him sitting in her kitchen played, and she stopped herself. That would just feel too weird.

"I could really go for something hot to drink about now," he said.

"Mmm . . . me too . . ." She closed her eyes and felt herself warm at the thought.

"I'll just be glad when this whole mess is over." He pulled a brittle leaf from a branch overhead.

"Have you gone back to work? You teach, right?"

He nodded. "Fifth grade. But no . . . I haven't gone back. I'm supposed to Monday. You?"

She swallowed hard. "I have a part-time job at the library. I'll go back next week probably. But I was working at the shelter, too. Volunteering anyway. We were trying to live on Adam's paycheck. I wanted to stay home with our kids."

Confusion clouded Garrett's eyes, and he looked down at her belly. "Are you . . . ?"

"Oh, no . . ." She quickly corrected his assumption. "We were trying, though."

"I'm sorry." He kicked at a pile of twigs.

She shook her head. "I'm thankful I'm not . . . now. That would have made this so much harder." It was true, yet the disappointment that she wasn't pregnant—may never be now—washed over her again.

He nodded, sympathy thick in his gaze, then

peered past her through the trees. "Hey, I think I see the trail."

He forged ahead and Bryn tromped after him to what had obviously been a maintained path at one time. The trail led them deeper into the woods. Time had cluttered the edges with roots and vines, but standing in the middle of the lane, she could see a walkway where trees had been cleared for a path. They followed it a block or two past the apartment buildings until they found themselves behind a gated development that backed up to the woods. There was little chance of those reporters tracking them to here. She felt her shoulders relax.

She reached out a hand for the leash. "Do you want me to take him for a while?"

"I don't mind. Unless you want to practice."

She looked up at him, trying to decide whether he was teasing. But he looked serious, and she decided it wasn't a bad idea, while she had him here to rescue her if Sparky took off again.

Garrett turned the lead over to her, then knelt beside the dog and took its eager face in his broad hands. "Listen, boy. You mind this lady. You hear me? I'm talking to you." He roughed up the dog's head with the manner of someone who'd been around dogs and had great affection for them. Sparky sensed it, too, if the wild wagging of his tail—and his entire hind quarters—was any indication.

She jerked on the leash and tried to mimic

Garrett's tone. "Come on, Sparky. Let's go, boy."

The dog tugged at the leash, testing her, but at Garrett's low command, Sparky quieted and trotted ahead. Bryn kept the rope taut. "Good boy," she said under her breath.

"Thanks." Garrett grinned down at her, sporting an ornery grin.

She laughed and rolled her eyes. "I was talking to the dog."

"How come I did all the work and he gets all the credit?"

"I'm sure you're a good boy, too." Once the words were out, she wanted them back. They felt flirtatious, and too flippant in light of everything that had happened.

But if Garrett noticed, he didn't let on. Instead he pointed ahead, changing the subject. "I think the trail comes out at the street up there. On Portmeyer, if I remember right. We can go around the block and back the long way to your street. They won't be looking for us there."

"Sounds good to me."

It felt good to get back in the sunlight. They let Sparky set the pace and walked briskly through Hanover Falls' older residential district. Beside her, Garrett was quiet, and Bryn took in the ivy-covered porches and the wide, leaf-strewn lawns and let herself imagine what it might be like to raise a family in one of the stately homes Adam had loved so much.

When they reached the development where her building stood, she wished for some excuse to keep from having to go inside the dim, quiet apartment.

Garrett seemed to sense her hesitation. "It felt kind of good to get out, huh?"

"It really did. Except for having to ditch the paparazzi. I'd sure hate to be a movie star."

"You got that right." He shifted from one foot to the other. "Well . . . I guess I'd better get back myself."

"Sure. Thanks again for rescuing me. I'd probably be in the lake about now if you hadn't come along."

He laughed. "I doubt that." He stretched out a hand and let Sparky nuzzle it. "Just use a firm voice and a firm hand. He'll learn to respect that."

"Got it. Thanks again." She fished her keychain from the pocket of her hoodie and searched for the right key.

Garrett scuffed the toe of his tennis shoe on the sidewalk. "Well . . . I'll see you . . ." He waved and took off down the sidewalk at a jog.

As the front door swung open, Bryn remembered she still had his scarf. "Garrett!" she called after him, but apparently he didn't hear her.

She whipped the scarf from around her neck. She didn't want him to think she'd kept it on purpose. She calculated the distance between him and the front door and thought about running to catch up with him, but it had been awkward enough to say good-bye the first time, and Sparky was champing to get to his water bowl.

She went inside and unclipped the dog's leash and filled his bowl. Garrett surely had other scarves. She'd get it back to him another time.

She shrugged out of her coat and hung it on a peg in the entryway. Reaching to loop Garrett's scarf over her coat, she first brought the soft fabric to her nose and inhaled the masculine scent it carried. *Adam.* The house echoed with his absence, hollow without him. She wasn't sure how she could spend another night here alone.

She buried her face in the scarf and gave in to the tears.

8

Monday, November 26

Bryn parked behind a white pickup on the gravel drive at Susan Marlowe's home a mile outside Hanover Falls' city limits. A minivan and another car occupied the space in front of the double garage, and she didn't recognize either. She got out and closed the car door, sighing. She wasn't sure what Susan had planned for the evening, but she hadn't expected a crowd. Whatever this was, though, it beat sitting home another lonely night.

The Marlowes' home was an older farmhouse with a wide wraparound porch. The exterior was dressed up like one of the colorful "painted ladies" row houses Bryn and Adam admired when they'd vacationed in San Francisco last summer. The white clapboard siding was trimmed in shades of deep rose, moss green, and brown. If anyone had described the paint scheme to Bryn, she would have thought it sounded garish. But nestled in the wooded acreage, surrounded by evergreen bushes and rock gardens, the house fit the landscape as if it were another pretty shrub.

Tonight the windows of the old farmhouse glowed with warmth, and the porch still wore Thanksgiving decorations with hay bales serving as tabletops for a colorful arrangement of pumpkins and gourds. Thanksgiving had passed almost without her noticing, thanks to Dad's offering of roast turkey from the deli. But Thanksgiving was essentially a one-day holiday. Now Christmas loomed before her—an entire season. She would have given anything to skip the whole next year on the calendar.

Sighing, Bryn climbed the porch steps and reached for the doorbell, but Susan opened the door before she could press the button.

"Bryn. So good to see you."

"Hi, Susan."

The rich aroma of coffee greeted her as Susan ushered her inside. Dressed in slim black pants and silk tunic, Susan wore a festive apron over the outfit, like something Bryn remembered her grandmother wearing at holiday dinners, but somehow Susan managed to pull off the look with panache. "Come in, come in . . ."

Hearing laughter float from the kitchen at the back of the house, Bryn allowed the knot in her stomach to loosen a bit. She'd been a little afraid she would be the only one to show up tonight. And more afraid of what they would talk about if there was a crowd. She knew the Falls well enough to know that the fire was still a hot topic around town, and this would be her first "public appearance" since the funeral.

She wondered if Jenna would be here. She hadn't talked to her friend since that day she'd stopped by the house. She'd tried to call a couple of times since that day but hadn't made it past voice mail. Jenna hadn't returned her calls, and her two-line replies to Bryn's emails later felt like brush-offs. Bryn missed her friend, but she could take a hint. She wasn't going to play the pushy, smothering girlfriend.

"May I take your jacket?"

"Oh . . . thanks, but I think I'll keep it with me. I'm kind of cold-blooded." And it would be easier to slip out early if she didn't have to search for her jacket in some back bedroom.

"Well, come on back to the kitchen. What can I get you to drink?"

"The coffee smells wonderful." She'd been in Susan's home on several occasions. The shelter director loved to entertain and always seemed to be hosting some kind of event in her home—whether it was a home sales party or a Christmas open house or just a small dinner party to thank the shelter volunteers.

Like the exterior, the inside of the house looked like something from the pages of a magazine. Open, yet cozy with Susan's artistic touches everywhere. It had always struck Bryn as odd that a woman who ran a homeless shelter would care so much about the decor of her own home. But maybe it made perfect sense. Susan no doubt enjoyed and appreciated her house more than most because she knew intimately what it was like to be without a place to call home. This place looked like the very definition of home.

She followed Susan through the foyer past a wide, open staircase and into the kitchen–great room combination.

"Bryn's here, everybody."

"Hi, Bryn." The group greeted her in unison.

She raised a hand in greeting and looked around the warm space. Garrett Edmonds leaned against the frame of the archway between the kitchen and great room. He threw a smile her way, then looked down, swirling the ice in his glass.

Lucas Vermontez, Manny's son who'd been injured in the fire, sat in a wheelchair near the kitchen table. Bryn hadn't seen him since that fateful night. He bore no visible wounds, but his handsome face was thin and wan. Emily, his mother, stood behind his chair and worried over him, smoothing his collar, refilling his Coke.

"We're just waiting for Jenna now," Susan said. "But why don't you bring your drinks, and we'll move to the living room? I'm sure she'll be here any minute, and then we can get started."

It appeared that Susan had gathered the survivors of the fallen firefighters of the Grove Street fire. What was she up to?

Bryn caught Garrett's eye, and he gave a subtle shrug. He didn't know why they were here either.

Susan poured Bryn coffee from a French press, and the group filtered into the front room. Candles were aglow on the coffee table, filling the house with a cinnamon spice scent—and taking Bryn's mind where it didn't want to go. She hadn't lit a candle since the night of the fire.

She chose an overstuffed chair near the fireplace and sat on the edge of the plump cushion, her back straight.

After ten minutes of uneasy small talk, Susan rose and went to stand in front of the hearth. "I'm not sure what happened to Jenna, but I think we'll go ahead and get started."

Bryn had never seen Susan look anything but poised and collected, but there was a slight tremor in her voice as she addressed them now.

"Thank you for coming. It's been a very difficult month for all of you . . . all of us. You have each been in my prayers over these last few weeks. When we become part of the rescue family, we know that we might be asked to make a sacrifice like we've each made. We come in hoping we're prepared, but when our worst fears come true . . ." She sniffed, her eyes brimming. "Well, it's not easy. I'll *keep* you in my prayers for a long time to come."

A murmur of uneasy agreement went up.

Garrett's gaze encompassed the room. "Has anyone heard anything new on the investigation?"

"I spoke with Chief Brennan yesterday," Susan said.

Peter Brennan had been the fire chief as long as Adam had been with the department. He was well respected in the community.

"Peter—" Susan hesitated, as if she'd slipped in referring to him with such familiarity. "Chief Brennan says they may never know for sure how the fire started, but they're working with several possibilities."

"Like what?" Garrett's tone held a challenge.

"Well, they seem to think Zeke Downing's disappearance leaves arson as a strong likelihood. But it could just as easily have been a coincidence—or was unintentional. Bryn can tell you that there were always clients trying to sneak a cigarette or mess with the thermostat or cook with a contraband hot plate. It could have been any number of things."

Bryn shifted uncomfortably in her chair. For a while she'd lived in dread of having to answer more questions. She'd only recently begun to breathe easier as the investigation appeared to be winding down.

"The newspapers keep talking about Zeke as if it's a foregone conclusion that he set the fire." Emily Vermontez spoke in her quiet, steady voice that carried a trace of a Spanish accent. "Why aren't they doing more to catch him?"

Garrett leaned forward. "Yes. Why else would the guy just disappear?" His tone was bitter, but he held his arms out in a way that was more imploring than combative.

"Oh, Garrett . . ." Susan sighed softly. "There are a million reasons any one of our clients wouldn't have wanted to stick around that night. It's not like they were going to collect insurance money or something. These people, if they're not dealing with mental illness or addictions, are there because they're in trouble with the law, or because they've had a falling out with family. There was no reason for any of them to stick around that night. The only thing they were thinking about was where they were going to sleep the next night, where their next meal was coming from—and it obviously wasn't going to be our shelter." She nodded in Bryn's direction.

"Bryn knows how skittish Zeke was about giving us his documents in the first place. People like that have a lot to hide, even if it's only in their own imaginations. The last thing Zeke would have wanted was to talk to the police or some newspaper reporter."

Susan brushed her hands together as if to dismiss the subject. She inhaled and her voice brightened. "Well . . . we should probably get started. You might have guessed why I invited you here tonight . . ."

Bryn let out a breath she hadn't realized she was holding. She and Garrett exchanged looks again. She didn't know why Susan had called them together, and she was glad she wasn't the only one in the dark. Maybe if she hadn't quit watching the news, she wouldn't be so clueless.

"You're probably aware," Susan continued, "that the city has expressed a desire to fund some sort of memorial for our husbands—and Molly, of course." She offered Garrett a sad smile. "For all of the fallen heroes. And that's what they are. Heroes. And because our loved ones were truly heroic, I hope you'll agree that they would be far more honored by a memorial that goes beyond a bronze statue or a plaque on some courthouse wall. What I have in mind is a living memorial of sorts."

"I know some of you have already given your efforts to the shelter." She looked pointedly at

Bryn. "How's it going with Sparky, by the way? Bryn took in one of our client's dogs," she explained to the others.

Bryn laughed. "He's a little . . . feisty. But we're managing okay."

Garrett caught her eye and gave her a knowing wink.

"I know Charlie really appreciates what you're doing," Susan said.

Bryn managed an embarrassed shrug. "I'm glad to do it." It was true. Sparky had provided a much-needed diversion—in spite of the fact that he could be trouble with a capital *T*.

"Anyway," Susan continued. "I'm hoping you all agree that getting the shelter back up and running again should be a priority."

Lucas shifted in his wheelchair, and his mother leaned over him, whispering something in his ear.

Susan seemed not to notice. "If you do agree, I'd like to ask the city to put the funds they would spend on some useless memorial into an account to fund the new shelter."

"New shelter?" Garrett's brow wrinkled. "Have you found a place to reopen the facility?"

Susan shook her head. "Not yet, I'm afraid. But only because we have no funds. The old building was minimally insured, and we won't have those funds anyway . . . at least not until the fire investigators finish their report. But thanks to the local churches and volunteers, we ran the first shelter on almost no budget. Once we have the building—and some beds . . . the bare necessities—we can go back to the way we were, with volunteers providing staff and meals."

Emily Vermontez straightened in her chair beside Lucas. "I'm not sure I understand what it is you are asking of us."

Susan's smile was smug as she rose and went to a large oak desk in an alcove created by the room's bay window. She picked up a folder and began distributing its contents around the room.

Bryn skimmed the two-page document. It was a petition of sorts, stating what Susan had just reported and verifying that the signee was in favor of a living memorial for the fallen firefighters.

Susan cleared her throat. "The shelter simply won't happen without some funding, and I know the city will consider the request much more strongly if all of us—the survivors—are on board. I'm not asking you to sign anything or make any commitments tonight. If you'd please just take this home and read through it, and then either get the petitions back to me or deliver them yourself to the city offices. Does anyone have questions?"

"Not to go back to a closed subject," Garrett said, "and I admit I haven't kept up with the news the last couple of weeks . . . but has anyone said when they think the fire investigators will have anything conclusive?"

Bryn's senses went on alert. ___ h___ made Garrett ask that question wher___ ___'d ___ready talked about possible causes of t___ ___?

Susan started to speak, then ___sitated. She looked around the room as if offering the others a chance to answer first. When no one did, she frowned. "Frankly, I doubt the investigators' report will turn up anything we haven't already heard in the news. Obviously, they consider Zeke Downing a person of interest. They think his disappearance is too much to be coincidental." She shrugged. "Whether they can prove it is another thing."

Garrett fanned his copy of the petition in front of him. "It seems a little unlikely the city would do anything concrete until they know the results of the investigation. I just wonder if we might be jumping the gun with this."

Bryn's breathing returned to normal but accelerated again when Susan glared at Garrett.

"I am not going to wait on that report." Susan's voice rose an octave. "Our clients are sitting on waiting lists in Springfield and even St. Louis. These are people—some of them—with family in this area. You can't put out birdseed in September and then quit feeding the birds in November!"

Bryn was still trying to decipher Susan's metaphor when the director proffered an explanation. "We offered a service and made our clients dependent on us. Now we've left them hanging."

"It's not as though you did it intentionally." Garrett's voice was soothing. "I understand your concern, S ... . I didn't mean to sound argumentative ... under how easy it—"

"Of course, Garrett. I'm sorry. I . . ." Susan put a hand to her mouth, obviously trying to gain control of her emotions. "I'm sorry."

Now Garrett looked embarrassed. "No apology necessary. I understand. It's a good cause. I'm not arguing that."

"All I ask is that you consider this." Susan held up a copy of the petition. "And . . . until we get the petition together, I'd ask that you please keep it within this group." Her gaze panned the room. "I'm sure I don't have to tell any of you that the media is still skulking around the Falls, looking for anything that smells like a story. I'd rather they not get hold of this one until we have something solid to tell."

Emily Vermontez shook her head and rolled her eyes. "I don't know about the rest of you, but I've about had it with the reporters. They had the gall to follow us into Luc's therapy session last week."

"I thought I was just being paranoid," Bryn admitted. "But I've been afraid to answer my phone."

The others murmured knowingly, and Bryn took comfort in discovering she wasn't the only one getting the calls.

Emily stood and tapped on the brake locks of her son's chair, looking pointedly at him. "Thanks for inviting us, Susan, but I think we need to be going." She took Lucas's copy of the petition from his lap and tucked it with hers into her purse. "We'll read this over and get back to you."

Susan sighed. With the two of them leaving, the meeting was essentially over almost before it began. "I'll get your coats." She hurried from the room, swiping at her cheeks.

An awkward silence settled over the four of them until Susan reappeared a moment later—dry-eyed—with two coats over her arm.

They watched as Emily helped her son with his sleeves. The young man hadn't spoken two words the entire evening and had sat mostly with his head bowed as if he were dozing. Or praying.

Susan held the door while Garrett helped Emily maneuver Lucas's chair through. Bryn took the opportunity to collect empty drinking glasses and carry them to the kitchen. When she was finished, she gathered her purse and went out onto the porch where the others were calling out good-byes to the Vermontezes.

"I didn't mean to chase anyone off," Susan said, frowning.

"Oh, no." Garrett waved off her apology. "I needed to be going anyway. Papers to grade."

"Me, too. Thanks for having us, Susan. I'll get

back to you. I really appreciate you getting the ball rolling on this."

"Thanks, Bryn. And thanks again for taking Sparky in. Charlie was so relieved when I told him."

"No problem." She waved over her shoulder and hurried to her car, just wanting to get home.

But she heard footsteps behind her, and Garrett called after her. "A little white lie, huh?"

Keys at the ready, she turned to face him. "Excuse me?" Her breath formed puffs of steam in the cold night air.

"Back there." He hooked a thumb toward the house. "What you told Susan . . ."

She stared at him, her brain racing to recall what she'd said that would make him accuse her of being a liar.

9

Leaning against her white Honda Accord, fumbling with her keys, Bryn stared at Garrett, her brow knit, eyes narrowed. "I . . . I'm not sure what you mean?"

"I distinctly heard you tell Susan that Sparky was no problem." He grinned, remembering the image of her sailing along the riverwalk tethered to the black Lab's leash last week.

Even in the dim glow of the porch light, he

could see the hangdog smile spread across her face. "It wasn't a *complete* lie. He is getting better. Slowly."

He laughed. "Glad to hear it."

"Yep, he only dragged me three blocks today before I reined him in."

Garrett put his head back and laughed louder.

Her smile turned to a giggle. "Yeah, yeah, go ahead and laugh. But he really is kind of growing on me. At least he forces me to get out of the house."

"That's good." His smile faded and he reached to touch the sleeve of her coat, then caught himself. "Sorry . . . I just had to give you a hard time."

"I know. I probably wouldn't have been able to resist if the tables were turned."

They joked back and forth, laughing about that day they'd outfoxed the TV reporters. The conversation reached a comfortable lull, and he turned serious, glad for a chance to have caught her alone. "So, what do you think of Susan's proposal?"

"The 'shelter as memorial' you mean?" She chalked quotations marks in the air.

He nodded.

She shrugged. "Like she said, I think it beats a plaque or statue downtown. I'm just not sure the city will get behind it. If you saw how . . ." She studied the gravel beneath their feet. "Let's just say, if the city gets involved, there would be a few regulations we'd have to comply with that we weren't exactly up to code on before. And I'm not sure Susan would be willing to go along."

Curious, he eyed her. "Like what?"

"Like . . ." She gave a hollow laugh. "Like just about everything. Every single meal we ever served there was provided by a church or an individual. There's no way all the kitchens that food was prepared in would pass inspection. The menu wouldn't meet USDA guidelines most nights. And even though the upper floors of the hospital were handicap accessible, the majority of the shelter was housed in the basement. We cobbled a ramp together for Charlie—Sparky's 'dad.' He's in a wheelchair," she explained. "But it wasn't much more than a slab of plywood on the stairway, and if he'd ever overturned his chair on that—or if one of the able-bodied clients tripped on it—and the city was involved, they'd probably be sued for everything they're worth."

"Wow. I didn't realize. So I take it you're not in favor of Susan's suggestion?"

"It depends, I guess. If she's just asking the city for a one-time gift—start-up money or whatever—with no ties, then I think it could work. But Susan ran the shelter as a ministry, not an institution. She couldn't have kept the place open one week if she'd had to worry about state and federal regulations."

"I see your point." He tried to imagine how Susan must feel. "It must be hard. She didn't just lose her husband, she lost the thing she was passionate about, too. The rest of us can throw ourselves into our work—" He stopped short. "Sorry . . . I guess you're kind of in the same shoes as Susan Marlowe."

Bryn bit her lip. "I don't know. I'm not sure what I'm . . . passionate about."

"If you volunteered your time to the shelter, you must have felt pretty strong about it. That's not exactly the kind of thing people jump into for fun."

She closed her eyes, and a sigh escaped her throat. "I wish I could say my work at the shelter was my passion. And I did—*do*—have a special place in my heart for Charlie and some of the other clients I got to know. But, I don't know . . . I'm not sure I feel passion about anything these days." The words rolled out quickly, like she was confessing to a crime.

Hearing them, an odd sense of relief washed over him. "Thank you for saying that."

She peered up at him from beneath hooded eyes. "What do you mean?"

"It's how I've felt lately, too. I mean, I love my students, and I think teaching is where I'm still supposed to be. But . . . it all seems pretty meaningless without Molly." He looked at his shoes. "Everything, not just teaching."

Bryn nodded, and Garrett recognized the same glaze of sadness in her eyes that he saw when he looked in the mirror every morning.

She pulled her coat tighter around her. "I keep waiting for it to get . . . better."

"Yeah. Me too. When do you think that might happen?"

She gave a humorless laugh.

"Listen . . ." He felt like he had the first time he'd climbed the ladder to the high dive and stood poised to jump. Did he dare ask her? But he'd already opened his mouth. May as well take the plunge. "Do you want to go get a cup of coffee?" He made a show of looking down the wooded lane that was Susan Marlowe's driveway. "I don't think the paparazzi is tailing us tonight."

That earned him genuine laughter. "Coffee sounds good."

He brushed off the guilt that tapped him on the shoulder and nodded toward his truck. "You want to ride with me?"

Bryn looked toward the house, where lights still glowed behind the windows. "It might be easier if I just follow you."

He knew how she felt. He couldn't shake the feeling that he was cheating on Molly. And maybe it was too soon to be asking any woman to coffee, but it sure beat going home to an empty house again.

He drove slowly, checking the rearview mirror

every few seconds to be sure Bryn was behind him. The Falls didn't have a lot of choices when it came to coffee shops, but the lights were on at the Java Joint, and there were a couple of cars out front. He turned in and chose a parking spot across from the building, leaving an empty stall in front of the shop for Bryn.

She eased the Accord into the space while he stood waiting.

Soft jazz drifted out the door when he opened it, holding it for Bryn. She ordered a hot chocolate. He decided on decaf and paid for both.

"You didn't have to do that," she said, looking embarrassed.

"I know, but I wanted to."

"Thanks." The smile she offered him didn't do anything to assuage the guilt that was still sitting on his shoulder.

They stood at the counter watching the barista fix their drinks. Once the warm cups were in hand, Bryn gravitated to a table in the corner at the back of the shop. She took the seat with her back to the door. He pulled out the chair across from her, feeling uneasy being here with a woman who wasn't his wife. And hoping he didn't run into fifty people he knew here tonight.

But business was apparently slow on Monday nights, and after ten minutes, no one at all had come in, let alone anyone either of them knew. He got caught up in their conversation and forgot to worry about being seen with a woman who wasn't Molly.

Bryn was back on the subject of resurrecting the homeless shelter. "I really hope Susan can make it work."

"Would you go back to volunteering there if she does?"

"Probably. I guess it would depend on what I end up doing about a real job. I really need to find something full-time. But yes, I think I'd want to work in the shelter again. A little like getting back on the horse . . ." Her voice trailed off, and he knew she was thinking about the night of the fire.

"I guess it would be kind of scary? Going back?"

"A little. But it's not like it'd be the same building . . . probably not even the same site."

His face must have reflected the skepticism he was feeling. She tilted her head and studied him. "What?"

He shrugged. "Nothing."

She gave him the same look Molly would have at that kind of answer. "Your expression doesn't look like it's nothing."

"I just don't see the community getting behind this. Between the assault and the fire—"

"You knew about that?"

"The assault?"

She nodded, her brown eyes growing darker.

"It was in the papers." A frightening thought

struck him. "That . . . it wasn't you, was it? That the guy tried to—"

"Oh, no. No, it was another volunteer. But—" she frayed the edge of her napkin between her fingers, "Adam didn't want me to have anything to do with the shelter after that happened."

"I don't blame him."

She blew out a little breath, sounding frustrated. "I was safe there. That guy's probably in jail."

"No, he wasn't. Not according to the newspaper, anyway."

"Maybe, but there are a hundred others like him out there. And in a higher concentration at a shelter, unfortunately. You don't know who you can trust."

"But that's true walking down Main Street in the Falls!"

He leaned back from the table, holding up his hands in mock surrender.

"Sorry." She gave him a wry smile. "For a minute there I felt like I was having the same old argument again."

"He said the same thing? Adam?" Garrett hadn't known Adam Hennesey well. He'd always thought the guy came off as a little cocky, but Molly had liked Adam, and Garrett trusted her assessment of people.

Bryn nodded, tearing up.

"Sorry . . . I'm sorry. Let's change the subject."

"No, it's okay. I should have listened to him. He

was just worried about me. Once we started talking about having a baby, he turned into a big fat worrywart. Maybe if I'd listened . . ." She wept softly, dabbing at her eyes with a paper napkin.

Garrett looked away, wishing he could kick himself. What was he thinking? "Listen, Bryn . . . I'm sorry," he said again. He reached to touch her arm, then drew his hand away, feeling awkward.

She shook her head. "You didn't say anything wrong. I'm just . . . I get this way a lot lately."

"Don't think I don't understand."

"I know you do. Thanks." She blew her nose on the napkin and looked up at him. "So you don't think the shelter has much chance of reopening?"

He took her cue to change the subject. "I just think people are going to be a little leery after everything that's happened. And I think most people are convinced the fire was arson—I don't think people are going to be too crazy about bringing that element back to town. I've heard enough buzz at school . . . I think people are relieved to be rid of the place."

Her eyes widened, the flecks of gold in them sparking. "They surely don't say that to you?"

"You mean because of Molly?"

She nodded, looking aghast.

"That probably didn't come out right. I'm not saying anybody is glad the fire happened so we could get rid of the deadbeats, the more that they're seeing this as one good thing that's come of the fire."

She looked up at him from beneath dark lashes. "You sound like you agree."

He thought for a minute, not wanting to insert his big foot in his mouth again. "It's hard for me to get too excited about reopening the place where my wife died. Like you said, I know it won't be the same exact spot. But I'm finding it hard to separate the two. I know we have a need for a place like that, though. I don't think anyone is disputing that."

"Yes. It's sad that in a town this small we would need a shelter."

"And that's just it. I think the people who are opposed to reopening the shelter have the idea that if we don't open a shelter, the homeless will just go away. But it doesn't work that way. 'The poor you will always have with you . . . ,'" he quoted.

"The Bible, right?"

"Hey, I'm impressed. It's in the book of John. Deuteronomy, too, and twice in Matthew."

Her perfectly shaped brows went up in unison. "Now *I'm* impressed."

"Don't be." He gave a little laugh and tried to look appropriately humble. "It was in the sermon at church yesterday."

"Ah. Okay, I'm not quite so impressed. But hey,

it shows ʹɾ   re paying attention." She smiled. "Where ᴄ you go to church?"

"We—I . . . we . . ." He groped for the right pronoun and finally gave up. "Molly and I had just started going to Community Christian. Mike Mitchard is the pastor."

"Yeah, I know. That's where we . . . went."

"Really? I haven't seen you there."

She looked sheepish. "We weren't exactly regulars. I haven't been since . . ."

She didn't need to finish the sentence. He nodded. "It was hard for me to go that first time, too . . . After Molly—" He felt himself choking up and dragged in a breath, trying to stave off the emotion. "But with her working so many weekends, I came by myself quite a bit. I had my posse to sit with."

Bryn wrinkled her nose. "Posse?"

"That's what Molly called my teacher friends. She used to always say I had more girl friends than she did." He affected a cringe. "It was true. She had the guy friends and I had the girl friends."

She looked at him askance.

"Take it easy. Most of my women friends are old enough to be my mother. Or at least an older sister. And I do have a few guys I play basketball with—and baseball in the summer. Don't worry, I'm a manly man."

She laughed.

But he wanted to be sure she understood. "My teacher friends . . . I don't know how I'd have made it through these last weeks without them. They're the best."

"You're really lucky, Garrett."

"I'm blessed is what I am."

She frowned. "How can you say that . . . after what happened?"

"What happened doesn't change the fact that God has blessed me with some very dear friends."

She sighed. "Jenna—Zach's wife—and I were friends."

"Were?"

Sadness shadowed her features. "Except for a couple of emails, I've only talked to her once since the funeral."

"How come?"

Bryn stared up at a painting on the wall above the windows. "I don't know. I know part of it is that she's been staying with her in-laws, and the two of them went to visit Zach's sister some-where on the West Coast for a while. But even before then, she seemed to be avoiding me. Maybe I remind her too much of everything that happened. I just—" She shrugged. "I don't think things will ever be the same."

"She'll come around. Give her time."

She looked skeptical, and he shut up. He suddenly felt too weary for this conversation. They'd all lost so much.

"Do you . . ." Bryn seemed to consider something, then started again. "Do you think Lucas is okay?"

"Vermontez? Why do you ask?"

"I don't know. Tonight he seemed awfully . . . quiet. A little slow, even. Did you notice?"

"Slow, as in brain damaged?"

"I'm not sure. Not that I knew him that well before, but he was always so outgoing. Always smiling, pulling pranks."

He nodded. "Oh yeah, Molly was always coming home still laughing about some crazy thing Lucas had done. You don't think it . . . messed him up in the head or something, do you?"

"Oh . . . I don't think so. I think he's just—" Again, a shadow crossed her face. "I'm sure it's hard for him to accept that his dad is gone. Manny was everybody's hero. I'm sure he was all the more that for Lucas."

"I hope that's all it is."

"Grief looks different on everybody. And Lucas didn't just lose his dad. He lost his career . . . at least for a while."

"I wonder if they think he'll ever walk again?"

That faraway look she wore so often clouded her eyes again, as if she hadn't thought about that possibility before. "Dear God, I hope so . . ."

10

"*T*hanks for the hot chocolate." Bryn hitched her purse up on her shoulder and reached for the door, feeling self-conscious, almost like she was on a date and wondering if the guy would try to kiss her good night . . . or more.

She avoided Garrett's eyes as he held the door for her. Being with him made her realize how much she'd missed a masculine voice, a man's touch. It had been almost a month since anyone had kissed her, and right now she missed Adam so much she ached.

Despite the frigid night air, heat rushed to her cheeks at the thought. The parking lot was almost empty, and the door closed on the mellow jazz and opened on the sounds of late-night traffic. She looked at her watch. *10:15.* They'd been here for almost two hours. The minutes had flown, and she'd enjoyed the time with Garrett immensely. For the first time in a long time, she'd felt halfway normal. Sure, they'd talked about the fire and about Adam—and Molly—but it wasn't what she'd come to think of as "grief talk" so much as just sharing their thoughts and experiences. It was a relief to be with someone she didn't have to explain everything to.

More than anything it was nice to laugh again.

She liked that about being with Garrett. With him, she could laugh without feeling guilty. She had a feeling he felt the same about her.

"Thanks again for the drink—" She stopped short, realizing she was repeating herself.

Garrett seemed not to notice. "Good luck with the job search."

"Thanks."

He backed away to his car, waving and watching, she knew, to be sure she got safely in her car. Like Adam would have done. She fumbled with her keys, opened the door, and hurried to climb behind the wheel.

But she didn't want to go home. It was bedtime, but she knew sleep wouldn't come. Especially after the caffeine she'd consumed. Sparky would probably want to go out. But she'd let him out before she left for Susan's, and he'd never had an accident in the house. He could wait a while.

Watching the blinker on Garrett's truck in her rearview mirror, she turned the opposite direction and meandered through the mostly empty streets of town. Almost without thinking about where she was going, she realized she was tracing the route to the homeless shelter—or at least the site where it had been. Since the night of the fire, she'd rearranged her route to avoid the scene of the tragedy. Between the television and newspapers, she'd seen enough images of the ruins to last a lifetime.

She considered turning around in a driveway and hightailing it out of there, but now seemed as good a time as any to get it over with. Maybe under the cloak of night, it would be easier than in stark daylight.

Slowing the car, she peered through the windshield, watching for the boxy building that had always been her landmark. A strange sense of disorientation overtook her when she realized she was directly in front of the lot where the shelter used to be. The sky gaped empty in front of her like the space a missing tooth used to fill. The skeleton of steel beams was gone.

She started to turn into what had once been the parking lot, but police tape stretched across the driveway between two iron rods staked on either side, blocking her way. She pulled forward and eased her car along the curb.

According to the papers, after the fire inspectors had finished their work, the city had dozed the site, hauling off what debris hadn't been burned up or buried in the crater the explosion had forged.

Bryn turned off the engine and sat, waiting. For what, she wasn't sure. If she thought too hard—about how this was the last place she'd seen Adam alive, about how many heroes had lost their lives on this hallowed ground, about the last hours she'd spent inside that building . . .

She rolled the car window down, hoping the brisk air would force the thoughts away. Instead the acrid scent of charred wood stung her nostrils and carried her back to that night. She closed her eyes, but the images played on. The crack of the flames, the roar of the explosion, the shouts of the rescue crews were as clear in her ears as if it were happening all over again. She squeezed her eyes tighter, but the images wouldn't leave. One by one, she saw the bodies being carried from the building and lined up in the parking lot.

For one panicked moment, she was paralyzed. By force of will, she moved her hands to her face and forced her eyes open with her fingertips. Her hands trembled, and her breath came in uneven gasps. She never should have come here. She had to get away from this place. *Now.* She fumbled for the keys, but her hands were shaking too hard.

A sound from the direction of the ruins made her look up.

A streetlamp half a block away provided the only light, but a shape moved amid the canted shadows on the ground. Her heart stuttered, and she quickly rolled up her window and started the car. But reason won out and instead of driving off, she put the car in reverse and backed up a few feet, aiming her headlights at the lot.

A short-legged, squatty dog stared back at her, its eyes glowing in the reflection from the head-lamps. She gave a short blast of the horn, but the animal just stood there, hunkered down like it was challenging her.

She backed around to the entrance of the parking lot and considered driving through the tape. But, afraid the debris from the building might puncture a tire, she stopped at the edge of the drive, angling her headlights for a better look.

The dog stood like a soldier guarding his post. It had a broad chest and a low-to-the-ground build, like a bulldog breed, but its face looked skinny and its eyes were hollow. This dog was hungry, maybe starving. She glanced around the interior of her car, wishing she had some food to toss the animal.

She tooted the horn again. The dog trotted forward, stopped ten feet in front of her car, and cocked its head at her.

She knew this dog! It was Boss, the little bulldog Zeke Downing had kept at the shelter. In spite of his starved appearance, the pup had grown since she'd seen him last, but she was almost positive it was Boss. His brindled coloring was the same, and something about the way he looked at her made her think he recognized her, too. Surely he hadn't been hanging around here since the fire.

Bryn peered through the windshield. There were a few lights on in the houses of a neighborhood to the south, and she could see the faint glow of neon from downtown to the west. But across the street in the office parking lot where they'd huddled the night of the fire, not even a streetlamp illuminated the night.

She opened the car door and climbed out, keeping the door as a shield between her and the dog. "Boss? Is that you? What are you doing out here, boy? Are you hungry?"

He gave a little whine and took a tentative step toward her, his head down in submission. All fear vanished, and Bryn closed the car door and approached the dog. She spoke his name softly. "Come here, Boss. It's okay. You know me, don't you, boy?"

When she was close enough, she held her hand out, palm down, and let the dog make the first contact. He pushed hard against her hand with his muzzle, whimpering excitedly now.

"You're hungry, aren't you? Poor baby . . ."

The stubby tail started to wag, and Bryn dropped to one knee to take the pup's face between her hands. She felt around his neck. No collar. Susan had made Zeke get Boss's shots up to date, and buy a collar for his tags. Still, she was almost positive this was the same dog.

Scratching behind his ears, she talked to him the way she talked to Sparky.

Sparky. Oh, brother. What had she gotten herself into? No way could she take Boss home. Besides the fact that she was already pushing it to have one dog in the development, Boss and Sparky had a history. She was worried enough about how she'd work out the schedule with Sparky once she found a full-time job. But maybe two dogs would be better than one. They could keep each other company.

An image of Charlie and Zeke Downing trying to break up the fight between their two dogs outside the shelter made her toss out that idea. Maybe her dad would take Boss. At least until they could find another home for the pup.

She smoothed a hand down his back and cringed, feeling the greasy, clumped fur—and worse, the jagged crenellations of his spine beneath her palm. She had to get some food into this little guy.

The pup didn't resist as she wrestled him into her arms. She carried him to the car and put him on the floor mat in the backseat. When she got behind the wheel, he pushed his nose between the front seats and nuzzled her elbow.

As she started out of town to her father's house in the country, she checked the clock on the dashboard. It would be after ten thirty by the time she got there. Dad was probably already in bed. Besides, the more she thought about it, the more she realized it was a bad idea to ask him to take the dog. He was in a constant battle to keep his blood pressure down, and that had caused other health issues. Though Dad rarely talked about his condition or complained about his pain, she'd snooped in his medicine cabinet and knew that besides his blood pressure medicine and nitroglycerin tablets, he was taking a prescription for his heart. She would never forgive herself if something happened to Dad because of trying to take care of Boss.

But she didn't dare try to take the dog to her place. Maybe she could leave him in the car overnight while she decided what to do. She looked over her shoulder at Boss, who now rested his saggy jowls on the backseat. A dark stain of drool spread out underneath him. No way. She wouldn't *have* a car by morning if she left Boss inside it.

Garrett? She wasn't even sure where he lived. She and Adam had been to a Super Bowl party at Garrett and Molly's apartment a couple of years ago, and she thought he still lived in the same complex, but she couldn't remember which building. She dialed 4-1-1 and asked for his information.

"I can dial that number for you," the operator said.

She hesitated. Did she really want to drag Garrett into this? Would he be willing to consider taking in a stray? But before she could talk herself out of it, she told the operator, "Yes, please."

11

"*H*ello?" His voice warmed Bryn somehow.

"Garrett? Hi. I hope I didn't wake you. It's Bryn," she added quickly.

"No, just doing laundry. What's up?"

"I have a . . . huge favor to ask."

"Okay . . ."

"You're going to think I'm crazy, but is there any way you'd consider taking in a cute little puppy?"

"Excuse me?" The smile she heard in his voice gave her hope.

"I, um . . . sort of adopted a stray on my way home."

"What?" He sounded bemused.

"I picked up a stray dog, a little bulldog pup. He's really adorable, but um . . ." She worked up her most winsome pleading voice, knowing she needed to tell him the truth about Boss. But she'd let them meet first, let Garrett warm up to the pup before she sprang the history on him. She cleared her throat. "The thing is, he and Sparky have a history, and I don't think there's any way I can bring him home. I can take him to the pound tomorrow . . . if you don't want to keep him. Long-term, I mean. But the Humane Society shelter's not open now, and I don't dare leave him in the car all night. But he's starving, and I just can't leave him here without—"

Garrett's laughter interrupted her desperate prattle. "You said he's little, right? And cute?"

"He's still a puppy."

"But a bulldog?"

"Well, a mutt probably, but he looks like a bulldog. Mostly."

His tone became guarded. "Not a pit bull, I hope?"

"No . . . no, of course not. Just a regular bulldog. A really cute one."

"So you said." Silence, then a sigh. "Bring him over. He can stay—"

"Thank you, Garrett. I owe you one."

"Wait a minute. Let me finish." She heard the grin in his voice. "He can stay the night. But I'm not making any promises. And I don't have anything to feed him . . . except maybe some leftover chili."

"No! Good grief, no. Not chili." Now it was her turn to laugh. "That would *not* be a good idea. I'll stop by the grocery store on my way and pick up some dog food. Thanks, Garrett. You're the best."

He gave her his address, and fifteen minutes later he met her at the door of his apartment barefoot, with a stainless-steel mixing bowl in hand. "This work?"

"Perfect." She tucked the bulky pup closer to her body, trying to make him look as small and cute as possible. "Garrett, meet Boss."

"You named him already?" He set the bowl down on the floor and scratched the pup under the chin. "He looks a little ragged."

She ignored his question—and the guilt it made her feel. "I don't think he's eaten in a long time. He's in desperate need of a bath, too. Sorry." She thrust the bag of supplies she'd bought at him.

"There's food in there . . . and a dog brush . . . I'm not saying you have to— I mean, *I* can clean him up."

He peered into the bag and looked up. She was relieved to see humor behind the suspicious look he cast her.

"First things first. He's starving. Here . . ." He ripped open the bag of dog food and filled the bowl.

Boss wriggled in her arms, drooling on her sleeve. Somewhere in the apartment a TV commercial jingle played. They watched while the pup noisily devoured the contents of the bowl.

"Poor little guy." Garrett rolled the top of the bag closed. "If you'll help, we can give him a bath as soon as he finishes eating. Molly'll have a cow if I let him on the furni—" He clapped a hand over his mouth and his face went red. "I don't know where that came from. I—" He shook his head.

Bryn grasped for something to say to dilute his distress but came up empty.

"Man! Sorry." He raked a hand through his hair. "That was weird."

"Hey," she said softly. "I do it all the time. It's hard to . . . remember. To let go."

"Yeah." He looked at the floor.

She knelt to pat Boss's head. "I'll help you give him a bath. But if it's anything like Sparky's first bath, it'll be more like a shower."

"I'll go run the tub. Come on in." He led the way through the entry into the apartment's combination living-dining room. He motioned toward a pit group arranged around the big-screen TV. The evening news droned softly from surround-sound speakers. "Have a seat."

Bryn sat on the edge of the cushion, looking around the room while Garrett went down the hall. She heard the sound of the bathtub filling and cabinets opening and closing.

Everywhere she looked she saw Molly's touch on the apartment. From the basket of artfully arranged sea glass on the end table beside her, to a collection of hand-painted pitchers lined up on a shelf over the antique pine dining table, it was obvious a woman had decorated the apartment, and lived in it. It was also obvious, by the over-flowing laundry basket on one end of the table and the stack of dirty dishes—several days' worth—on the coffee table, that a woman's touch had been missing for a while. She wondered what Garrett would have thought of the touches of Adam in her home.

She heard a familiar click behind her and turned to see Boss. His toenails made the same sound on the hardwood floor as Sparky's. She jumped up and scooped him into her arms. "Hey, boy. You can't be in here until you've had a bath."

"What's that?" Garrett's voice drifted down the hall over the running water.

"Oh . . . I was just talking to Boss," she hollered back.

"The water's ready if he's done eating." He appeared in the doorway. "Right this way."

Lugging Boss, Bryn followed him down the hallway into a bathroom that looked like it was used only by guests. Plush decorative towels hung from the racks, the sink and mirrors were spotless, and the throw rug in front of the tub bore only the fresh indentions of Garrett's bare feet. If Molly would have been upset about a dog in the living room, she would have had a conniption seeing him in here. "Um . . . do you have some old towels we can use?"

"Oh." He glanced over his shoulder at her. "I didn't think about that."

"I'm talking ragged-and-ready-to-be-thrown-away old. This dog is filthy." She held Boss away from her body, revealing a dog-shaped smudge on her pale blue shirt. She wrinkled her nose. "*Uggh!* He stinks, too."

He laughed, seeming himself again. "Let me see what I can find."

While Garrett went for towels, she sweet-talked Boss, kneeling beside the tub to gauge how receptive he was to the idea of a bath. He sniffed the air and leaned toward the water, his tongue lapping. Poor dog was probably thirsty, too.

Holding him in her lap, she tested the water with one hand. It felt about right, so she lowered him into the tub. The minute his paws hit the porcelain, he started slipping and sliding like a skater on ice—only not quite as gracefully.

"It's okay, Boss . . . Settle down, boy," she cooed, trying to calm the frantic pup.

"How's it going there?" Garrett's voice behind her startled her—and Boss.

The pup dived into the side of the tub, attempting escape, except his stubby legs were too short to gain him purchase on the slippery porcelain. He toppled over backward into the water, flailing like an overturned turtle.

Bryn looked over her shoulder to see that Garrett was laughing so hard he could barely stand. He dropped to his knees beside her, and together they tried to right the dog, but Boss shot out of their grasp like a slippery bar of soap. That made Garrett laugh all the harder. It proved contagious, and soon Bryn was doubled over beside the tub.

No thanks to the two of them, Boss finally got his footing, but instead of standing still, he shook himself violently. A spray of lukewarm water hit Bryn full in the face. She gasped, rubbing her eyes with one hand and trying to fend off the spray with the other. That sent Garrett into spasms again.

"You're not a lot of help, you know," she shot over his head, still trying to get a grip on Boss.

Red-faced and hair damp, Garrett made a feeble

effort to hold the pup still in the water. "I've got him," he said. "You get the shampoo."

Bryn reached across the tub for the bottle of salon shampoo. "You sure you want to use this on a dog? This stuff isn't cheap."

"Go for it." Garrett adjusted his grip on the wet dog. "Just hurry."

Bryn wrinkled her nose. "Ugh. You *really* stink."

"Hey, I took a shower."

She laughed. "Not you, dummy. Him." Breathing through her mouth, she rubbed her hands into a lather. "Is there anything worse than wet dog fur?"

"Oh, I'm sure we could come up with—"

Bryn ribbed him with an elbow. "That was a rhetorical question."

"Sorry."

The ornery smile he gave her was so like Adam, it nearly knocked her backward with memory. Sobered, she worked in silence, massaging the suds through the dog's wiry coat.

They had to drain the filthy water and refill the tub twice, but working together, they scrubbed the little bulldog until he practically squeaked.

With one hand on the dog, Garrett rummaged in the cupboard under the sink until he came up with a plastic St. Louis Cardinals drink cup. "Here, you can use this to rinse the last of the soap out."

He held Boss while Bryn filled the cup with warm water from the tap and poured it slowly over the dog's fur. Once he settled down, Boss seemed to rather enjoy the bath.

Boss set Garrett to laughing again when he shook himself dry just as the last sudsy water rolled down the drain. Lifting Boss from the tub, he nodded toward a stack of old towels he'd brought in. "Can you reach one of those?"

"Sure." Bryn fashioned the towel into a sort of sling, and Garrett deposited him into it.

"You got him?"

"If he'll hold still," she said, wrestling to wrap the corners of the towel around the wet dog.

"Here . . ." He tucked a terry cloth corner under Bryn's elbow. "You want me to take him?"

She transferred the dog into Garrett's arms. "I'll go get the brush." She jogged down the hall and retrieved the pet brush from the grocery sack. Back in the bathroom, she spread out another towel on the floor between them, and Garrett slowly lowered Boss onto it, then patted his fur with the first towel. Boss stood there looking bedraggled. He swung his blocky head from her to Garrett and back, as if he was trying to figure out what they intended to do with him. But he didn't try to escape while they worked on him, Garrett rubbing him dry, and Bryn coming behind with the grooming brush.

Garrett leaned in and took a whiff of the dog's

fur. "Well, you still stink, Boss, but not quite as bad as before."

Bryn eyed the bottle of expensive shampoo. The doggie odor wasn't completely gone, but the scented shampoo did improve it some.

"Hang on . . ." Garrett disappeared but was back a minute later holding up a small red air freshener candle and a book of matches. He set the candle on the counter by the sink, tore a match from the book, and struck it. "This should help." He touched it to the wick. It caught and flared once before settling into a warm glow. The faintest whiff of cinnamon wafted through the room.

Memories bombarded her and heightened her fear of how Garrett might react once he learned who Boss had belonged to. She felt on the edge of panic.

But Garrett rescued her. He caught her eye over the wet dog between them, a gleam lighting his own blue-gray eyes. "Okay now, let me see if I understand. You were on your way home tonight and you just happened to run into a stray bulldog? What'd you do, go home by way of the city pound?"

"No . . ." Dismissing the strange sense of panic, she dipped her head and tried to look appropriately sheepish. Might as well get it out in the open. "I drove by the shelter—Grove Street—on my way home."

"The homeless shelter? The burn site?" He looked askance at her. "That's not on your way home."

She shrugged, not sure if he would understand what had drawn her to the site of Adam's death. "I haven't been there since—that night. I thought . . . maybe it would be easier in the dark. I just wanted to get it over with."

She breathed out a sigh of relief when she saw the understanding in his eyes. She told him how she'd parked at the curb and seen something moving in the shadows. "I thought it looked like Boss, and then when he let me get close enough, I knew it had to be him. He surely hasn't been there all this time, but he must have come back looking for Zeke. Poor little guy," she said again, reaching down to scratch the pup's head.

"Zeke? Wait a minute . . . what do you mean?" Garrett's voice turned hard. "This was Zeke Downing's dog?"

12

"Is this some kind of sick joke?" Garrett stared at Bryn. Why would she have brought that man's dog here? To his home? "Why would you think I would be willing to—" He didn't know what to say. What could she have possibly been thinking?

"Garrett." She closed her eyes. "I am so sorry.

But I couldn't just leave him out there. He was already in the car before I realized I couldn't keep him myself—because of Sparky," she explained. "I swear to you, I didn't even think about the . . . connection—to Zeke . . . to Molly—until I was halfway over here. All I was thinking about was finding a safe place for him. I almost took him to my dad's, but he hasn't been well, and you . . . you were the next person I thought of. I guess, since we'd just been talking . . . I knew you liked dogs. At least you seemed to get along with Sparky the other day, and I figured you'd still be awake—" She stopped short, as if she'd suddenly realized how she was rambling. "I'm sorry, Garrett. There's no excuse for me being so thoughtless."

It was clear her mistake and her apology were sincere. He chewed the corner of his lip, feeling bad for going off on her that way. It was only a dog. "I'm sorry. It was . . . an honest mistake."

"I— shouldn't have . . ." She bowed her head, picked up the bag of dog food, and stuffed it in the sack with the other things she'd bought. "He can sleep in my car for tonight. I'm sure he'll be fine. Just let me take this stuff out to the car, and I'll be back to get him."

Garrett looked down at the dog. It had cleaned out the bowl earlier and was pushing around the few bits of kibble that had fallen on the floor with its tongue. "Are you sure this is his dog? How do you know?"

"I'm pretty sure. He's got the same markings. And—" She shrugged. "I don't know. His collar is gone, but he looks like the same dog. And he seemed to remember me."

He made a snap decision. "He can stay."

Bryn shook her head. "No. I'll take him. I understand why you're upset."

"It's not the dog's fault." That was true. She'd been kind not to have pointed that out. But if he thought it out too far, it still gave him pause to think about having the dog in his house. That man—Zeke Downing—was responsible for Molly's death.

A new thought struck him. "You don't think the guy is hanging around town, do you?" Why else would the dog have been at the site?

She shook her head. "Look at him, Garrett. He's skin and bones. Nobody is looking after him."

"Yes, but without the shelter, Downing doesn't have any place to mooch his meals. Or feed a dog . . . He could still be in town. This might be something for the police to go on."

"But surely Boss wouldn't have come to me so easily if Zeke was there, would he? He probably was scared to death by the fire and all the sirens that night, and then came back looking for Zeke." She shivered and rubbed her arms. "It gives me the creeps to think of the guy being out there."

"He could be, though. We need to tell the cops."

Bryn fidgeted with the grocery bag. "Tonight? You think I should call them right now?" She looked at the floor.

"I suppose it could wait till morning, but I think they should at least know that you found the dog. You said he's missing his collar? You're sure he had one?"

She nodded. "The only way Susan would let the guys keep a pet is if they had their shots up-to-date and wore their tags. She had enough people on her case without getting on the bad side of animal control."

"I wonder how he lost the collar."

"He probably just slipped out of it. Look how skinny he is."

"Was Zeke's name on it—on the tags, I mean?"

"Probably. Sparky's tags have Charlie's name on them. And the address of the Grove Street Shelter. Susan let them use that since the city requires a permanent address."

"But maybe he took the dog's collar off so it couldn't be traced to him. The paper quoted Susan saying Downing was reluctant to produce his ID—when he checked in to the shelter."

"Oh, he was. I remember." Bryn looked thoughtful. "Susan wasn't going to let him stay. It's policy that clients have to have at least one form of ID. And have a photo taken for our files and for the office bulletin board. Just Polaroids, but you'd have thought we were putting Zeke in front of a firing squad when Susan got that camera out. She had to take three shots before she got one with him facing the camera."

Garrett shook his head. The man was guilty as sin. And if they didn't catch Molly's murderer soon, he would be tempted to hunt the man down himself. "I think we need to call the police. I'll make the call if you want me to."

Bryn nodded, but her eyes held a distant sheen and her mind seemed to have wandered to some far-off place.

He went to the phone and dialed 9-1-1. The dispatcher answered immediately, and Garrett gave him the details about Bryn finding the dog.

"Can you hold the dog overnight?" the dispatcher asked.

"Yes. He'll be here." He gave his address. "I teach at the middle school, but if they need to see the dog, I can come home from school during my prep period tomorrow."

When the dispatcher had all his information, Garrett set the phone back in the charger and relayed what they'd said to Bryn.

She nodded but looked like she was near tears. He put a hand lightly on her shoulder. "Don't worry. I'll be nice to him." He reached to give Boss what he hoped was a convincing pat and tried to muster a smile, but judging by the look she gave him, he'd failed.

• • •

Thursday, November 29

"Mr. Edmonds, can I go to the library?"

"I don't know, Jillian . . ." Garrett tilted his head and feigned a stern look at the fifth grader. "*Can* you?"

Jillian Payne flashed a sheepish grin. "I mean, *may* I go to the library?"

"Yes, you may. Just be sure to sign out."

She dashed to the bulletin board by the door and slipped the card bearing her name into the library slot.

His classroom was uncharacteristically quiet this morning, and it was a good thing. He could scarcely keep his mind on his students, for thinking about that stupid dog Bryn Hennesey had picked up Monday night. It was Thursday and he still hadn't heard from anybody since his call to the dispatcher. The authorities apparently didn't think the dog was significant. But if he didn't hear from somebody by the end of the day, he was going to call the police himself.

Bryn seemed convinced this was the dog Zeke Downing had kept at the homeless shelter. Without a collar or tags, he doubted there was any way to prove it, and he didn't know how the dog itself might serve as evidence, but he'd at least had to report it. The fact it had shown up at the site of the shelter could mean that Downing had been there, though Bryn thought it was more likely the dog had come back in search of his master.

He didn't want to admit that her idea made more sense. But this was the first ray of hope he'd had that they might be closer to finding the man responsible for Molly's death. There wasn't a prison dark enough or a sentence long enough for Zeke Downing as far as he was concerned. Even if he hadn't started the fire on purpose, the man was a coward not to have stayed and helped fight the blaze. He hadn't even owned up to the lives he'd been responsible for.

"Mr. Edmonds?"

He forced his thoughts back to his classroom. His students had not received his full attention recently. Physically, he'd come back to work two weeks after Molly's death, but since then, his mind was too often anywhere but this classroom. "What do you need, Gage?"

"Are we gonna have homework tonight?"

"Do you *want* homework?"

The room erupted in a chorus of high-pitched *no*'s.

Garrett laughed and scratched his chin for effect. "I'll take that as a no. Okay. No homework. But then you can't complain if I pile it on for the weekend, right?"

"Mrs. Blakely never gave us homework."

His substitute had done a good job keeping the

143

kids caught up, but she'd spoiled them a little, too.

"Well, I could probably arrange to have her come back," he teased.

The same chorus of *no*'s did his heart good.

"We want *you,* Mr. Edmonds." Michaela Morrison's moony smile made him regret his fishing expedition.

"Then you get homework, I guess."

They groaned, but they were smiling.

The students worked quietly while Garrett graded some papers, but after a few minutes, he heard loud throat-clearing. He looked up to see Michaela with her hand raised, supporting her arm with her opposite hand, as if she'd had her hand up for a long time.

He curbed a grin. "Yes, Michaela?"

She tilted her head and eyed him. "Are you still sad about Mrs. Edmonds?"

Garrett felt like he'd been punched in the gut. The rest of the class came to full attention, all eyes forward and glued on him, waiting. He gulped and grappled for an answer. As he so often did with these kids, he tried to remember his own middle school years—how he would have wanted his teachers to handle situations.

He scraped his chair back and came around to lean on the front of his desk. Michaela looked like she thought she might be in trouble, and he sought to put her at ease. "That's a fair question,

Michaela." He sighed and nodded slowly. "Yes. Sometimes I still feel sad."

"Do you cry?" Gage's question was a challenge.

Giggles fluttered through the room, and Garrett waited until he had their attention again. "You know, guys, it doesn't matter how old you are, or whether you're a man or a woman or a kid, when you feel sad about something, sometimes you can't help but cry. That's normal."

Gage ribbed Mark Lohan. "I bet you'd blubber like a baby, Lohan."

Mark shoved back. "Would not."

"Bet you would."

"Cut it out, guys." Garrett waited for the two boys to settle down. "Believe it or not, sometimes it *helps* to cry. Even for us guys." He winked at Mark, but what he really wanted to do was go somewhere and have a good cry.

Michaela raised her hand and waved it in the air, but she didn't wait to be called on. "Are you gonna get married again?"

He wasn't crazy about the direction this conversation was taking. "I don't know, Michaela."

"Mama says you will. She says you're smokin'."

"Mr. Edmonds does not smoke. Do you, Mr. Edmonds?" Mark defended him.

Gage howled. "That's not what she means, you idiot. She means—"

"Guys, guys . . . whoa!" Garrett pushed off the desk. "We're getting *way* off track." He went to the whiteboard and erased the math problems that were still there from this morning. It was only an excuse to turn his back to the kids until his face cooled off a little. "Back to work. Take out your science books."

He got through the lesson without his thoughts wandering, but when the secretary's voice came over the intercom system, his heart lurched to his throat. "You have a call, Mr. Edmonds. Can you take it now?"

"Did they say who it was?"

"Um . . . yes, they did . . ." Judy's hesitation told him it was the call he'd been waiting for. "It's *Mr.* Perlson."

He'd been stupid to ask, and silently blessed the secretary for not referring to the police chief as Chief Perlson in earshot of his students. "I'll take it in the hallway, Judy. Thanks."

He panned the room with a stern expression, hooking a thumb in the direction of the door. "I'll be right out in the hall if anyone needs me. You guys keep the noise level down to a dull roar, okay?"

They murmured their agreement, and Garrett went two doors down to the phone that hung on the wall between the third- and fourth-grade classrooms. The light was blinking, indicating that his call was holding on an outside line. The door to Lucy Brighton's classroom next door stood open, and before he picked up the phone, he quietly pulled it shut.

He picked up the receiver and turned toward the wall, keeping his voice low. "This is Garrett Edmonds."

"Mr. Edmonds, Chief Perlson here. I understand you called the dispatcher last night. Something about a dog?"

"Monday night, actually. But, yes. A friend found a dog—a bulldog—at the Grove Street Shelter that night. She thinks the dog belonged to the homeless man you're looking for . . . Zeke Downing."

"What did you say your friend's name was?"

He hadn't said but didn't see any harm in giving the police chief Bryn's name.

"Hennesey. The wife of the fireman?"

"Yes." He explained about her finding Boss.

"But you say the dog wasn't wearing a collar?"

"No. But Bryn feels pretty certain it's the same dog. She volunteered at the shelter. Was there the night Zeke Downing was admitted . . . the night of the fire, too."

"Yes, I remember talking to her that night. Her and the director . . . what's her name? Marlowe, I think . . . What makes Ms. Hennesey think the dog belonged to Downing?"

Garrett tried to explain, but his hope dimmed at the skepticism in the chief's voice. "If there's no

ID on the animal, we don't really have anything to go on. You say the dog had tags at one point?"

"Yes, but he looks like he's half starved. I'm guessing the collar just slipped off after he lost weight." He mentally rolled his eyes. He was starting to sound like Bryn. "We thought it might mean that Downing is still hanging around here."

He heard what sounded like coffee being slurped on the other end of the line. "I suppose we can talk to some of the neighbors . . . see if any of them saw the dog after the fire—or recently. Can you hang on to him for a few days?"

"Yes, of course." His hopes were on a roller coaster. At least it sounded like they were going to check into it. It might be a lead.

"I'll let the fire investigator know you found him. I doubt they'll need to see him, but at least—"

"Do they have any new leads?"

"If you read the papers, you know what I know."

Laughter from down the hall punctuated the air. His students were getting rowdy. Garrett gave the chief the number of his cell phone and hurried back to the classroom.

After the students were dismissed, he went down to the office to make some copies. Judy dropped hints that she was dying to know about his phone call from the police, but he didn't give her the satisfaction. But when Kathy Beckwith, the fourth-grade teacher, asked how his day had been, he confided in her about Bryn finding the

148

dog. He didn't say where. "She already has a dog, though, so I got elected." He shrugged.

"She asked you to keep it? That was pretty cheeky." Kathy's grimace made Garrett feel the need to defend Bryn.

"She took in one of the shelter client's dogs. She found it—" He caught himself before he revealed where she'd found Boss. And that they'd had coffee together that night. Kathy and his other female colleagues would read more into it than was there—and they would not approve. Never mind that a few of them had already tried to set him up with a friend or a cousin or a little sister. "To be honest," he said, "the dog's kind of growing on me."

It was true. Boss had become his shadow since that night, and it was nice to have someone to talk to when he came home every evening. Even if it was a four-legged someone.

13

Tuesday, December 4

The phone was ringing when Bryn unlocked the door. She eased the bag of groceries onto the kitchen table and let her purse slide off her shoulder to the floor. Sparky danced around her, yipping, as she picked up the phone.

149

"Bryn? It's Garrett."

"Sparky, hush!" She took a deep breath and steeled herself. "Hi, Garrett." She hadn't heard from him since the night she'd taken Boss to his house. She'd been tempted to call him to see how things were going, but every time she thought about picking up the phone, she was afraid it would only make it easier for him to ask her to come and take Boss off his hands.

With each day that went by, she'd breathed a little easier, thinking he must have decided to keep Boss. But she worried that the police didn't seem to think the dog's appearance at the shelter site had any significance. Every news story she'd read or heard still called the inspectors' conclusions "inconclusive."

She forced her attention back to the phone. "What's up? Is everything going okay with Boss?"

"He's doing just fine. Getting a little meat back on his bones."

"Oh, good. I'm glad."

"That's why I called, actually."

Here it came. He was going to ask her to come and get Boss.

"I wondered if you'd want to take the dogs for a walk. I got away early today, and it's so nice out this afternoon, I just thought . . ."

She released a breath. Maybe Boss was growing on him. But considering his invitation, she wondered if he remembered why she'd brought Boss to his house in the first place. She opened her mouth to remind him, but the thought of time with Garrett made her swallow her protest. The dogs might kill each other, but it would be worth it for a chance to see Garrett again. "I'd like that. Do you just want to meet at the riverwalk? At that curve where you rescued me that day?"

He laughed. "Sure. Ten minutes?"

"I'll be there."

"Great. But I'll have my hands full. You're on your own with the leash this time."

"I think I've got a handle on it." *Unless Sparky remembers Boss.*

She threw up a prayer and went to put the groceries away and collect Sparky's leash.

She almost lost her nerve on the way to the riverwalk. Garrett hadn't sounded upset on the phone, but what if he was still angry with her for bringing Boss to his place? He had every right to be. Maybe he'd invited her so he could break the news that he wasn't willing to keep Boss.

But when she rounded the corner to the spot where Sparky had run away with her, there was Garrett, and he wore a smile that said he remembered that day, too.

Boss lifted his head and sniffed the air, and Bryn tightened her grip on Sparky's leash, but though the Lab's ears perked up at the sight of the bulldog, he stayed at her side, tail wagging. "Good boy."

Bryn couldn't believe the change in Boss in only a week. She handed Garrett Sparky's leash and went to her knees to love up on the pup. "He looks so much better!" Boss had filled out quite a bit. His eyes had lost the dull sheen they'd held that night she'd rescued him, and his coat was shiny and smooth, as if he'd gotten a good brushing every day since his bath at Garrett's.

"He's eating me out of house and home, but he does look better, doesn't he?"

"He really does." She stood, brushing the dog hair off her hands. "Thanks again for taking him, Garrett. I hope he hasn't been too much trouble."

A glint came to his eye. "No trouble . . . I'm taking out a second mortgage to pay the dog food bill, but otherwise, we're good."

"Sorry." She shot him a sheepish smile.

He looked down at the dogs, who were cautiously sniffing each other. "I thought you said these two had issues."

She shrugged. "They nearly killed each other the first time they met."

"Maybe this isn't Downing's dog after all."

She shook her head and opened her mouth to dispute him. For some reason, she felt certain this was Boss. But if it made Garrett feel better to think otherwise, she wasn't going to argue. "Do I dare ask if you're considering keeping him?"

"For good, you mean?"

She nodded.

"Well, the police asked me to hang on to him at least until they complete their investigation. But I've thought about what happens after. He *is* kind of growing on me."

She smiled at that, then remembered what he'd said about the police. "They called you back? What did they say?"

He told her about his conversation with the police chief. "It took the guy almost three days to get back to me. I don't think he's too interested. But he did say he'd let the fire investigator know we found him." Garrett bent to run a hand down Boss's brindled coat. His demeanor was almost possessive, as if he meant to reassure Boss he wouldn't let anyone hurt him. For some odd reason, the simple act endeared Garrett to Bryn.

He straightened and untangled Boss's leash. "You ready?"

She nodded and they set out on a leisurely stroll, letting the dogs set the pace. By the time they'd gone half a mile, Sparky and Boss seemed to be enjoying each other's company—as much as Bryn had to admit she enjoyed Garrett's.

"So, how's the job hunt going?" Garrett asked.

She shrugged. "I've had a couple of promising interviews, but to be honest, I'm hoping the library will just give me more hours so I don't have to find something else."

"Is that a possibility?"

"It is, but they don't seem to be in any hurry to make a decision. In the meantime the bills are piling up, and I'm well on my way to maxing out our—" She caught herself. "*My* credit cards. But the thought of starting a new job—starting all over somewhere new—about does me in."

"I understand. Well, I'll pray the library makes you an offer soon. What do you do there? Just a librarian?" He held up a hand. "Wait . . . that came out wrong. I didn't mean *just* a librarian. I meant—"

She laughed. "It's okay. I do a little of everything. Shelve books, repair books, send out fine notices, whatever needs doing."

"Uh-oh." He winced. "I suppose that means you know I'm in hock to the library to the tune of $7.54."

"You'd better take care of that before Myrna puts out a warrant for you." She laughed, but it wasn't exactly a joke. Myrna, in an effort to make a point, had actually done just that with a patron last year. Unfortunately, the man was a professor at one of the private colleges in Springfield and had been up in arms about the action, calling it defamation of character. The *Hanover Falls Courier* had published dozens of letters to the editor on both sides of the issue. Ultimately the charge was dropped when the man produced the overdue book and paid a fine, though Myrna still took every opportunity to inform patrons that she was merely following the law.

"Oh, yeah . . . I heard about that. Probably wouldn't be a good example for my students, huh?"

She gave an exaggerated shake of her head. "Not at all."

"Okay. *Note to self: take care of library fine.*"

"You teach sixth grade, right?"

"Fifth."

"Oh. I bet they love you."

He eyed her as if he wasn't sure she was serious.

"No, I mean it," she said. "I remember fifth grade. I guarantee all the little girls have crushes on you and all the little boys want to grow up and *be* you."

"Oh, brother." He rolled his eyes. "I sure hope not. And no, actually, all the little boys want to grow up and be firefighters like my wife."

Bryn smiled and tested the water. "She's a hero to them."

"Yeah, yeah . . . tell me about it."

His answer surprised her. It must have shown in her face.

"Listen," he said, "it wasn't exactly easy being a middle-school teacher married to a firefighter wife. I got razzed about that plenty."

"By your kids? Your students, I mean?"

"Them, my family, the guys I play basketball with . . . and pretty much the rest of the civilized world. All in good fun, of course." He grinned.

"Oh, come on . . . really? But I'm sure you were man enough to take it." She punched him lightly on the arm, the way she would have Adam when they were bantering. He felt solid and warm and real. A rush of affection overwhelmed her—for Adam, but for Garrett, too. Maybe *more* for Garrett.

He didn't seem to notice. "I came to terms with Molly being the hero . . . but it took a while." The way he shrugged told her he was serious. "And now it's my turn to be her hero."

She wasn't sure what he meant by that. "I'm sure you *were* her hero, Garrett."

"Depends on how you define hero, I guess." He looked out over the river and changed the subject. "You want to walk again tomorrow?"

There was nothing she wanted more.

"Weather's supposed to be nice again." His expression looked like Sparky's when he was hankering to go for a walk. Like he thought he had to convince her.

But she didn't have to think twice. "I'd like that. Do you want to just meet here again?"

He nodded. "Same time, same place."

They started to part ways, but she felt compelled to say what she'd been about to say when he changed the subject. "You know, Garrett, being a hero isn't always about saving lives and leaping tall buildings in a single bound."

He studied her, then kicked at a stone on the

sidewalk. "Maybe. But now I have a chance to make a difference. To somehow make sure justice is done. And I'm not giving up until I know every stone has been turned to find whoever started that fire. I owe that much to Molly."

A weight settled in the pit of her stomach, and she couldn't quite put her finger on the reason.

Or maybe she could.

14

Saturday, January 5

Bryn spotted the sign for North Broadway and turned onto the narrow street. She gripped the steering wheel and took a couple of deep breaths. She hadn't been to Springfield since the last time she and Adam had come in to see the new James Bond film.

She'd somehow gotten it in her head that once she got through Christmas, things would get better. But she'd taken Sparky and gone out to her dad's on Christmas Eve, and if anything it seemed like the memories of Adam had grown stronger. She spent the night there, and Dad had gone out of his way to make Christmas Day festive, but she'd spent most of the day trying to hold back the tears, or when she couldn't, trying to keep Dad from seeing her grief.

She'd suspected he was doing the same, and it startled her to realize that even after three years, Mom's absence still left a huge hole in Dad's life. Hers, too. Would she still be aching for Adam three years from now? Longing for what they'd had together? The thought was unbearable. She'd ended up going home before dark on Christmas Day. She'd crawled under the covers, wishing she was a bear and could sleep until spring.

But every morning she woke up, and the reality hit her all over again: Adam was gone. Forever. And her life would never be the same.

Peering out the side windows, she searched for a number on one of the run-down older homes and abandoned office buildings. She'd never been in this part of town, even with Adam. It wasn't a part of the city the bureau of tourism would have steered visitors to, and she was thankful it was daylight and that she had Sparky with her.

She glanced over her shoulder to where the dog was sprawled on the backseat. He wore a blue bandanna around his neck, compliments of the groomer Bryn had taken him to yesterday. He watched her, panting, as if anticipating a reunion with Charlie. Would Sparky recognize his old master?

Bryn was eager to see Charlie again, and for him to have a chance to see Sparky again, but she worried a little that he might expect to keep the dog. Of course, she'd inherited Sparky in the first place because this shelter didn't allow its residents to keep pets. But she'd promised Charlie that she'd bring Sparky for a visit, and she'd waited longer than intended. She just hoped seeing Sparky didn't somehow set Charlie back—make his situation worse instead of better.

She'd called ahead and talked to the director, who informed her that Charlie would be at the shelter any time of day. They'd given Charlie a part-time paid position at the shelter, which not only covered the small fee they charged for residency, but gave him a place to be during the daylight hours when the shelter was officially closed. Good for Charlie. Except this probably meant he wouldn't be coming back to Hanover Falls, even if Susan got a new shelter up and running in the near future.

She didn't know if they'd told Charlie about her call, or if he would be surprised to see her, but the shelter manager had welcomed her to come and bring Sparky, as long as the dog stayed outside the building.

The rambling whitewashed building from the photo on the Internet appeared on her left, and she parked at the curb and turned off the car. She reached over the seat and scratched Sparky's ears, then adjusted his bandanna. "You stay here, boy. I'll bring Charlie out to see you."

Sparky barked his protests as she locked him in the car. Ignoring him, she looked up and down the street before crossing pavement pocked with potholes. There were two entrances to the building, and it took her a minute to decipher the hand-lettered signs plastered to the door. She chose the first door and tried the bar handle. It didn't give, so she rapped loudly on the glass.

A red-bearded man with matching wild curls escaping his thick ponytail appeared in the inner doorway. He jogged to the door and unlocked it for her. He wore hospital scrubs and flip-flops. A rush of memories assailed her. She remembered her first night at the Grove Street Shelter when a grad student from a Springfield college had showed up to take the night shift dressed similarly. Bryn had assumed he was checking in to the shelter as a resident and had been thoroughly embarrassed to realize the man was a volunteer.

If she'd learned anything in her time at the shelter, it was that you couldn't judge a homeless person by the way he looked. While a few—like Charlie, Tony X . . . and Zeke Downing—fit the stereotype, many of the residents wouldn't have gotten a second look if they'd strolled through the grocery store or walked into the public library.

"Come on in," Red said. "You must be Charlie's friend."

"He told you I was coming?"

"Are you kidding? That's all he's talked about since I came on this morning."

"How's he doing?"

"No complaints—well, unless I'm whipping his tail at gin rummy."

Bryn smiled, remembering. "I've got his dog out in my car. I promised him I'd bring Sparky to visit."

"Ah, Sparky. The famous wonder dog."

"You've heard about him, too, huh?"

Red winked. "Ad nauseam."

Bryn laughed. "He's a good dog."

"Yeah, well, it's too bad they won't let the guys have pets here. Gives 'em something to live for, you know? Somebody who depends on them."

She nodded, looking past him, suddenly feeling a little nervous about seeing Charlie. Though she'd kept up with Charlie through Susan, she hadn't seen him since the night of the fire. What would they talk about? She didn't want to rehash the events of that night. She hoped Sparky would keep the conversation centered on happier things.

"Come on back . . ." Red turned and strode through the inner doorway, then did a quick about-face. "I'm Tim, by the way." He held out a hand.

She shook it, and after a glance across the street to check on Sparky, she followed.

The room beyond was twice as big as the dining room and kitchen at the Grove Street Shelter had been. The furniture looked like something from a doctor's waiting room. Bookshelves on one wall held a sparse offering of paperback books and board games. A big-screen TV hung in one corner, and several rows of tables and mismatched chairs took up the opposite end of the room. For the first time Bryn realized what a task Susan had ahead of her trying to get the shelter reopened and furnished.

Tim went to a corner of the room that opened onto another hallway. He cupped his hands around his mouth and hollered down the hall, "Hey, Charlie? You got company."

Bryn heard the familiar squeak of Charlie's wheelchair and stepped forward to meet him halfway.

He appeared around the corner, a question mark in his expression. But then his caterpillar brows lifted and his eyes lit up. "Well, ain't you a sight for sore eyes!"

"Hi, Charlie." The catch in her voice took her by surprise. "Long time no see. How are you doing?" She went to him and bent over his chair, taking his gnarled hand in hers.

"Well, I'm better now. I didn't think you'd really come."

"I told you I'd bring Sparky for a visit."

"What's that?" He put a hand to his ear and fiddled with his hearing aid.

Bryn repeated herself.

He dipped his head. "I didn't think you meant it."

"Of course I meant it, Charlie."

He looked past her. "How's the old fella doing?"

"He's out in the car. And he was none too happy I made him wait, either."

Charlie's shoulders shook with silent laughter—or maybe he was crying. She didn't risk looking at him to find out but went around behind his chair. "You warm enough? Or do you want to get a heavier coat? It's pretty nippy out there this morning." The words were already out when she realized Charlie may not have a heavier coat than the letterman-type jacket he was wearing now. She was pretty sure he hadn't been wearing the heavy down coat he'd owned at the Grove Street shelter when they'd evacuated the night of the fire . . . unless he'd had it tucked into his chair somewhere.

He reached under the lap robe covering his knees and whipped out a pair of gloves. "It's so blame cold in here I'm bundled up all the time anyway." He glanced in Tim's direction and raised his voice. "Ain't that right, Tim?"

"Just trying to keep the place open, Charlie. I could turn it up a few degrees and pay your salary to the electric company, I guess . . ."

Charlie waved him off. "Forget I said anything."

"Uh-huh . . . that's what I thought. Now, go see that dog of yours."

Charlie took his hands off the wheels of his

chair, tucked them beneath the lap robe, and looked over his shoulder at Bryn. "Give me a shove, will you?"

She pushed his chair through the door as Tim held it for them. "Just knock when you're ready to come back in. I need to keep this locked."

As she rolled his chair down the sidewalk to the street, Charlie reached up and patted her hand. "So, how are you doing, sis?"

"I'm hanging in there." She put a hand over his and bowed her head, not trusting her voice. "It's been nice to have Sparky. He was a handful at first, but he's a good dog."

"That he is. Oh . . . speak of the devil." He pointed toward her car, where Sparky sat with his nose pressed against the driver's-side window.

They crossed the street and Charlie wheeled his chair beside the car. "Hey, boy." His voice broke and Bryn pretended not to notice, fishing through her purse for the car keys. "Why don't you park behind my car, Charlie. I'll get him out." She nodded toward the empty parking spot behind her Accord, then opened the front door.

Sparky bounded out of the car and almost bowled Charlie over with his enthusiasm. He stood on his hind legs and put his front paws on Charlie's shoulder, licking his master's face. Bryn's throat closed, watching the reunion.

When Sparky finally settled down, Charlie sat there with one hand on the dog's head and, with his other, wiped his face with the sleeve of his jacket. "That blame dog slobbered all over me."

Bryn suspected his own tears provided some of the moisture he was swiping at.

She leaned against the trunk of the car and laughed while Charlie played with the dog, throwing a stick for Sparky to retrieve and wrestling with him from his chair. While Sparky romped up and down the sidewalk across from the shelter, Bryn caught Charlie up on the news from Hanover Falls.

"You still working at the library?"

"Oh, yes. I'll probably be there till I die. I'm trying to get Myrna to give me some more hours."

"The old battle-ax ought to have work for you now that I'm not there to help her out."

"I think she's waiting to get the okay from the board."

"Red tape. Story of my life." Charlie clucked sympathetically. He lifted himself up by his forearms and settled in the seat again. "I wanted to talk to you about something."

Something in his voice made Bryn straighten and pay attention.

"I know Susan is trying to get the shelter up and running again in the Falls, but . . . I don't think I'll be coming back."

Bryn waited, guessing what was coming next.

"They've been real good to me here. It's a better situation than I had in the Falls. They've got work for me that pays my way. And I can stay in one place, not have to make that trip back and forth from the library every day, rain or shine. I'm no spring chicken, you know." The smile he gave her broke her heart.

"We'll miss you, Charlie."

"Nothing says you can't come and see me once in a while. Bring that mutt with you, too." He lifted his head to where Sparky was frolicking in a pile of crisp yellow leaves. "He's yours now."

"Oh, Charlie—"

"Now, don't tell me you can't keep him."

"No. I'll keep him. He's grown on me. But I'm sorry. I wish you could have him here."

He waved her off. "Yeah, well . . . if wishes were horses and all that rot. Besides, you need him worse than I do." He snapped his fingers and whistled Sparky over. Cradling the dog's head in his hands, he roughed him up and hugged him close. Sparky seemed to sense something was up, and he stood still for the show of affection.

"You behave for this young lady, you hear me, dog? She'll take good care of you. You've been a good friend." Charlie stroked the silky ears, making no effort to hide the tears that swelled his eyelids, then rolled down his leathery cheeks.

"Thank you, Charlie." Bryn swallowed, searching for the right words. "He sure is going to miss you, but we'll come and visit."

"You think you will. You'll mean to. But you've

got a life to live. You need to go live it. But thanks for coming today. I—I didn't think you'd come."

"Of course I came. I've thought about you a lot, Charlie." She was glad she could truthfully tell him that. "I'll come. Maybe not as often as I'd like, but Sparky and I will be back to see you." She determined in that moment to keep her promise. "And hey, in the meantime, I think . . . I think he's pretty happy with me."

"Sure he is, sis. Who wouldn't be happy with you?"

15

Friday, January 11

"May I help you?" The woman behind the desk looked at Garrett expectantly.

He shuffled his feet and looked at the carpet. "I'd like to speak with the fire inspector."

"Does it matter which one?"

"Oh . . . I didn't realize there was more than one in this office."

"We have two here in Springfield, and Bob Trenton is in the Poplar Bluff office."

"I'm looking for whoever covered the Grove Street fire—the homeless shelter fire in Hanover Falls."

She tilted her head, studied him. "Actually, they all three worked that fire, but Morley was lead."

"Is he in the office today?"

The receptionist offered a crooked smile. "*She* is in. It's *Andrea* Morley. But don't call her that. She's Andi—with an *i*—even professionally. I take it you don't have an appointment?"

Garrett shook his head, trying to cover his surprise. He recalled newscasters referring to an "Andy" Morley in reports about the investigation, but it had never crossed his mind that Morley might be female.

Garrett gave the receptionist his name. "I called earlier this week . . . about your hours. But no, I don't have an appointment. My wife was one of the firefighters who . . . was killed in that fire."

Recognition—and that familiar sympathetic expression—lit the woman's eyes. She picked up the phone. "Let me see if Andi has time to see you. Have a seat."

"Thanks." Garrett had no sooner taken one of the chairs by the window than the receptionist beckoned him to the hallway, then ushered him into the first office on the right.

"Come in, Mr. Edmonds." A tall brunette rose and reached across her desk to shake his hand.

Garrett had expected a burly former fireman. It took him a minute to get used to the attractive forty-something woman who greeted him. Dressed in black pants and a crisp white shirt, she motioned for him to take the chair in front of the desk. "How can I help you?"

"I'm just trying to get some information about your investigation of the Grove Street fire. It's been two and a half months, but unless I've missed a news report somewhere, there still haven't been any announcements about what caused the fire." It was too late to take back the accusatory tone in his voice.

The investigator picked up a ballpoint pen from her desk top and clicked it off and on. "That's because we haven't reached any conclusions. Believe me, we will let the public know as soon as we have anything conclusive to report."

"Can you tell me if Zeke Downing is still a suspect?"

She hesitated. "His disappearance from the scene of the fire certainly gives us reason to think he may have been involved."

"Did someone let you know that I found his dog—or rather my friend did—at the burn site?"

"Yes, Chief Brennan called about that."

"I still have the dog at my place."

She looked surprised at that. "Like I told the chief, when we found the collar, we thought it probably meant—"

"Wait a minute . . ." Garrett leaned forward, resting his forearms on the edge of the desk. "You found Boss's collar?"

She nodded. "Some neighborhood kids found it

on the embankment behind the shelter. We figured Downing ran with the dog but ditched the collar because of the ID it contained. Of course, when the dog showed up, that kind of challenged that theory." She folded her hands and steepled her index fingers. "But he must have dumped the dog somewhere along the way. He may have heard the police were looking for him and been afraid the dog would give him away. If it's the same dog, it wouldn't be surprising for it to make its way back to the shelter."

"Yes, that's where my friend found it," Garrett confirmed.

The investigator looked confused. "Chief Brennan said it was the wife of one of the firemen who found it."

"Right. That's who I meant . . . Bryn Hennesey. She's the friend I was talking about." It felt awkward describing Bryn that way, as if he'd been trying to conceal their relationship when he first mentioned her. "Bryn feels sure it's the same dog."

The investigator shrugged. "Well, none of that really changes anything. We're still on the lookout for Downing. We'd like to question him. But I don't want to get your hopes up. As I've told reporters, the damage from that fire was extensive. In ten years as an investigator, I've never seen that kind of devastation. It's a miracle they were able to get the bodies out of there at all, let alone that same night—" Her shoulders slumped, and Garrett watched the realization of what she'd said register in her eyes. He wanted to alleviate her pain, but felt paralyzed.

There were no miracles that night. He didn't know where God had been while Molly was breathing her last agonizing breath, but no miracle had happened for her. Or for him.

Andi Morley closed her eyes and held up a hand. "I'm sorry. I am so sorry. That was a stupid, thoughtless thing to say."

Garrett shook his head. "It's okay." He knew she hadn't meant anything personal by it. But it *wasn't* okay. He scooted his chair back and stood, bowed his head briefly before meeting her eyes again. "I appreciate your time. How long . . . before the investigation is closed?"

She rose and came around her desk to extend her hand again. "I lost friends in that fire. I promise you we won't close the file until we're certain there is nothing else to discover. I give you my word."

"Thank you." He turned and walked out the door, feeling her eyes on his back.

He hurried through the front office without speaking to the receptionist. Out on the sidewalk he squinted against the afternoon sun. He wasn't sure what he'd expected to learn here today, but he'd felt compelled to talk to the investigator personally. He'd left school early to get to

Springfield before the investigators' offices closed.

Now it looked like the whole thing might have been a colossal waste of time. What did he think he could accomplish by talking to them anyway? He felt so helpless. But maybe it was time to let go. Leave justice up to God. But there had to be something he could do to find justice for Molly and the others who'd died with her.

Monday, January 14

Garrett swiped at the fogged-up bathroom window with his shaving towel and peered out to the woods behind the apartment complex. An inch of fresh snow lay over everything, and the morning sky was gray and heavy with the promise of more. The view was stunning. Like a page from an art calendar. But the temperatures had dipped into the teens, and Garrett's spirits fell with them.

But not for the reason his fellow teachers would guess. He'd survived his first Christmas without Molly. Bryn Hennesey had made that surprisingly easy.

But he was depressed because after a month of relatively mild winter weather, the days had grown colder. The ponds had frozen over, and the riverbanks were crusted with ice. Snow from a week ago was still piled on the side of the road.

Now with more snow on the way, Bryn would no doubt call and say it was too cold to go for their walk. And the time they spent together had become as necessary as his morning coffee. As necessary as breathing, if he was honest.

He and Bryn had met at the riverwalk with the dogs almost every day since the first of December, and her sweet company had done more to heal his grief than any other antidote he could imagine. While he was with her, he forgot about how sad he felt. Forgot about anything but the way she made him laugh, the way she made him forget.

They hadn't talked about where their relationship was headed, both careful to keep their time together casual. They'd exchanged text messages and a few lighthearted emails, but other than walking the dogs—something they both had to do anyway—they hadn't planned anything that either of them might construe as a date. They were just friends.

Still, he knew other people probably suspected it was more. And maybe it was.

It had only been two and a half months since he'd lost Molly—and since Bryn had lost her husband. But after long walks and heart-to-hearts, he sometimes felt he knew Bryn as well as he'd known his wife.

Was it so crazy to think he and Bryn might feel something for each other? If anyone understood what he was going through, Bryn did. Likewise, he empathized with her grief like no one else could. Theirs was a unique situation, and it only stood to reason that their timeframe for becoming more than friends would be different than the average grieving person.

They'd both felt free to talk about the marriages they'd had—both good, solid marriages, although from the things Bryn shared, it sounded like she and Adam had struggled more than he and Molly ever did.

Bryn didn't like being alone and until she'd found a purpose in her work at the homeless shelter, she'd resented her husband's hours. He hadn't been crazy about Molly being gone for long stretches either, but even before he'd met Molly, he'd never minded being alone. He'd filled the days she worked an extended shift helping with school events, painting the apartment, and reading everything he could get his hands on.

He and Molly had only been married a year and a half. Maybe their time of discontent would have eventually come, the same as it had for Bryn and Adam. Bryn had told him that she never doubted she and Adam would have worked things out. "Everything I griped at him about seems so petty now," she'd told Garrett one chilly night as they walked together. "I thought he was being possessive and controlling, but I see now that he was

174

just trying to protect me. I wish I could go back and appreciate that more. I wish I'd told him . . ."

"I think he knows," Garrett had said, trying to reassure her. He liked to think that he and Molly would have had a long and happy marriage had things been different.

He splashed water on his face, trying to rinse away the thoughts. He didn't want to think about Molly. He wanted to think about the future. About Bryn.

The two of them talked about everything under the sun, but they'd skirted around the subject of their relationship. And he didn't want to ruin things by bringing up something she might not be ready to talk about.

When he finished dressing he flipped on the TV and went to let Boss out of his makeshift kennel in the laundry room. In the background the meteorologist was saying something about school closings. "Hey, boy. We might get to stay home today."

Boss cocked his boxy head and looked up at him as if trying to interpret what he'd said. Garrett scooped a cup of dog food from a plastic storage bin and poured it into the mixing bowl— the same one he'd presented Bryn with the night she'd brought Boss over. The night he and Bryn had started becoming friends.

He stopped in front of the TV and did a double take at the list of school closings scrolling by at the bottom of the screen. This storm must be amounting to more than they'd forecast. While he filled the coffeemaker with water, he kept one eye on the television screen.

There it was. *Hanover Falls: no school district-wide.*

Three months ago, the announcement would have made him and Molly whoop with joy. They would have crawled back into bed. They would have made love and fallen asleep in each other's arms, relishing the rare chance to sleep in. Later they would have shared the newspaper over coffee and bagels and watched the snow pile up on the deck rail just outside the French doors, the way it was now.

He would curl up on the sofa in front of the fireplace with a good book, watching Molly putter around the house in her pajamas, her hair all wild around her angel face.

A wave of longing churned through him, so strong it made him nauseous. *Bryn.*

He shook his head. No. *Molly.* He'd started to get them mixed up in his mind: Bryn and Molly. It frightened him a little.

He went to see if the newspaper was on the front stoop. Boss left his breakfast and followed him through the foyer, toenails tapping on the wood floors in the entryway. The lid on his postal box bulged. He couldn't remember when he'd last gotten the mail. Two days at least.

He'd get it tonight. Or tomorrow. Since November's avalanche of sympathy cards he had learned to avoid the mailbox until it couldn't hold another envelope and the mail carrier started to complain.

Though it was seven a.m., the sky was almost black. A streetlight flickered, trying to decide whether it was morning or not. Giant wet flakes were illuminated in its glow, and though it was bitter cold, the wind was almost nonexistent. It reminded him of a morning last winter when he and Molly had skated on the frozen pond at Ferris Park.

Boss took a tentative step onto the snowy stoop. He tossed his head and caught a snowflake on his tongue. "Come on, buddy, do your business. It's too cold to stand out here all day." Boss obliged and trotted back inside. Garrett followed him and shut the door behind him, but as he turned, his gaze landed on the coatrack beside the door. Two pairs of skates hung over the pegs by their laces. The idea that formulated almost instantly filled him with joy.

He stomped the snow off his shoes and went back to the kitchen. Before he could change his mind, he picked up the phone and dialed Bryn's number.

Her voice was drowsy.

"I woke you up, didn't I? Sorry."

"It's okay." He heard something clatter on her

end and pictured her groping for her glasses on the nightstand. "Is everything okay?"

"Do you have to work this morning?"

"Um . . . no. Not till this afternoon. Why?"

"What size shoes do you wear?"

"What? Garrett, you are making no sense. Are you even awake yet?"

He laughed. "Just answer the question."

"Not that it's any of your business, but I wear an eight-and-a-half. Or sometimes a nine," she mumbled.

"That'll work."

"What are you talking about?"

"Get up, get dressed—dress warm, in layers. And put on two pairs of socks."

"What in the world is going on? Where are you?"

"I'll pick you up in thirty minutes."

"Huh? It's Monday. Don't you have school?"

"Look outside."

"What?"

"Just haul your lazy bones out of bed and look out your window."

He listened to the rustle of sheets and heard her groan as she crawled out of bed.

"Oh! It snowed! It's beautiful!" Her voice held the same awe he'd felt when he first saw the fresh-fallen snow a few minutes ago.

"Coffee's brewing as we speak. I'll pick you up in half an hour."

"But I'm not . . . my hair is a mess and I'm—"

"You're gorgeous. And besides, nobody will see your hair. You'll be wearing a stocking cap."

"I will?"

"Yes, you will."

"And where exactly am I going?"

"It's a surprise. Seriously though, it's cold out there. Dress warm. Layers." He hung up before she could argue and chuckled at the certainty that she was arguing anyway, even as she hung up her own phone.

Rummaging in the coat closet, he found a couple of his old sweatshirts. He spread them out on the kitchen table and took scissors to the long sleeves, lopping them off to make sweaters for the dogs. Knowing Bryn, Sparky probably already had a nice doggy sweater, but he'd take them both just in case. That ought to be good for a laugh, trying to get those two mutts into sweatshirts.

He found the Thermos under the kitchen sink, rinsed it out, and poured in hot coffee from the carafe. He searched the cupboard for something edible and came up with a box of stale granola bars. He didn't eat the things, but Molly had liked them, so maybe Bryn would, too.

In the hallway he pulled his ice skates and Molly's white ones—his gift to her their first Christmas—from the coatrack. Guilt nipped at him, but a sense of excitement at being with Bryn again quickly replaced it.

"Come on, Boss. Come on, boy. We're going to see your buddy. Yeah, boy, we're going to go see ol' Sparky."

Boss wagged his whole body in anticipation. Garrett loaded the breakfast things into his pickup, swept the snow off the windshields, then came back for Boss. He slipped the leash from its hook by the door and stooped to clip it to Boss's collar.

He bent to scoop the dog under one arm, surprised by how muscular Boss had gotten. Tossing the skates over his shoulder, he threw off the last shreds of guilt, too. Molly was gone, and God had put Bryn in his life for a reason. Hadn't he prayed for help, for a way to get through his grief? God had answered with a beautiful friendship. He refused to feel guilty for rejoicing in that divine provision.

16

Keeping one eye on the clock, Bryn slicked on lipgloss and ran a brush through her hair. A dark lock sprang back above her temple like a stubborn cowlick while the other side of her hair lay flat and lifeless against her skull. She twisted the mess into a low ponytail and tugged a bright orange knit stocking cap—one of Adam's—over her head. She turned away from the mirror, not wanting to know how awful she looked.

In the garage, Sparky rose from the fleece nest bed she'd bought him and trotted to greet her. Poor dog. He looked fine, but it was cold enough out here that she could see her breath in front of her. He might get to sleep in the house tonight. While he went outside, she filled his dish and got him fresh water. He didn't waste any time outside, and while he ate, she ran back into the house to gather her coat and gloves and to watch for Garrett.

He had something up his sleeve. Knowing him, he just wanted to play in the snow. She could see why Garrett was a good teacher. He was still a kid himself. It was a quality she'd loved about Adam, too.

She filed through a tangle of coat hangers in the hall closet looking for her hooded sweatshirt with the Southeast Missouri State logo on it. Not finding it, she settled for a light jacket to layer under her down coat and stuffed two pairs of gloves in her coat pockets. Standing on tiptoe, she scoured the top shelf of the hall closet for her favorite scarf, a thick red wool that had been Mom's. Not finding it, she went to search her bedroom, but without success. It had probably fallen back behind the boxes of Christmas decorations and stuff she meant to take to Goodwill. She didn't have time to dig for it now, but she'd clean the closet out this weekend. When had she last seen it? She hadn't needed it with the recent warm weather, but she had to find it. The scarf was one of the few things she had of her mother's.

She remembered Garrett's black scarf that had hung in the laundry room since that day he'd loaned it to her at the riverwalk. She'd kept meaning to return it, and always forgot. She grabbed it now and looped it around her neck. She could "borrow" it again this morning and give it back to him when he brought her home.

The doorbell rang, and she opened it to an abominable snowman that looked a little like Garrett. She laughed and stooped to peer up under the hood of his jacket. "Is that you in there?"

Only his upper lip, nose, and those steel blue eyes peered out from the hood and the plaid flannel scarf around his throat and chin. But the eyes were smiling. "You ready?"

"I will be—as soon as you tell me what we're doing."

He looked over his shoulder to the street. "What do you think? It's snowing. We're going to go play in the snow."

"Aha! I was right."

"About what?"

"Never mind." She peered over his shoulder to where his pickup was parked, the exhaust hovering over the street in a cloud. "Is Boss with you? You want me to bring Sparky?"

"Boss would never forgive me if you didn't."

"Okay. Hang on, I'll get him."

Sparky danced for joy while she tried to clip his leash to his collar.

Garrett opened the passenger door for her and a mellow country ballad wafted from the truck's cab. Boss was perched on the front passenger seat like he owned the vehicle.

"Are we going far?"

"Nope. Just across town."

"Okay. We'll ride in the backseat. That might be easiest."

Garrett didn't argue, and Bryn nudged Sparky up onto the narrow bench seat and slithered in behind him. The cab was toasty warm, and outside the snow had turned the world into a sparkling vacuum. Garrett's truck rolled almost soundlessly along the street, the engine muffled to a soft purr by the cushion of snow. Only the intermittent scrape of windshield wipers marred their silent cocoon.

Bryn inhaled through her nose, detecting only car exhaust and doggie breath—and the slightest hint of Garrett's piney aftershave. Maybe it was from his scarf wrapped close around her throat, but he was close enough she could almost bury her nose in his shoulder. She pushed the image away lest she be tempted to act on it. "Hey, I don't smell coffee. I thought you mentioned coffee. I can't function till I've had my coffee."

"Hold your horses . . ." Laughing, he reached to the floorboard and came up with an old-fashioned red plaid Thermos. He handed it back to her, then produced two clunky pottery mugs from the console. "You might want to blow the dog hair off of those before you pour."

"You have that problem, too? How can one dog shed that much hair? It's gross. My house is one big hairball."

"Worth it, though." Garrett patted Boss's head. "Aren't you, boy?"

Relief rushed through her veins again at the fact that Garrett had become so fond of Boss. That he hadn't held it against her for bringing the dog to him that night.

She'd quit reading the papers, but around town, the news of the fire had died down. Though Garrett was tracking the investigation carefully and he'd told her that it was ongoing, there were apparently few clues since the damage had been so extensive. Whenever he started talking about the fire, she tried to change the subject. She was ready to move on. She wished the investigators would just close the files and be done with it.

The pickup fishtailed on the slippery street, and Bryn gripped the seat in front of her.

"Sorry about that."

"That's okay. I needed something to get my heart pumping this morning." She blew out each cup and wiped the rims with her shirttail, grateful for the distraction. She hadn't liked where her thoughts were taking her. Especially not in Garrett's presence.

Balancing the mug between her knees, she loosened the cap of the Thermos. "Okay, I'm pouring. Try to keep the vehicle somewhere between the two ditches if at all possible."

She filled a mug half full, breathing in the fragrant steam. Handing it over the seat to him, she met his eyes in the rearview mirror. "Where are we going anyway?"

He raised his eyebrows mysteriously. "Patience. We're almost there."

She poured herself half a mug, and they sipped in silence for the next few blocks until Garrett slowed the truck and turned onto the lane that led to the old city park. "See that box on the floor beside you?"

"Yes?"

"Open it and see if those will fit. The white ones."

She nestled her empty mug on the floor and slid the lid off the box to reveal two pairs of ice skates, a scuffed black pair, and a smaller white pair. Immediately she knew they were Molly's. "I've never skated before, Garrett. At least not for a long time." She watched him from her spot in the seat behind him, trying to gauge his response.

"I know. You said."

Had she? She didn't remember.

"I'll teach you. It's a good day to learn. The snow will cushion your fall."

"Do I look like a klutz to you?"

He shrugged and ducked her playful backhand.

Smiling to herself, and not minding so much that the skates were Molly's, she scooted to one end of the narrow bench seat and slipped one of her hiking boots off. Sparky eyed her, his huge head cocked to one side.

She unlaced a skate and tugged it on. "They'll work."

"Good."

She took the skate off and slipped back into her boot.

A few sledders had left scars on the hill on the east end of the park, but the rest of the park was a pristine sheet of snow. If not for the few inches of the posts that marked off the lane, they would have had a hard time finding the roadway. They located the pond only because of the dock jutting out of the snow.

Garrett put the truck in low and crept toward the water's edge. "I'm not worried about the ice holding us, but I don't want to test it with the weight of a pickup."

He cut the engine and opened his door. Boss jumped onto his lap and sniffed the frigid air. Laughing, Garrett started to lower him into the snow. "Oh wait. I almost forgot." He lifted him back onto his lap, shut the door, and reached

186

under the seat again. "Here." He handed what looked like a sweatshirt back to Bryn.

"What's this?"

"For Sparky."

She unfolded it and started laughing. "You're going to make me put my dog in a Missouri State sweatshirt?"

"You have a problem with that?"

In reply, she burst into the fight song of her alma mater, Southeast Missouri State, stumbling over the words after the first bar.

Garrett laughed. "Too bad you don't know the lyrics. But, sorry. I didn't know. Here—" He pulled another sweatshirt from under the seat. "I'll trade you. You have anything against Old Navy?"

"Not at all."

"SEMO, huh? I never would have pegged you for a Southeast gal."

"Hey! What's that supposed to mean?"

"You just don't look like a Redhawk, that's all."

"Ha! Spoken like a true MSU Bear."

"And what's *that* supposed to mean?"

"Nothing." She shot him a smug look.

She slung the offending sweatshirt at him and unfolded the Old Navy one. "Come here, Sparky. Let's see if this contraption fits you." She put the shirt over his head and lifted his paw, trying to stuff it into the cutoff sleeve. "Offensive logos aside, this was a pretty clever idea. Where'd you come up with it?"

He tapped the side of his head. "What can I say? I'm just borderline brilliant."

Sparky cooperated while she lifted his other paw. She pulled the rest of the shirt down around his middle and leaned back to survey the result. Sparky cocked his head as if striking a runway pose, and Bryn laughed and clapped.

In the front seat, Garrett wasn't having quite as much luck getting the other doggie sweater on Boss.

"Here, let me help." Bryn hauled Sparky across her lap to the other side of the bench seat and crawled out of the truck. She opened the passenger side door and clucked for Boss to come. Garrett handed her the sweatshirt, and between the two of them, they managed to wrestle the stubborn bulldog into it.

When he was ensconced in the ill-fitting "sweater," Boss gave Bryn a grumpy look. She turned his head so Garrett could see, and that set them both laughing.

With the dogs dressed for the snow, Garrett grabbed both pairs of skates and carried them over to a snow-covered picnic table. He brushed one end of the bench clean and patted it with his gloved hand. "Sit . . . I'll help you with your skates."

She obeyed, slipping off one boot at a time as he knelt in front of her and helped her into the skates. He wore a serious expression. She wondered if he was remembering the last time he and Molly had gone skating together. Was it here at the park? Had he helped his wife with her skates like this?

She grasped for something to say. "Can you skate on top of snow?"

"The pond was clear yesterday. I don't think this will be too bad. At least not yet." He looked at the sky. "I guess we'll find out, huh?"

"I guess."

He finished lacing her skate and gave her ankle a pat. "Is that too tight?"

She put her foot down, testing. "It's fine."

He patted his knee. "Next."

She wiggled out of her other boot and offered him her foot.

A few minutes later, she stood on wobbly ankles clutching the edge of the picnic table while Garrett put his skates on.

The dogs raced each other down to the pond, and Bryn held on to Garrett's arm as they half clomped, half skated to where the ice met the banks.

"You're positive it's safe?"

"I read it in the paper."

"You believe everything you read in the paper?"

He rolled his eyes. "Now you sound like my mother. And no, I don't believe everything I read in the paper." His face darkened. "Not since the fire."

"I know. Me neither." She felt herself tensing, wishing the subject hadn't come up. She didn't want to talk about that day. Didn't want to spoil the magical mood of this moment.

Garrett must have thought the same thing, for he grabbed her hand and tugged her onto the ice. "Let's go."

Squealing and flailing to regain her balance, she let him pull her along. "Slow down, Garrett. I haven't skated since I was a kid."

"It's easy. And you were going to prove that you're not a klutz, remember?" He let loose of her hand and spun on the ice, facing her and skating backward away from her. The snow that settled on the ice was powdery, and his skates sliced through it like a knife blade through powdered sugar.

She put her hands out in front of her and shuffled her feet, feeling wooden and clumsy.

Garrett laughed, spun 360 degrees, and skated back toward her. "Give me your hands."

She let him take her hands and pull her across the ice.

"Try to relax. You're more likely to fall if you're all tensed up."

"I'm likely to fall no matter what." Her laughter came out warbled.

"If you fall, you just get back up. How hard is that?"

"Easy for you to say. Oh . . . !"

He sped up, tightening his grip and holding her gaze. "You're doing fine. Relax. Bend your knees and lean forward a little bit." He tugged gently, pulling her closer to him. "Take tiny steps. Don't try to pick your feet up. Just let them glide . . . find the rhythm."

She sucked in a frigid breath, forced her muscles to relax.

"That's better . . . see there, you can do it."

Gradually her whole body found the rhythm, and soon they were almost dancing on the ice, matching each other's gait step for step. New snow swirled around them, and Sparky and Boss romped beside them. Bryn couldn't stop smiling.

Garrett smiled back, and in one smooth motion reversed, came alongside her, his hand at her waist. She became acutely aware of the weight of his arm around her. He took her hand, and even through the thick gloves they both wore, she could feel his warmth, his strength. She'd forgotten how much she'd loved holding hands with Adam. How safe and loved it had made her feel.

Her toes were starting to go numb, and her face stung with the moist air, but she didn't care. She wanted this day to go on forever.

17

*F*rom the banks of the pond, Garrett stood laughing as the dogs ran circles around Bryn. She cut through the powdery snow, turning circles on the ice, improving by the minute, but still a bit wobbly solo on her skates. *Molly's skates,* his conscience corrected. He brushed the thought away like a bothersome cobweb and finished lacing his boots.

He was worn out and the snow accumulating on the pond was making it harder to skate, but Bryn seemed to have boundless energy. She'd caught on quickly and her delight in this newly acquired skill made him feel the way he did when the light came on in one of his student's eyes after solving a pesky long-division problem.

It had been a good day. Bryn's company always made him feel he could carry on another day, that there was something worth living for, even though Molly was gone. Recently he had dared to entertain the idea that he and Bryn might end up together. It was too soon for either of them, but Bryn made it easy to think of her as more than a friend. Much more.

He'd grown more cautious, distant even, with the other teachers at school, wanting to avoid any more attempts to set him up with eligible young women. He wasn't ready to tell them about Bryn. Besides, what was there to tell? He didn't really miss the times he and Molly had hung out with other young couples from church or from the firehouse. She'd been the gregarious one in their marriage, always planning a party or a get-together with friends. She'd often accused him of being a loner, of never needing any friends but her. He didn't deny it. And now, if he couldn't have Molly, he'd found the only friend he needed in Bryn.

He rubbed his hands together, trying to warm them. The snow was still coming down, and he flicked a few flakes off the sleeves of his down coat. "Are you about ready to go? It's freezing out here."

"Not if you keep moving." She glided toward him, smiling, turned a rather clumsy pirouette, and skated away with Sparky and Boss in pursuit.

He rose and slung his skates over his shoulder. "I'll be in the truck . . . drinking coffee."

At that she skated back to the edge of the pond and clomped up the slippery bank. "Okay, okay . . . but I was just getting the hang of it."

"We'll come back soon so you can practice." He extended a hand and helped her up the slippery bank. He loosened the laces of her skates and pulled them off. She changed into her boots, and they trudged back to the truck with the dogs nipping at their heels.

With the dogs in the backseat together and Bryn in the passenger seat beside him, he started up the truck. The radio came on, and Kenny Chesney crooned a love song. Fitting. Garrett turned up the volume and put the heater on full blast.

Bryn unscrewed the cap of the Thermos and divided what was left of the coffee between their two mugs.

He popped the steering wheel up and sat sideways in the seat, facing Bryn as he pulled off his damp gloves. The frigid air from the heater gradually warmed, and he rubbed his hands in front of the vent.

She placed her mug beside his on the dashboard and did the same. "That was fun," she said, grinning like one of his fifth graders. She lifted her mug in a toast.

"It was." He scratched Boss behind the ears and took a sip of coffee. "You were getting pretty sure on your feet out there, too."

"I was, wasn't I?"

"I was talking to the dog," he deadpanned.

Bryn looked flustered for a minute, then he saw the memory dawn in her eyes, and she burst out laughing. "Oh, touché. You've just been dying to get me back with that, haven't you?"

He chuckled, peering at her over the rim of his mug, loving the way she looked right now with wisps of dark hair floating around her face and her cheeks rosy from the cold. Loving having her here in the truck with him. Wishing he didn't have to take her home in a few minutes, that she could just come home with him and forget about the rest of the world.

He'd only had Molly for a few years, but they'd made it till "death do us part." That was almost forever.

"What are you thinking about, so serious there?"

He looked up to see Bryn studying him, her eyes still laughing. He didn't want to spoil the mood. Didn't know how to answer. He drained his mug, buying time. The warm liquid felt soothing on his throat. "I'm thinking that I . . ." But he wasn't thinking. He was acting, almost unconsciously, not willing to let rational thought keep him from what he wanted in this moment.

Holding her gaze, he set his coffee on the dashboard and took Bryn's mug from her. Her hands were cool to the touch, and he rubbed them briskly between his own, warming them both. He edged closer to her on the bench seat and brushed a strand of hair away from her face.

She looked at her lap, fidgeted with the scarf at her throat. But when her eyes met his again, he knew that she wanted this as much as he did.

He reached up and tucked a strand of hair back under her cap, drawing her close. Her lips were warm and soft, and her mouth fit his the way it had in his dreams.

Her arms went around his neck, and she kissed him back. When he finally pulled away, he couldn't stop touching her, tracing a finger down her nose, outlining the cupid's bow of her lips, cupping her smooth cheek in the palm of his hand.

He leaned to kiss her again, and she responded in a way that made him think he needed to put this truck in gear and take the woman home. To her house. Before he did something he would regret.

He forced himself to let her go. Fumbling under the steering column for the mechanism that put the steering wheel back in position, he slid back to his side of the cab. He dared to look over at Bryn and saw that her eyes were brimming with tears.

"I'm sorry," he said simply.

"I'm not."

Her words took him aback. And didn't fit with her tears. "I . . . I don't know what I was thinking." He put a hand on the gearshift.

"You really don't?"

"Huh?"

"You really don't know what were you thinking? Are you sorry? I . . . I don't think that was an accident."

He shook his head, too upset to speak. She was right. A guy didn't just accidentally kiss a woman, did he? He sure hadn't left home this morning *planning* to kiss her. But here they were. Why would he risk what they had, risk losing the only friend who understood what he was going through, just because he'd been wanting to kiss her for two weeks now?

"Bryn, I had no business doing that." He held up a palm and pasted on a sheepish smile. "Can we just . . . pretend that didn't happen?"

"Garrett . . ." She dropped her head and picked an invisible speck of lint off her ski pants. But when she looked up again, there was a spark in her soft mink eyes. "What if I told you . . . I've been wanting you to do that forever?"

He siphoned a breath and opened his mouth to remind her that she used the word loosely . . . her definition of *forever* couldn't mean longer than ten weeks. It was too soon. *Too soon.* For both of them.

But instead of speaking the words he should have spoken, words that would put them back to where they'd been this morning—nothing more than dear friends—he moved back across the seat and folded her into his arms, kissed her over and over again, hungry for the taste of her.

This time it was she who pushed him away, breathing hard, her shoulders lifting with each quick breath. Her hands went to her mouth, as if shielding her lips from him. Her cheeks glowed pink, and above her hidden mouth, her eyes held a smile. But her slender fingers trembled. And not from the cold. It was obvious she was as shaken as he was.

He slid back under the steering wheel and put the truck in reverse. The snow was falling faster now, piling up in the streets. Sometimes he bucked against all that his faith required of him. Chastity, for instance. The thought made him feel guilty, but it didn't change the fact that, right now, he wanted nothing more than to take this beautiful woman home with him and spend a snowy day making love to her in front of the fire at his apartment.

The temptation was almost more than he could bear, and he had a feeling she felt it, too . . . that all it would take was one word, and she would come inside with him. Or at least want to.

But because of Molly, he knew the reward of waiting, knew that as wonderful as acting on his desires might feel in the moment, he would regret it later.

He pressed the accelerator pedal and gripped the steering wheel harder. The pickup fishtailed on the ice, and Bryn reached both hands out, steadying herself on the dashboard.

"Sorry."

"I'm not."

He gave a nervous laugh. "I meant my driving."

She snickered.

He gave her a sidewise glance. Their eyes met, and they both dissolved in laughter.

When he pulled up to the curb in front of her

townhome a few minutes later, she put a hand on the handle of the car door, then turned to Garrett and narrowed her eyes. "I'm not sorry, Garrett. I'm not."

He gripped the two ends of the scarf she wore and tugged her close for another kiss. "Me neither."

"I'll call you, okay?"

"Okay."

He let loose of her scarf, then did a double take. "Hey, isn't that mine?"

Bryn gave a little gasp, then giggled and dipped her head, unwinding the scarf. "I . . . meant to give it back. Really. You loaned it to me . . . that first day on the riverwalk. Remember?" She handed it to him. "Sorry."

"I wondered where that thing was." He took it from her but put it back over her head and wound it around her neck, giving her one last kiss. "You keep it. I have another one."

She didn't argue with him but wrapped the scarf tighter, hugging herself. Almost like she wished it was him.

18

The phone rang not ten minutes after Garrett dropped Bryn off. She had just dried Sparky off and was heading to the shower to get ready for work.

Caller ID displayed Garrett's number. She smiled and picked up the phone. "Hello?"

"Hi." She could hear the smile in his voice.

"Hi. What's wrong? Did you change your mind about the scarf?" she teased.

He laughed. "No, but I wondered if you'd changed your mind." His laughter died. "About us."

"What do you mean?"

He exhaled into the phone and his words came out in a breathless gush. "It's just that . . . I know you're going to start thinking through everything that happened today—between us. And it's not going to make sense. It's going to seem like we were just acting on our loneliness. Like it's way too soon for either of us to be thinking about having anyone else in our lives."

He paused. But when she didn't say anything, he rambled on. "If you call up one of your girl-friends, she's going to freak out and say, 'Are you crazy?' and if you tell your dad, he's going to try to convince you that I'm taking advantage of you, and how could I possibly care about you when I've barely had time to grieve my own loss and how could you even think about another man when you've just lost your own husband and—"

"Garrett—" She closed her eyes and a picture of Adam materialized behind her eyelids. A wave of longing—for her husband—washed over her, stronger than any grief she'd felt in the beginning. *Oh, babe . . .*

She forced her focus back to Garrett's voice, not wanting to go where her thoughts threatened to carry her. Garrett rambled off his list of the thousand and one reasons—all good, *reasonable* reasons—that they shouldn't be together.

And he was right. Her father *would* say those things, and if she told her friends—the few she'd kept in touch with since the fire—they would coo well-meaning platitudes. But she would see the judgment in their eyes. Especially Jenna, whose own loss was identical. She could already hear her friend's lecture—or the one she would have given if they were on speaking terms: *It's way too soon, give yourself some time to grieve, don't jump into anything for at least a year . . .*

Bottom line, all the advice would mean the same thing: *what* could you possibly be thinking?

"Garrett." She tried again to get a word in edgewise.

"Huh?"

She forced a laugh. "I know all that. Okay? And you're right. Everyone will probably tell us it's too soon. But how can they know that if they haven't been where we are?"

"That's what I was thinking."

"We won't do anything stupid. We'll take it slow."

"We will?" He laughed. "I mean, we *will*."

"Right." How they were going to take it slow when all she wanted to do was kiss him again, feel the warmth of his arms around her . . . she didn't know. She cleared her throat. "Is that the end of your speech?"

"Why?"

"Some of us have to go to work, you know."

"Oh. Sorry. The library's open?"

"As far as I know. Myrna hasn't called anyway. The president has to declare a national disaster before she'll close the place. I think she thinks we're the post office or something."

"Huh?" She could almost picture him scratching his head.

"You know: neither snow, nor rain, nor gloomy night or—however that goes."

He laughed. "I think it's 'gloom of night.' But hey, I say good for her. At least the kids will have someplace to go since they're out of school."

"Oh, great. The place will be overrun with little rug rats today."

He gave a dastardly villain laugh. "Lucky you."

"You could come and help, you know."

"No, thanks."

She realized she'd been hinting, and for a split-second she felt the sting of rejection.

But he clucked his tongue. "Woman, why do you think I brought you home from the park when I did? I don't need the temptation of you and me in some dark corner behind the stacks."

She warmed to the words and let herself flirt. "Why'd you call me, then?"

His sigh dripped with feigned exasperation. "Did you not hear the twenty-two-point lecture I just delivered?"

"I heard *blah blah blah blah.*" She smiled into the phone.

But Garrett's tone was serious. "I just want you to think about what happened. I don't want you to think I seduced you—well, maybe that's not the word I want."

"No," she agreed. "You were the quintessential gentleman."

"You obviously didn't read my mind."

She chose to ignore that. They were skating dangerously close to a topic they'd best leave alone. The truth was, she wasn't sure how she would have responded if he hadn't been such a gentleman. It frightened her to realize that. She moved to a safer topic. "I had a wonderful time, Garrett. Thank you."

"I did, too. I just want you to know that if things . . . are going too fast . . . I don't want you to have regrets. I didn't mean to rush you. I can slow down if you want me to. I know it seems soon. After . . . everything. But don't you think it's possible that God brought us together exactly because we each know what the other is going through?"

"That's crossed my mind, too."

"Maybe this is His way of answering the prayers I've prayed—for comfort, for a way out of the loneliness." He gave a snort. "I didn't mean to make it sound like just any warm soul would do. Nothing is coming out right."

"It's okay. I know what you mean. I've thought the same thing." That wasn't quite true. She couldn't bring herself to tell him that she hadn't been able to pray since that night. She wasn't mad at God—at least she didn't think she was. But for some reason, she hadn't been able to reach out to Him the way she had when Adam was alive.

But how could she tell Garrett that? He seemed so close to God. Odd, since he'd told her he wasn't sure he'd even really believed in God before Molly died.

"Molly was the one who had the faith in our marriage," he'd told her one day as they walked the dogs on the riverwalk. "I was just along for the ride. But after I lost her . . . I don't know . . . for the first time, I think I understood why God was so important to her. Knowing she's in heaven has made me look at everything differently. For the first time I understand what she meant when she talked about loving Jesus, following Him. And how she always lived with the idea that this life isn't all there is."

Garrett had looked at her with that brooding, serious expression he wore too often. "I don't know how I could have missed it before—when it was right in front of my eyes every day. In Molly. In the way she lived with such purpose. I don't understand why God took her and let me live. But I don't want to waste the gift."

She wished she could feel what he felt. She'd been raised in a home where prayer was like breathing. Especially when Mom got sick. She'd felt close to God even then. Felt like she could pray and He heard her. Knew she could talk to Him and He cared about what she had to say. But something had changed the night of the fire. While it seemed wrong to compare her personal loss, the fire had burned up more than what photographs or newspaper stories or cemetery plots could measure.

Maybe it was about trust. But how could she ever trust again, after something as horrible as that night? She wasn't blaming God. She didn't believe He had caused the awful events of that evening. But if He was all powerful, all knowing—if God loved her—He had, at the very least, *allowed* it to happen. She couldn't reconcile that.

It was too hard to think about. She envied Garrett's peace.

"I really should go get ready for work." She cradled the phone to her ear, not wanting to lose the closeness she felt to him right now. "Thank you for calling, Garrett. I heard your sermon. I think I know what you're saying. We'll . . . talk about it more, okay? We don't have to decide something right now, do we?"

"I guess not. I just wanted to make sure I didn't scare you off. I don't want to lose you because I was stupid."

She curbed a smile. "Oh, so now kissing me was stupid?"

"No! That's not what I—"

"Kidding . . . I'm kidding." She feigned what she hoped was a convincing laugh.

"You'd better go get ready for work."

"Didn't I just say that?"

"I'm hanging up, you big goof." He laughed and she could picture the exact smile he was wearing—one corner of his mouth tilted upward while his teeth teased his bottom lip.

She disconnected and set the phone in its cradle. She adored that man. They would proceed with caution. Neither of them wanted to ruin what had turned into the most precious friendship she'd ever known. Her conscience made her insert *next to Adam.*

But she wasn't sure it was true.

19

At work that afternoon, Bryn couldn't stop smiling. There were a few rowdy kids in the children's library, but she volunteered to shelve books there, just so Myrna wouldn't grill her about the goofy grin she couldn't seem to shed.

In bed that night she smiled up at the ceiling. It was like strong medicine to smile again. She'd shed enough tears to last a lifetime. She thought about what Garrett had said on the phone after he dropped her off. She didn't care if the whole world thought it was too soon. She would defend her friendship with Garrett to anyone. She didn't care what her dad would say. Or what Garrett's family might think. The more she considered Garrett's words, the more they made sense.

What they had together was a gift from God. They had each lost the most precious person in their world, they had both experienced the horror of being left alone in the prime of life. God had sent her a person who understood her grief intimately because it matched his own. Identically.

Something compelled her to slip from beneath the covers and fall to her knees beside the bed. She folded her hands and bent her head, the way her mother had taught her to pray. The memory warmed her. Like coming home.

"Thank You, God," she whispered into the quiet of the night. "Thank You for drawing me here. I'm so sorry I haven't turned to You for help. I'm so sorry I've ignored You. I want to have the kind of faith Garrett has in You, Lord. I know I need to stay close to You. Please heal my broken heart. And thank You. I think You've already begun to do that . . . through Garrett. Oh, thank You for putting him in my life, Lord. I don't know what I'd do without him."

The tears came, cleansing and healing. Tears of gratitude. And, strangely, a new wave of love for Adam. She'd let petty things come between them. She hadn't always been kind to him, hadn't demonstrated her love nearly well enough. And she hadn't been honest with him. It was wrong for her to have snuck around, working at the shelter when he'd asked her not to. He'd only done it because he loved her, and he wanted her to be safe.

"I'm so sorry, Lord. Please forgive me." Though the air in the room was chilly, a rush of warmth went through her. She hadn't felt God's presence like this in so long. Convicted, she continued to pray, whispered words that rushed out without effort. And this time, the words didn't seem to stop at the ceiling, but instead they rose to heaven, and she somehow knew they were heard and understood.

"Oh, God, I want to be right with You. No matter what it costs. Please show me what You want for me, what You have planned for my life. And thank You again, Lord, for putting Garrett in my life."

When she crawled back into bed a few minutes later, she closed her eyes and floated in a cocoon of peace like she hadn't experienced since she was a little girl. Something had changed within her. She couldn't have described it if her life depended on it. There were no words. But she knew she would look back on this moment and know that something of great value—something eternal—had happened the moment she truly opened her heart to God.

She felt herself drifting off, in that twilight place between consciousness and sleep. Her mind replayed the day with Garrett, his laughter, the sweet kisses they'd shared. As if she were actually back in the warmth of his car, she felt him tug at her scarf—the one she'd "borrowed" from him. He pulled her toward him for yet another kiss.

But something happened, and Garrett disappeared. The scarf around her neck turned from black to red, as if it had been dipped in blood. She looked down, rubbed the soft wool between her fingers.

But it wasn't Garrett's scarf around her neck. It was her mother's. Where had it been all this time? She thought she'd lost it. She held it to her face, expecting, for some strange reason, that it would smell like Garrett. But it smelled of smoke and sweat and fear.

She clutched at her throat, trying to shed the scarf. It fell in a puddle at her feet. Onto the ancient tile of the second-floor office. She looked around her. She was back at the Grove Street Shelter. The room still reeked of that man's body odor, despite the fact that he'd left the room twenty minutes ago.

Another scent tickled her nostrils. Cinnamon. Sweet and warm.

The flame flickered and waned, then flared again.

A knock sounded. "Come in," she muttered. She held her breath against the stench, thinking the client had returned to stink up her space again. It was bad enough that he'd waited until after midnight to check in. Susan's policy was no admissions after eleven p.m. He was lucky she'd made an exception.

But instead it was Charlie at the door. "Hey, Charlie. What's up?"

"What are you doing up so late, sis?"

"We had a late admission."

"Oh." He rolled his wheelchair back and forth in the narrow space between the desk and the door—his version of pacing. "Wanna play some cards when you're done there?"

She looked at the papers covering her desk. Then at Charlie. He was agitated, she could tell. He often got that way for no reason. Probably some form of post-traumatic stress from his years in Vietnam. He managed it pretty well, but sometimes if he couldn't sleep, he started thinking too hard.

"My call. Gin rummy. Best two out of three. But then you have to promise to get some sleep."

"You're on." His grizzled grin told her she'd done the right thing.

She scooted her chair back. The paperwork could wait a few minutes. "Seven-card, no jokers."

"Whatever you say, sis. I'm not picky about which game I beat you at."

"Ha ha," she deadpanned, coming around from behind the desk. The office was warm, and she realized that, oddly, her mother's scarf was somehow wrapped around her neck again. She slipped it off and traded it for the small purse she carried to work. She ran the red scarf through her hand and lopped it over the hook on the back of the door. The paneling and wide woodwork suggested this room had probably been a private office—belonging to one of the doctors, or perhaps the administrator. The hook had probably held a lab coat or suit jacket back when the hospital had still been in business.

The cinnamon candle on the desk winked at her, then settled into a steady glow. She inhaled through her nose. Maybe it was her imagination, but she could still smell that man's B.O. She would let the candle burn while she played a couple hands of gin with Charlie. Make the air halfway breathable so she could finish filling out the intake forms and clean off the desk for tomorrow night's volunteers.

Blow it out! Blow it out now!

With one hand on the doorknob, she waited for Charlie to maneuver his chair through the wide doorway. Charlie was saying something. Something that made her laugh, but she couldn't hear his words. Why was she laughing? Slowly she watched her hand pull the door shut and place the key from her lanyard in the lock.

No! Go back! Don't leave it burning! Go back! Go back!

Something was pressing down on her chest. She couldn't breathe. She struggled to open her eyes, but her eyelids were glued shut. She tried to push the door open, but her arms were dead weight. She willed her leg to kick the door open. Nothing. She couldn't move. Paralyzed. She could barely seize her next breath.

Something was wrong. Something was terribly wrong.

20

Tuesday, January 15

*B*ryn sat upright in bed, trembling, frantically trying to shake off the dream. That had to be what it was. Just a dream.

The clock on her nightstand glowed the hour. Ten minutes after one. She'd watched the clock change to midnight from her knees beside the bed. The memory flooded back—the sweet time she'd spent praying, feeling as if God had reached down and touched her, let her know He heard every word.

That was barely an hour ago. But enough time to fall asleep. Enough time for her mind to manufacture that horrifying nightmare. She threw the blanket off and swung her legs over the side of the bed. Getting her bearings in the dark room, she stumbled to the bathroom and flipped on the light.

She went to the sink and splashed cold water on her face. Rubbing her cheeks briskly with a rough hand towel, she felt herself come awake. She leaned forward and studied her face in the mirror, lifted her shoulders, taking in a deep breath.

Her mind swam with the images of the nightmare. She rarely dreamed, and almost never had nightmares—at least not ones she remembered in the morning. But this was all so real. She could hardly separate the dream from memory. In her dream Charlie had come up to the office at the Grove Street Shelter just like that night. In fact, their conversation in her dream was almost word-for-word the way it had really gone.

She started. Her mother's scarf. It had been in the dream. The black scarf Garrett had loaned her had morphed into her mother's scarf. Didn't that prove it was a dream?

She reviewed the events of the dream in her mind, terrified to revisit the way it had made her feel, but at the same time desperate to sort out the details—sort fact from fiction.

And then, in a flash, it all came clearly. Her mother's scarf. The reason she hadn't been able to find it was because she'd left it in the office that night. She'd left it there because she intended all along to go back to the office. And she *had* left that candle burning. Not just in her dream, but that night.

She staggered back out to her bedroom and slumped onto the bed. Everything in her dream was exactly the way it had happened in real life. It wasn't a dream, it was a memory. A vivid memory of everything that had happened that night. Of what she'd known all along, but had been too terrified to explore. Too terrified to admit.

Worse, they might have had earlier warning that night, might have been able to get the fire out before it got out of control, but the smoke detector in the office had been disabled. And it didn't take a dream for Bryn to remember— vividly—that *she* was the one who'd disabled it. Her actions had seemed so innocuous the night she'd done it. Her intentions had never been sinister.

You will know the truth, and the truth will set you free.

"Oh, dear God." She could barely breathe the words. "What have I done? Oh, God, what have I done?" Every ounce of strength went out from her, and she slid to the floor at the foot of the bed, feeling as paralyzed as she had moments ago when the dream had awakened her.

It was true. It was *all* true. And she was responsible. She'd never had a chance to go back and blow out the candle. Because that candle had somehow started a fire. *She* was responsible for the fact that they'd had no warning until it was too late. How could she have hidden it . . . from everyone? Even from herself?

"What do I do, God?" She gasped as the gravity of the truth rolled over her. She was the same as a murderer. Those lives—Adam's, Captain Vermontez, all of them—were on her head.

Molly. "No! Oh, no. Please, God . . ." A wave of nausea deluged her. How could she ever face Garrett with this truth? All this time everyone had been looking for Zeke Downing, looking for someone else to charge with the deaths of five heroes.

And it had been her. All along it had been her.

How could they ever forgive her? Could even God forgive her?

She groveled on the floor at the foot of the bed, tearing at her hair in anguish. She saw no way out, no possible way that God could redeem her. That this could ever be made right.

She struggled to her knees, steadying herself with palms flat on the mattress. She cast about the room, frantic. If her eyes had landed upon a means of ending her life—a bottle of pills, a gun—she might have grasped it in relief. The thought left her breathless. She didn't want to go on. But she couldn't end her own life. She could never do that to her father.

But she wished she could fall asleep and never wake up. She slumped against the bed. "Help me, God. Help me."

Like the rain of ashes and debris from the inferno, the thoughts plagued her. She would have to tell her father. It might kill him, send him into heart failure. But how could she keep it from him? There was no way.

And of course Garrett would have to know. That would end everything between them. He had made no secret of his desire to see the arsonist punished to the full extent of the law.

She wasn't an arsonist. But her actions had resulted in no less a tragedy. Was what she'd done punishable by death? Her blood ran cold, and she dropped her head. But that would be a gift, wouldn't it? Death would be a far more merciful sentence than living with what she'd done.

Who could she tell? Where could she go to reveal her secret? And how could she explain why she'd waited so long to confess? She hadn't known. She hadn't remembered until now. But would they believe her?

You will know the truth, and the truth will set you free.

Her breath came in short gasps. She *had* known.

Deep inside—someplace she'd buried deep and toiled to forget—the truth had dwelled all along. She had known. But the truth had been too terrible to face, even in secret.

The truth will set you free.

How could the truth set her free? No. The truth might put her behind prison walls. Possibly put her to death.

"What are You trying to do, God? I don't understand," she wailed. "Why did You bring that memory back now? What difference will it make? It won't bring those people back. It doesn't change anything, God."

The truth will set you free.

The words came as clearly as if He had spoken them aloud. The truth *would* set her free. She could never forgive herself if she wasn't honest. She had to confess her role in the fire that had killed Adam and the others. She somehow knew that, as well as she now knew what had happened that night. She had manufactured memories of blowing that candle out. She wanted to believe it so badly that she'd created images in her mind, somehow convinced herself. And then she'd filled her time with other things so that she didn't have to think about what she'd always known.

But now that her dream revealed what actually happened, she had no choice but to turn herself in. She could never bring Adam back. Or Molly, or any of them. But she had to pay for what she'd done. She could not live with herself if she didn't.

Clutching the bedcovers, she rose on legs like Jell-O and went into the bathroom. She turned the shower as hot as she could make it and stood under the sharp needles.

Half an hour later, when she stepped from beneath the spray, she knew what she had to do.

21

Garrett checked his cell phone again as he unlocked his apartment. He'd texted Bryn three times since he got up this morning and called both her home phone and her cell. When she didn't answer either, he left two voice mail messages and an email. She hadn't responded to any of them. When she finally got all those messages, she'd probably accuse him of stalking her, but this wasn't like her. He usually got an almost immediate response if he texted her.

A sinking feeling went through him. He'd been afraid all along that she would start to think too hard about what had happened in the park, start to second-guess how their friendship had moved to a new level after he'd kissed her.

She'd said she was happy with the change. She'd made a point to tell him that on the phone. Still, he knew once she started thinking it through that she might have second thoughts, might decide that it was too soon. He'd had similar thoughts himself. That's why he'd called her last night after he got home. He wanted to reassure her that he wasn't willing to risk their friendship by running ahead of her. But maybe she didn't believe him.

Things had gotten pretty hot and heavy between them. The kind of intensity Molly called "no turning back." Once, he and Molly had run into Molly's best friend while they were shopping at the mall. Michelle was with a guy she worked with—someone she'd always told Molly was "just a friend"—but it was obvious by the way they were pawing each other that they'd turned into more than friends. When they were out of earshot, Molly had rolled her eyes. "Well, there goes a perfectly good friendship."

"Why do you say that? Looks to me like they're better friends than ever."

But Molly stopped in her tracks, put her hands on his shoulders, and turned him around. "Look at them." She pointed down the corridor at the arm-in-arm couple. "Don't you get it, Garrett? There's no turning back now. They can never go back to being friends. If this doesn't work out, they'll never be able to get back what they had before."

He'd argued with her. But deep inside he knew she was right. Was that what Bryn was worrying about right now? That they'd already gone too far? That they'd already ruined a perfectly good friendship?

He culled a pile of catalogs and credit card offers from the mail and tossed them in the trash can under the kitchen sink. He had to convince her somehow. He'd have to take it slow, keep his paws off her for a while. Prove to her that he was willing to back off a little for the sake of preserving what they'd had before today.

But oh, it would not be easy. The thought of being with Bryn again did a number on his heart rate. Smiling, he fished his cell phone out of his pocket, flopped on the sofa, and dialed her number again.

Wednesday, January 16

The phone started ringing. Again. Bryn froze. It would be Garrett, and she couldn't talk to him. Not yet. Maybe not ever.

She shifted in the hard chair at the kitchen table, then turned back to the stack of envelopes on the table in front of her. The sheet of paper beneath her hand was blank.

She'd called Myrna and told her she was sick and wouldn't be in to work. It wasn't a lie. She'd never felt so sick in her life—mentally, physically, emotionally. She hadn't been able to keep down what little she'd tried to eat, and she could barely stay upright.

Nevertheless she had sat here with barely a break since early this morning, writing letters of apology to everyone she could think of, explaining what had happened, how she truly had not remembered her role in the fire for certain until last night, that she would give her own life a thousand times if it would bring back the brave firefighters who'd died that night, and that while she was prepared to take whatever punishment the law required for her act of extreme negligence, she knew that in the eyes of these heroes' loved ones, it would never be enough.

She'd bent to the task, writing by hand, making each note personal and unique, not willing to do this by rote. She didn't have mailing addresses for each person on her list, but she would find them and mail the letters tomorrow morning.

One by one, she turned over each sealed envelope on the stack, admiring the handwriting she'd taken such care with, and then feeling sick that she could think of such a trivial, self-centered thing at a moment like this.

As she read each person's name, she said a prayer for them—that God would comfort them, that they would accept her apology and somehow find the mercy within them to forgive her.

Jenna Morgan. Her friend. It hurt more than she'd admitted, even to herself, to have lost her friendship. It didn't matter now what Jenna's reasons for drifting away were. This letter would seal the distance between them in a way that could never be repaired.

She'd written separately to Bill and Clarissa Morgan, Zach's parents. She'd never met Jenna's in-laws, but she'd seen their name in news stories about the fire. Now she prayed for them, weeping as she imagined them opening her letter and reading words that couldn't help but reopen the wound of losing their son. Jenna would probably read their letter, too, and share their pain all over again.

She turned over another envelope. Emily Vermontez, Manny's wife. And another letter to their son, Lucas, who'd not only lost his father, but had lost the use of his legs—at least temporarily—in the fire.

Her hand lingered when she turned over the envelope that bore Susan Marlowe's name. Susan had been her friend, too, someone a few years older, someone she looked up to. Bryn ached, thinking how betrayed Susan would feel when she learned the truth. She had lost the husband she adored and now she was left to comfort two sons who were taking the death of their father very hard. Like salt in an open wound, the fire had also destroyed the very building that housed the ministry Susan had poured her heart into.

Bryn had written separate notes to the Marlowes' sons, Davy—David, Jr.—and Danny, and included them in Susan's envelope. She didn't know Susan's boys either, but she knew the elder, David's namesake, had struggled greatly, wanting to drop out of college and come home. Perhaps her letter would allow Davy a small measure of closure on his father's death.

Not since she'd begun to write the letters in the early hours of this morning had she had second thoughts or been tempted to keep quiet about her role in the fire. She knew—beyond a ghost of a doubt—that she was doing what God had led her to do. That she could never live with herself if she didn't do everything in her power to make amends.

But now, looking at the fresh sheet of paper in front of her, she broke down. It took all her strength to pick up the pen again. She held the point over the paper, and in a shaky hand she wrote "Dear Dad." She put the pen down and wadded up the tear-smudged paper. With a groan of anguish, she tossed it into the trash can under her desk.

She couldn't let Dad read this in a letter. She had to tell him in person. Today. She needed to be with him to soften the news. But how could news like this ever be made more palatable?

Maybe she would spend the night at his house before she turned herself in tomorrow. She trembled, thinking about how distraught Dad would be, how disappointed in her. She prayed his heart could hold up under the strain. She would never forgive herself if hearing her news sent him into heart failure. But she couldn't *not* tell him.

A new thought brushed at her conscience, and the beginnings of a letter to Adam took form in her mind. She imagined the words scrawled across a sheet of paper. *Dearest Adam, can you ever forgive me?*

Wiping away the new onslaught of tears, she pulled out a fresh sheet of paper.

For Garrett. For the living.

To write his letter would be the hardest thing she had ever done. At first, she'd thought she would tell him in person. If the tables had been turned, she would have wanted Garrett to come to her and make his confession face-to-face. But as she'd relived their conversations in her mind over the past few weeks, she remembered Garrett's bitter words against "whoever" was responsible for the fire that killed Molly.

Maybe she was being cowardly in this respect, but she could not bring herself to face him, to see the look of love that had been in his eyes for her the first time they'd kissed, turn to disgust. After he knew the truth, he would never want to see her again. It would only be torture for him to have to look at her after he knew what she'd done.

She drew in a breath and steeled herself to write words that would end—forever—one of the dearest friendships she'd ever known.

22

"Hi, Dad . . ."

"Bryn! Come in, come in. What are you doing in this neck of the woods? I wasn't expecting you."

"I know. I should have called." She was losing her nerve fast.

"Nonsense. I just finished drinking some hot cocoa. Can I make you a cup?"

"No. Thanks."

"Do you want something to eat? Have you had dinner?" He closed the door behind her and headed for the kitchen.

"No. I'm not hungry. I . . . Daddy, I have something to tell you."

He turned to face her, cocked his head, and studied her. "And I bet I know what it is." A slow smile painted his face. "It's that Garrett fellow, isn't it? The guy you've been walking those dogs with?"

"No . . . Dad. It's . . ." She looked past him to his cluttered living room, suddenly not sure her legs would hold her. "Let's sit down, okay?" She plopped into a chair.

But Dad fluttered around the room like a little old woman, picking up newspapers, stacking food-crusted dishes to one side of the coffee table. "I think I know what you're going to say, Bryn Abigail, and I know what you think I'm going to say, so let me just save you the time." He crossed his arms and leaned against the doorjamb between the living room and kitchen. "You're in love with this man, and you think I'm going to tell you it's too soon."

Bryn opened her mouth to protest, but Dad was on a roll.

"Under other circumstances I might tell you just that, Bryn. But for some time now, you've had a cheerful catch in your voice and a spark in your eyes every time you mention that boy's name."

The love in her father's eyes made her want to weep. How on earth could she tell him what had happened? She needed to do it now, but she couldn't make her voice work.

And Dad rambled on. "You're too young to be in mourning for too long. If you love this guy, you have my blessing. I know you wouldn't jump into something you weren't sure about. I trust you."

She sat on the edge of the sofa, paralyzed. Oh, if only what Dad thought she'd come to tell him were true. In that moment, she loved him more than she could express—for giving her permission to love Garrett, for understanding, for trusting her. *Trust*. That thought took her breath away. For what she must tell him now would destroy that trust.

"Oh, Daddy . . ." She fought to keep from crying. "I wish it were that. I wish it were good news. But . . . it's not."

"Bryn? Honey, what's wrong?"

"I've done . . . I did something terrible. I didn't mean to." Overwhelmed again by what she had to confess, her voice caught on a sob. "Oh, I'm so sorry."

Like a flash her father was at her side, his arm around her. She drew strength from his presence. "What is it, honey? What's wrong?"

She heard the fear in his tone and wanted desperately to be able to take it back. But she couldn't. "I've been keeping a terrible secret— even from myself. I tried to tell myself that I hadn't done anything, but no matter how I wanted it to be true, it . . . it just wasn't. And now, I have to make it right. I have to, Dad."

"Make what right? Bryn, you're not making any sense."

"The fire . . ." She shot up a prayer for her father's heart. "The fire that killed Adam, that killed all those men . . . it was my fault."

"What? You're talking nonsense, Bryn. What on earth are you saying?"

"I left a candle burning . . . in the office at the shelter. That's what started the fire that night. I didn't mean to. I was going to go back and put it out. But then Charlie asked me to play cards with him and—" She stopped short. Over and over, she'd had to correct her thoughts, remind herself that she couldn't lay the blame anywhere else. Not on Charlie, not on the man with the body odor, not on a lack of sleep, and certainly not on Adam, who'd started their fight and put her in a fragile frame of mind. None of those things were an excuse for her mistake. "I never should have left it."

"Bryn?" Dad stared at her. "Are you sure?"

In agony, she could only nod.

He put his head down, ran the fingers of both hands through his hair again and again. Finally he lifted his head and stared across the room at nothing. "But you don't know that's what started the fire."

"I do know, Dad."

"How *could* you know? It . . . it could have been anything."

"Daddy . . ." She drew another labored breath. "They know the fire started on the second floor. And that's not all . . ." Flushed with shame, she told him about disabling the smoke detector in the office.

Her father slumped in the chair, exhaled a heavy breath. "But they—the paper said something about mattresses."

"That's why the fire was so intense, yes. Because all those mattresses from the hospital were stored there. But that's not what started the fire."

Her father sat shaking his head, seeming to absorb all that. Finally he put his elbows on his knees and looked up at her. "Why haven't you said anything before now?"

She told him about her dream, about how she'd suppressed the memories, even tried to manufacture a memory of blowing the candle out.

"How can you be so sure the dream is more real than the memories you made up? What's the difference?"

She hung her head. "I know the difference. I just know."

When his shoulders slumped, she knew he believed her. He closed his eyes for a minute before he met her gaze again. "So what are you going to do?"

"I have to tell someone. I have to confess."

"Bryn, you can't be sure it was you. Wait until the investigators have finished their work."

"No, Daddy. It's bad enough that I've waited this long. I have to tell someone. If I wait until it comes out in the report—" She didn't have a clue how to finish her sentence.

"But . . . who would you tell? You can't just walk into the police station and . . . We need to hire a lawyer. You have to be very careful. This is serious, Bryn. You can't just march in and claim you did it. You could go to jail! Maybe you're wrong."

She shook her head. "I've written letters to all

the families, apologizing. Now I need to turn myself in. I'm so sorry. I am so sorry." Grief flooded her as she realized how profoundly this would affect her father. And as she realized that he might be right, she also realized there was a very real possibility that she might go to jail for what she'd done.

"Bryn, I'm going to call someone. An attorney that Eberfield has used sometimes. He's a good lawyer."

She closed her eyes. "I can't afford a lawyer. *Any* lawyer, let alone a good one."

"Don't you worry about that. I'll take care of it."

"No, Dad. I'm *guilty*. What can a lawyer do with that? I don't want to try to get out of it. I want—I *need*—to pay the consequences. I couldn't forgive myself if I didn't."

"You're just saying that because you've lost Adam." He pushed up from the sofa and started to pace. "You're depressed, Bryn. But honey, you have to fight this. You have so much to live for."

She smiled softly. "I don't think I'll get the electric chair, Daddy."

His face went gray. "Don't even joke about something like that."

She went to him and put her arms around him. Love for her father welled inside her. She hated that her actions had caused him such grief and shame. Hated that more than anything about this whole mess. A quick image of the stretchers lined up outside the burning shelter corrected that thought immediately.

"Do you want to go with me?"

His eyes grew wide, and he glanced at his wristwatch. "Are you going *now*?"

She took a deep breath. "First thing in the morning. I . . . I can't go through the weekend with this on my head."

"Of course I'll go with you. And you stay here tonight."

She nodded. She had her things in the car, knowing Dad would insist on her staying once he knew what she planned to do.

Bryn tried to imagine the scene tomorrow—her father holding her hand as she told the police everything. It would be so much easier with him beside her. And yet it broke her heart to think of putting him through that.

A sob convulsed her. She stood quickly. She couldn't let Dad see her break down. "I'm going to the bathroom," she choked out, forcing her voice to steady.

He nodded, a faraway look in his eyes.

Bryn almost ran down the hall to the bathroom. She closed the door, locked it, and slumped to the floor, pressing her back against the cool tiled wall.

She yanked a bath towel off the rack and buried her face in it, trying to stifle the sobs. "Oh, God,

I don't understand! How could You let this happen?" she whispered.

The truth will set you free.

She heard the timeless words again, and with them came a tentative peace.

23

The guest room at her father's house was the small bedroom at the back of the house that served as his den. Exactly a year after Mom died, Dad had moved out to the country. Bought this little ranch-style house on three wooded acres twelve miles from the Falls. She'd hated like crazy to see him sell the house she grew up in, but he'd insisted it was too hard to have memories of Mom everywhere he turned. And she understood. She'd found it difficult to visit him at the old house after Mom died. She could only imagine how empty it must have felt to Dad.

She smoothed the blankets Dad had spread on the saggy old fold-out sofa, turned out the light, and crawled under the cool sheets. Out in the kitchen, she heard Dad running water, opening and closing cupboard doors. Then she heard him walk—shuffle was more like it—down the hallway, stop by her door for a moment, then move on to his room.

After tossing and turning for twenty minutes,

listening to the clock on the wall above the sofa tick off the seconds, she threw off the covers and felt her way to Dad's desk. She groped for the switch on his desk lamp. The lightbulb cast a yellow puddle on the old desk blotter. Bryn remembered it from his office in the house where she'd grown up.

Quietly she slid open one of the side drawers, looking for paper. She found it where he'd always kept it. Pulling out that crisp sheet of white paper brought sweet memories of Daddy sitting at his desk after work, fresh from the shower, smelling of shampoo and a freshly laundered shirt. She would creep up beside him, not wanting to disturb him as he bent his head over the desk, sharpened pencil in hand.

Years later she figured out that Dad's evening "business" consisted of working the crossword puzzle in the *News-Leader.* She smiled at the memory and chose a pen from the Eberfield & Sons mug on his desk.

Yet as she wrote the date at the top of the page, she sobered. The pen may as well have weighed a thousand pounds for its burden in her hand. Still, she was afraid words would fail her tomorrow, so she set the point to the page and wrote out her confession.

I, Bryn Hennesey, wish to confess my guilt in the fire at the Grove Street Homeless Shelter on November 1 of last year. Though it was completely unintentional, I believe my negligence caused the fire that killed my husband, Adam Hennesey, and four other firefighters.

She stopped and stared at the words, overcome with grief. Seeing her confession spelled out in black-and-white brought home again the gravity of what she had done. She studied the words, aware there was probably a way to word her confession that would leave loopholes and give her a chance of avoiding conviction.

Dad wanted her to hire an attorney. But no attorney in the world could change the fact that she was guilty. She didn't want to get out of punishment for what she'd done. Besides, there was no punishment that could ever right what had happened that night. Even death—could she have offered her very life—could never balance out the five lives the fire had taken. The people her carelessness had killed were valiant heroes. She was a coward, who didn't deserve one day of the happiness she'd enjoyed.

She thought of that magical morning at Ferris Park with Garrett, of the joy that had filled her just being with him. She had been so wrong to let him think she was a friend. Though she didn't understand how the human mind worked, surely she had known the truth all along. Surely somewhere, deep inside, she'd been aware that she was to blame for the tragedy. What was she thinking, allowing Garrett to trust her, be her friend, maybe even fall in love with her?

And how could he help but hate every cell of her being when he found out what she'd done?

She picked up the pen and continued to write. She had to remain rational. She had to face the truth . . . and then face whatever consequences came with it.

Thursday, January 17

A yellow slice of sunlight painted the matted carpet in the den. The familiar, comforting aroma of Dad's Folgers wafted under the door, and Bryn heard her father rummaging around in the kitchen.

She must have managed to finally fall asleep, but she had seen the hands of the clock announce every hour until five o'clock. It was seven now. She'd felt dread last night, despair even, but now she just wanted to get this day over with.

Would she be sitting in a jail cell tonight? Sleeping there? She didn't know. But neither did she fear what might happen. It was in God's hands now, and by the time the sun set tonight, she would have done everything in her power to bring the truth to light. There was immense relief in that knowledge. And the tentative peace she felt only proved that she'd been living with a terrible, hidden knowledge since that fateful night.

She quickly showered and dressed and went down the hall to the kitchen. Dad was sitting at the table, his back to her, his head bowed. She hadn't realized how gray his color had become. She cleared her throat and his head jerked up.

"Good morning. I didn't mean to scare you." She forced a note of cheer into her voice.

"I've been thinking, Bryn. What if we wait until the fire inspector's report comes back? Maybe something will turn up to prove that it wasn't a candle after all. If you didn't remember until now, maybe it didn't happen the way you think it—"

"Dad. Please." She held up a hand. "I know you don't want this to be true, that you're desperate to find a way out. But . . . you're just making it harder for me. I've prayed about this. I know the truth. And I know what I have to do."

He pushed his chair back and stood, defiance in his stance. "I've been looking on the Internet. Do you know what the penalty for involuntary manslaughter is? You could go to jail, Bryn. Prison. There has to be another way. There has to be a way out. At least let them appoint you a lawyer."

She nodded. "Dad . . . I'm not looking for a way out. I'm guilty. I deserve to go to jail." She'd begun to think she deserved to die. But seeing the distress on her father's face, she offered him words that had comforted her in recent days.

"There may not be a way out, but there has to be a way through. I'm not afraid, Daddy, so please don't be afraid for me. I'll be fine. God will get me through whatever happens."

It made no sense, but in that moment, she realized that it was true. In this worst moment of her life, she felt as if someone had pulled her out of a raging river, set her on the solid shore, and wrapped a warm blanket around her.

But in a few minutes, she would willingly jump back in that river. She only hoped the current didn't carry her too far from home.

$\mathcal{B}$ryn had thought she was calm, but when she walked through the front doors of the Hanover Falls Police Station, her hands began to tremble.

Dad must have sensed her fear, for he put a hand on her back, an uncharacteristic gesture for him. "I'm right here, honey."

She slipped the confession she'd written last night from her purse and sucked in a breath.

A female officer in uniform looked up from a desk as they walked toward her. "May I help you?"

She had no idea what the protocol was for this. "I need to speak to someone about—a crime."

"Are you the victim?"

She swallowed past the thickening in her throat. "No. I'm the one who—committed the crime."

"Excuse me?"

She held out the envelope. "I have a letter of confession here. Can you tell me who I should give it to?"

The woman pushed back her chair and rose slowly. She gave a nod toward Dad. "You her attorney?"

"No. I'm Hugh Terrigan. I'm her father."

Bryn thought there was pride in his voice. It surprised her. What she'd done had shamed him. But Dad's pride gave her strength.

The officer shook her head. "You're going to want her attorney present."

Bryn took a step forward, not wanting Dad to have to handle this. "I don't have an attorney. I'm guilty. I'm . . . not trying to get out of it."

"What is the nature of the crime?"

"I think you'd call it involuntary manslaughter?"

"You killed somebody?" She looked skeptical.

But Bryn nodded.

"Whoa . . . whoa . . ." The woman held up both hands, palms out. "Hang on a minute. I'll get Chief Perlson. Wait right here." She scurried around her desk and disappeared behind a door to her left.

Through a glass partition, they watched her weave through a maze of waist-high cubicles and stop at the desk of a man Bryn recognized from photos that had appeared in area newspapers after the fire—Chief Rudy Perlson.

Adam had worked numerous accident scenes with Perlson and had always spoken highly of the guy.

The chief looked up and caught Bryn's eye, gave a slight nod.

A minute later he ducked through the door in the partition and motioned to her. "Come on back." With a jut of his chin, he gave her father permission to come along with Bryn.

Two other uniformed officers and several women in street clothes looked up from their desks as Bryn and her father followed Chief Perlson to a sparsely furnished office in a back corner of the building.

"Officer Jamison says you want to confess a crime?"

Bryn nodded. "That's right." She held out the envelope. "I wrote out a confession."

He ignored the envelope, took a form from the desk drawer, and poised a ballpoint pen over it. "Name?"

"Bryn Hennesey." She spelled it for him.

He looked up, studied her like he might be con- necting that she was Adam's wife, but merely asked for her address and date of birth. When he'd copied them down on the form, he asked, "Do you have an attorney?"

"No, sir. I want to plead guilty."

He shook his head. "You're still going to want an attorney."

She glanced at her father, then back at the officer. "Do I have to have one?"

"Bryn." Dad cleared his throat. "Please listen to reason. Let them get you an attorney."

She looked up at the clock on the painted cement-block wall. *Ten o'clock.* Garrett would receive her letter today. She'd ignored several phone calls and text messages from him, knowing she couldn't pretend everything was fine if he hadn't read her letter yet, and too frightened to talk to him if he was calling in response to her letter.

Perlson cocked his head. "You do have the right to have an attorney present before you make a confession or answer any further questions. I'd strongly advise you to do so."

"I don't want an attorney. I just want to make my confession." If she couldn't get this over with now, today, she would go mad.

The chief shrugged and wrote something on the form. Looking up, he studied her. "So what is it you want to confess?"

Bryn laid the envelope on the desk and pushed it toward him, feeling as if she'd just stepped off the edge of a cliff into the abyss.

24

*B*ryn sat on the sofa in her father's guest room, a mixture of relief and terror swirling through her veins. She was home after a sleepless night alone in the Hanover Falls detention center.

Yesterday, after half an hour of filling out forms and being questioned, she'd been placed under arrest and escorted to a holding cell at the station.

Every time she thought about the shame of that moment, and seeing Dad's anguish at having to witness it, she regretted she'd let Dad come with her. Thankfully, Chief Perlson had managed to get her a bail hearing this morning, and the judge had released her "on her own recognizance"— whatever that meant. Apparently they didn't see her as a flight risk, so at least she hadn't had to spend the whole weekend in jail.

She'd wanted to kiss the chief for getting her out of there. She remembered how fondly Adam had always spoken of Hanover Falls' chief of police and she understood now. She suspected Perlson had felt the same about Adam, and she thanked God for the man's mercy toward her.

But she couldn't expect mercy from here on.

She'd committed a *felony*. The word rang in her ears.

She would appear before a judge on felony charges of involuntary manslaughter. The tragedy had drawn national attention. If Garrett's attitude was any indication, the community was hungry for vengeance and restitution. The judge would no doubt give them what they wanted.

"Ms. Hennesey, I can't advise you strongly enough to get a good attorney," the chief had said, "or at the very least let the court appoint one for you. This isn't something to take lightly. You do not want to be a pro se litigant . . . unless of course you don't mind the idea of spending the best years of your life in prison."

She'd been prepared for that. Time in the detention center at the very least. But probably prison. She deserved nothing less. Dad had harped at her about getting an attorney, and finally—for the sake of her father's heart and health—she'd agreed to talk to the lawyer Eberfield & Sons retained.

Dad somehow managed to arrange a meeting this afternoon in Judson Meyer's Springfield office. Bryn didn't have a good feeling about it. Either the guy was desperate for clients, or he was so eager for the publicity this case would bring him that he'd cleared his schedule for her. Neither scenario gave her much comfort.

A knock sounded at the door, and Bryn straightened and quickly wiped away the smudges of mascara she knew must rim her eyes. "Come in."

The door creaked open, and Dad stood there, studying her. "How you doing?"

She merely nodded, afraid she'd break down if she tried to speak.

He came in and sat on the sofa beside her. "You're doing the right thing, honey . . . talking to this guy. He's a good lawyer. He'll do right by you."

She didn't know what to do. She just wanted it to be over. "We should probably go, don't you think?"

He struggled to his feet. "I'll get our coats."

Neither of them spoke on the drive to Springfield. The radio played Dad's country music. If Bryn closed her eyes, she could almost imagine it was Garrett beside her, and everything else was just a bad dream.

"All right, then, Bryn. May I call you Bryn?" Judson Meyer appeared to be about fifty, with attractively graying temples, steely blue eyes, tailored suit, and a demeanor no doubt meant to instill confidence in his clients. But to Bryn, he looked too much like one of those sleazy attorneys from a TV commercial.

Her hands trembled uncontrollably. She pressed her palms together and put her hands under the table in a vain attempt to appear calm.

"I need to ask you some questions, Bryn, and I need the God's honest truth. If I'm going to represent you, I need to know everything you know, down to the smallest detail."

She met his eyes and nodded. At least they wanted the same thing in that regard. The truth.

"We'll waive the preliminary hearing. You know what the charges against you are." He explained the possible pleas she could enter at the arraignment. She could scarcely keep track of all the terms—plea bargain, no contest, pro se litigant, plead out. The phrases all melded together—and none quite sounded like they contained the truth, the whole truth, and nothing but the truth. *Help me, God.*

For an hour, the attorney volleyed questions at her—about her work at the shelter, about the events of that night, details about the candle, down to what color, what scent it had been. She answered his questions carefully, feeling removed from the situation—as if she were telling someone else's story.

She told him about her dream—or memory . . . she wasn't sure what to call it.

The attorney looked incredulous. "A dream? You're basing your guilt on a dream?"

She shook her head. "It was more than that. The dream just brought the memories back—real memories. I'm not imagining them."

"Did you purchase the candle?" Meyer asked,

seemingly giving up on his former line of questioning.

"No."

"Are you the one who brought it in to the shelter?"

"No."

"Who did?"

"Susan Marlowe, the director."

"The director of the homeless shelter? You're sure?"

"Yes."

He scribbled furiously on the legal pad in front of him. When he looked up, his expression was almost gleeful. "Even if you did leave that candle burning—and I'm not convinced that's the case—but even if you did, the candle should not have been at that shelter in the first place. And Ms. Marlowe no doubt knows that."

Bryn started shaking her head. "No. Susan had nothing to do with this. She made it very clear that it was just for the smell, to freshen the air. We weren't supposed to light it," she added quickly.

"You weren't supposed to? Were there regulations posted somewhere stating that?"

Bryn thought for a moment. "Not that I can remember. But there may have been. They had a training manual. It was probably in there." Her pulse stuttered. Had she said something that implicated Susan?

"Did Ms. Marlowe ever light that candle herself? Or any other candle at the shelter?"

Her breath caught. Could they arrest Susan for merely bringing the candles in? "I . . . have no idea." Let him take that however he would.

"Even if Ms. Marlowe didn't light the candle on occasion herself, it was completely irresponsible for her to allow it on the premises. Or, for that matter, for her to allow matches or other lighting devices on the premises. They served as a temptation. I'm surprised they got away with only having those cheapo smoke alarms."

Bryn didn't point out that they *hadn't* "gotten away" with it.

"Most of the clients smoked. Outside . . . well, once in a while when it was really cold out, they'd smoke just inside the entry . . . but still, there's no way we could have policed all the cigarette lighters and matchbooks. We had enough trouble keeping the booze and drugs out."

Mr. Meyer jotted something else on the legal pad. Bryn had given up trying to read his scribblings upside down—or any other direction.

"There's another angle we need to look at. According to the fire inspector's report, there were beds and mattresses stored on the second floor that were highly combustible. Either Ms. Marlowe, or a building inspector—somebody along the way—should have made sure those were removed from the premises. They constituted a grave threat in the event of fire."

She forced out a heavy breath. "Mr. Meyer,

you're trying to pin this on everyone except me. That's exactly why I didn't want a lawyer." She glanced at Dad, not wanting to hurt him but feeling she had to put her foot down. "*I* am the one who did this. I'm the one who should be punished. I'm not trying to get out of it. I'm not afraid of—whatever they decide to do to me. It's bad enough that I made such a terrible mistake, but if I tried to pin the blame on someone else, I might as well . . ." She didn't know how to finish the sentence.

Meyer cocked his head and studied her. "Ms. Hennesey, the DA has not garnered favor with the public recently, and he'd love a sensational case to hang his hat on. Do you *want* to be the sacrificial lamb?"

"I just want to tell the truth."

"The truth may well be that others are as much to blame as you are."

"No. They're not. I'm the one—the only one—who left that candle burning. Who tampered with that smoke detector. And I'll accept whatever consequences the law requires."

"If you plead guilty, you'll most likely go to jail."

She nodded. "I understand that."

He shook his head. "I'm not sure you do understand. I'm not sure you get how the legal system works. What happened is not entirely your fault. Not by any stretch of the imagination. There is no reason for the full penalty for what happened to fall on you. It is only right that others whose negligence contributed to this tragedy shoulder their deserved share of the burden."

Bryn thought about that. If none of them took full blame, if they each admitted that they had contributed in some small way, maybe none of them would be convicted.

Or maybe they would all be punished to the full extent of the law. She'd looked it up on the Internet. In Missouri the maximum sentence for involuntary manslaughter was twenty-two years. She'd done the math, and it took her breath away. Life would pass her by while she served her sentence. She could kiss marriage and babies good-bye. Or having a career. She would be in her fifties in twenty-two years. Older than Mom had been when she died.

Dad would probably die while she was in prison. Could his heart stand up under the strain if she was convicted, if she went to jail? She'd read that few people served such a lengthy sentence. Still, even if she only got half of the maximum sentence, it was a very real possibility that Dad would not be around when she was released. She shuddered. That thought was too much to bear. She erased it from her mind.

She didn't want to go to prison. But Susan couldn't go. She had two sons who needed her. Right now. Not ten, or even five years from now.

Davy, especially, was fragile right now. He might completely crack if something happened to his mother.

She didn't know about the building inspector Meyer wanted to implicate. Maybe Meyer didn't even know who that inspector was. But whoever it was, he or she no doubt had a spouse and children who depended on them. She had no one.

She straightened in her chair, took her father's hand. "Mr. Meyer, I wish to plead guilty. Like I said in the letters—" Her voice broke. "If there was any way in the world I could go back and undo this terrible—"

"Wait a minute." Meyer glared at her. "Letters?"

"The letters I wrote to the families. To apologize, to ask their forgiveness."

Meyer scraped back his chair and rose, towering over her. "Whatever you do—" He leaned across the table toward her, emphasizing every word—"do not send those letters."

Bryn glanced at her father, then up at the attorney. "I . . . already did."

Judson Meyer's eyes grew wide. His face crumpled, and he tugged at the knot of his tie and sagged into the chair behind him. "Do you have a death wish, Ms. Hennesey?" He turned to Bryn's father and threw up his hands, seemingly at a loss for words.

But words came for Bryn.

You will know the truth, and the truth will set you free.

The words—God's words that had echoed through her mind since she'd awakened from the dream—came to her again.

But what did they mean for her? What *was* the truth?

25

Monday, January 21

"*D*id you hear a word I just said?" Kathy Beckwith stood in the doorway of the teacher's workroom, arms akimbo, grinning at Garrett.

"I'm sorry . . . what?" Garrett shook off the mental cobwebs and forced his attention back to the fourth-grade teacher.

Kathy laughed. "You've got it bad, buddy."

He gave her a guilty grin and rubbed at the worn linoleum with the toe of his shoe. "I don't know what you're talking about."

She affected a huff that said, "Yeah, right." What she actually said was "I *said,* can I borrow your fraction dice this afternoon? We'll need them for a couple of days, if that's okay."

"Sure. No problem. Just send one of your students for them any time."

"Thanks." Kathy tilted her chin and studied

him, motherly concern clouding her pretty face. "Are you okay?"

"I'm fine."

"Women problems?"

Any other time, he might have made a joke about women definitely being problems, or he might have fed her some tidbit about his and Bryn's growing friendship, knowing she would encourage him, make him feel better about how quickly his relationship with Bryn had turned into something more—even if he hadn't revealed that to his fellow teachers yet.

But today he was in no mood. He was growing genuinely concerned about Bryn. Why hadn't she returned his calls? He racked his brain to remember if she'd told him she was going somewhere over the weekend, and came up blank. Not that she owed him a minute-by-minute schedule of where she would be. The thing was, for the past few weeks, between texting, email, and actually talking, he'd pretty much been able to account for her whereabouts at any given time.

Now, with no idea where she was and why she was ignoring him, he was growing more worried by the hour. After the romantic day they'd spent together at Ferris Park, the least she could do was tell him she was having second thoughts.

"Sorry, but I've got to run." He threw Kathy a wave as he left the workroom and headed back down to his classroom. His students would be back from PE in a few minutes, and he still had to set up a science experiment.

He checked his watch. If he hadn't heard from Bryn by the time he got out of school, he was going to try to contact her father. He wasn't even sure what the man's first name was, but he remembered Bryn joking once that her initials went from BAT to BAH when she married, and with her maiden name of Terrigan, they spelled BATH. How many Terrigans could there be in the Hanover Falls phone book?

After school, Garrett got in on a pickup game in the gym, but only a couple of the guys showed up, so they knocked off early. Afterward, he stopped by the store to pick up a few groceries. He gassed up his pickup and grabbed a pizza to take home for dinner. As he pulled into his apartment complex, he dialed Bryn again on his cell phone, not expecting an answer by now, but wanting to try one more time before he tried to contact her father. This time he didn't bother leaving a message.

The evening paper was on the stoop, and he grabbed it and retrieved several days' worth of mail from his mailbox in the foyer. He tossed everything on the kitchen counter and went to check the answering machine. Nothing.

He flipped on the television and listened to the end of some inane episode of *Oprah* while he poured a Coke and ate three slices of pizza. He glanced at the clock. Almost five. Bryn's father might be home from work by now. Wiping his fingers on a dishtowel, Garrett pulled the phonebook from a kitchen drawer. He thumbed through the white pages. Nothing for "Terrigan." Bryn had talked about her father living in the country, but either he had an unlisted number or he lived outside the area this directory covered.

He walked across the room and slid into his desk chair. Maybe he could find something online. He was typing "Terrigan" into Google when a blurb for the evening news grabbed him by the throat. A chirpy female newscaster was saying something about the Grove Street Inferno. He jumped up, grabbed the remote, and turned up the volume, but the station had already cut to a commercial.

It seemed like forever before the news came back on, but the Grove Street Inferno was the lead story, complete with the same photo illustration they'd used for stories about the fire back in November.

Garrett hurried over to the television and stood there, waiting, holding his breath. The fire investigators must have made an announcement.

The same newscaster looked into the camera, and Garrett could almost read her intent—to look gorgeous, intelligent, and serious, all at the same time. "In a surprising turn of events, a former volunteer at the Grove Street Homeless Shelter in

Hanover Falls has admitted to being responsible for a fire that killed five firefighters last November. Rudy Perlson, chief of police in this small south-central Missouri town, said the Hanover Falls woman turned herself in to authorities Friday, telling police she unintentionally started the blaze that destroyed the former hospital building that housed the facility.

Garrett's heart raced. A *volunteer*? He didn't remember Bryn talking about anyone else being at the shelter that night besides Susan Marlowe. Why was this person just now coming forward? How could someone have let everyone think it was that homeless man—Zeke Downing—all this time? At least this might explain why he hadn't heard from Bryn. They'd probably called her back in for interviews. Poor Bryn. He shot up a prayer that it wouldn't be too upsetting for her, having to relive the events of that night.

He sat on the edge of the leather sofa, his eyes glued to the television as familiar images from the fire filled the screen. TV stations in the area must have played the footage a hundred times in those days immediately following the fire. It had been shown across the country the first few days.

The woman's voice droned on with old details about the fire. "Stay tuned for more on this breaking story tonight at ten."

Garrett picked up the phone and dialed Bryn's number again. This time, when her voice mail picked up, he left a message. "Hey, Bryn, it's me. Wow . . . I just saw the news. I've tried to call several times, but I'm guessing now that you've been wrapped up in this whole ordeal. Did you know the woman who confessed? Hope it hasn't been too bad for you. I guess . . . I guess it's good we'll finally have some answers. Anyway, I'm thinking about you and praying for you. Call me as soon as you can. I don't care if it's late."

He hung up the phone and sat with his head in his hands. Always, when he'd thought about this moment—the moment when the person responsible for Molly's death was caught—he'd expected to feel an overwhelming sense of relief. But that didn't happen now. He felt numb, almost disappointed.

They'd said the woman had confessed to "accidentally" starting the fire. If that was true, why had it taken so long for her to come forward?

There would probably be another rash of news stories and reporters calling for interviews—wanting reaction from the families of the fallen firefighters. He'd be so glad when this was all over. But maybe once the person responsible for the deaths of Adam and Molly was behind bars, it would give Bryn and him both the closure they needed. And allow them to start a new, happier chapter of their lives—together.

26

7he teaser for the ten o'clock news played over the closing credits of some TV drama. Garrett had left the television on only because he didn't want to miss the news. The nighttime anchor read the same blurb from the evening newscast and the program went to a commercial.

Garrett had tried to reach Bryn twice since he'd heard the news and still no answer. *Why isn't she answering her phone?*

The commercial break ended, and the anchorman appeared on the screen. "Tonight we have shocking new information on the November fire that destroyed a homeless shelter and left five firefighters dead in Hanover Falls, Missouri. A woman who served as a volunteer at the Grove Street Homeless Shelter in this south-central Missouri town has admitted to being responsible for the fire."

So it wasn't Zeke Downing after all. *Incredible.* Garrett sat forward on the couch, punching the remote to turn up the volume.

"Hanover Falls' police chief, Rudy Perlson, said Bryn Hennesey turned herself in to authorities on Friday morning, telling police she had accidentally left a candle burning in the second-floor office of the facility the night of the fire.

Perlson says Hennesey, whose husband, Adam Hennesey, was one of the firefighters killed in the blaze, was released on her own recognizance and is awaiting arraignment on possible charges of involuntary manslaughter."

Garrett stared at the television.

Bryn? Something was wrong here. The Bryn he knew wasn't capable of what they were blaming her for. There must be some mix-up with her name. The same nausea and denial he'd felt when they'd told him that Molly was dead battered him now.

If this was true, why hadn't Bryn told him? How could she have kept something like this from him?

The anchorman droned on, and Garrett struggled to focus on the man's words.

"District Attorney Gordon Arrington declined to comment on whether felony charges would be filed in the case, but Fire Chief Peter Brennan said Hennesey's confession is consistent with findings of the state fire inspectors. That final report has not been released, and preliminary reports said the extensive damage to the facility made fire investigators' findings inconclusive, but investigators confirmed the fire started on the second floor of the former hospital building."

Peter Brennan appeared on camera, and a microphone was thrust in his face. Pete was standing in the break room at the fire station. One glimpse of that room brought the memories whirling back. Evenings when he'd picked up sandwiches at the deli and taken supper to Molly and the guys. And late one night when, bored, she'd talked him into coming to the station to play Scrabble. She'd beat his socks off, too. Not that he'd cared. He'd just been happy to be with her, glad it was his company she'd craved even though she was surrounded by half a dozen beefy firemen.

He sat, glued to the TV screen, still in shock, yet hungry for details. Not willing for what he was hearing to be true. The anchor said Bryn had been released. Why? And where was she? Probably at her father's.

All this time she'd pretended . . . ? At least now he knew why she hadn't returned his calls. He struggled to piece together what he knew, but nothing made sense. Not Bryn's confession, not the fact that the fire had been her fault, and certainly not the fact that, for weeks, she'd behaved with him as if nothing in the world were amiss.

But if this was true, why had she bothered to get close to him? It didn't make sense. Did she think a relationship with him could somehow offer her some sort of immunity?

He thought, for the thousandth time, of their time together at the park. Even the weeks leading up to today. Bryn had been so open and honest with him—or at least she'd made him believe that. They'd talked about everything. She'd told him that she felt guilty about Adam being there that night because she'd talked him into pulling an extra shift so they'd have money for Christmas shopping. And Adam hadn't known she was there. Had she only told him those things to cover up her real reason for guilt?

The weather came on and Garrett punched the remote, leaving the room in silence. He had to find out what was going on. He glanced at the pile of mail and newspapers on the kitchen counter and dragged in a breath. The TV station had the story in time to run it on the five-o'clock news. Maybe there was a story in tonight's paper as well. This was front-page worthy if anything was. He yanked a rolled-up paper from the heap and unfolded it. Yesterday's paper. He pulled another one from the pile, sending the whole mess sliding to the floor.

He growled in frustration and knelt to scoop the jumble of papers into a pile. A pale blue envelope caught his eye, and he picked it up. Bryn's handwriting. It was postmarked yesterday.

Heart racing, he rocked back on his haunches and tore open the envelope. The date at the top of the page was also yesterday's date.

Dear Garrett,
I'm having trouble finding the words to say what I must say. I don't know how I could ever

make you understand, but I have to try. Please know that I never intended to hurt you. You were the dearest friend I had in the world, and among all the other massive regrets I have, losing our friendship—as I surely will once you've read this—is one of the things I regret most.

I don't know where to start except at the beginning. And it seems like the beginning of the end was yesterday morning when I awoke from a dream and realized the dream was more than that—it was a memory. A memory of what really happened the night of the fire. A memory that, I swear to you, I had somehow suppressed until yesterday. When I tell you what I remembered, I think you'll understand how my mind allowed me to shut it out. Whether you can ever forgive me is another thing.

The letter went on for another page in Bryn's small, elegant cursive. Garrett leaned against a cabinet door and read that first page over again, trying in vain to make the words mean something rational. Finally he let the page fall to the floor, smoothed out the second page, and read on.

I hope you know me well enough to know that I would do anything to go back and change what happened that night, change my responsibility in it all. But I can't do that. So I will do the only thing I can do. Tomorrow I will go to the police and turn myself in, and I will accept whatever consequences the law— and God—require of me.

I am so sorry, Garrett. That I am responsible for Molly's death is almost more than I can bear. If I could give my own life in exchange, I would do it a thousand times over.

I know that I can't expect you to remain my friend, but I hope that somehow, with time, you will be able to find it within yourself to forgive me for what I did.

Again, he reread the words. The syllables formed in his mind, but they may as well have been a foreign language for all the sense he could make of them. After what seemed like an hour, he eased himself up from the floor, crumpled the letter into a ball, and tossed it across the room in the direction of the trash can under his desk.

He'd been a fool, and Bryn had played him for one. Maybe not intentionally, though it was pretty hard to swallow that she hadn't known she was guilty until this so-called dream.

Overcome with grief and anger and a thousand other painful emotions, he stood and forced one foot in front of the other. He'd sought God about his friendship with Bryn. He'd been sincere. He just hadn't counted on her betraying him. The truth was, he'd let Bryn stand in the way of a healthy grief.

Now it was as if he'd lost Molly all over again . . . except this loss came with a heavy dose of betrayal. If it was possible, that pain cut deeper even than the loss of his beloved wife. And this time, he wasn't sure he could hold up under the unbearable sadness.

27

Sunday, January 27

Bryn hung up the phone and slumped into a chair at the table in Dad's kitchen. The house was quiet with her father at work and Sparky in the backyard.

Ten days had gone by since she'd turned herself in to the police. Her arraignment was set for February 19, and her attorney had said if she insisted on pleading guilty, she'd be sentenced immediately and possibly be given the maximum sentence. She was prepared for the worst. Though she had several weeks yet to endure this awful limbo, she'd quit her job.

Myrna had given her time off immediately once the news broke that Bryn had submitted her confession, but Bryn sensed the library director would have preferred she bow out altogether.

She'd called Myrna at home moments ago and hadn't missed the relief in her voice when Bryn told her she would be sending a letter of resignation tomorrow.

Bryn needed the money her library job had provided, but she was sensitive to the fact that it had not been good publicity for the struggling library when it came out that Bryn was employed there part-time. Perhaps it would smooth matters over if the director could say that Bryn Hennesey had tendered her resignation. Dad had assured her to let him worry about the money for now. She didn't have a choice.

After the police released Bryn, Dad had gone with her back to her house to pack some clothes and to load up Sparky and his things. She'd been here at Dad's house in the country ever since. She was grateful now for the quiet of the place, and grateful that she hadn't had to face anyone since.

Sparky was in doggie heaven, with free run of Dad's backyard. In the evenings after work, Dad was building a dog run off the garage so Sparky could be outside even if no one was home.

She thought about Charlie and knew she needed to let him know that she'd moved—at least temporarily. She didn't know if he would have heard the news about her confession as far away as Springfield, but in case he did, she didn't want him worrying about Sparky's fate.

She'd have to get the contact information for

the shelter in Springfield off her computer when she went in to the Falls today for groceries. She'd considered bringing the computer back with her. Dad had a desktop—if you could call the beast that—but she'd had nothing but frustration trying to use the ancient thing. She'd just begun to realize how much of her life was contained on the compact computer she and Adam had shared. Besides her address book and phone numbers, her calendar was on that computer, not to mention all the websites she'd marked as favorites.

Here at Dad's she'd mostly spent her time reading, walking in the woods behind the house, cooking for Dad, and praying. She'd poured her heart out to God, praying daily, hourly for forgiveness, and then praying for the families of the men who'd died that November night.

For some reason, during these quiet moments before God, she found herself reliving her life with Adam. She'd recalled each moment of their courtship, of their wedding day, and remembered all over again how in love she had been with her husband. It was hard not to regret the time they'd wasted arguing over things that shouldn't have mattered—didn't matter at all now. But it was healing to think of Adam with love, to reflect on his life, and what he had meant to her. She was proud of him, and for the first time she appreciated the hero he had been. Why hadn't she ever been able to see the way he put his life on the line every day. It broke her heart that she'd never expressed her pride in him to his face.

She thought of Garrett, too. And prayed for him. Prayed that he could somehow go on with his life. That was a hard one. She knew it wasn't possible, but she caught herself too often day-dreaming that they'd somehow mended the chasm between them, that they were friends again. Sometimes she allowed herself to replay the sweet times they'd shared together. The brief kisses they'd shared. But that only depressed her more. How could he ever forgive her?

She hadn't heard back from even one of the people she'd mailed a letter of apology to. That fact was disturbing—and more than a little frightening. Had the DA gotten hold of each of them, hoping for that sensational case Meyer had talked about? Or worse, was there not one of them who could forgive her?

Dad and Judson Meyer were still trying to talk her out of pleading guilty, but how could she plead anything else? To do so was tantamount to lying. Even pleading "no contest" implied that she was making excuses for what she'd done. More than that, she did not want this case to go to trial. She wanted it over. Even if it meant she had to go to prison—a thought she hadn't dared entertain for too long—at least this wouldn't be hanging over her head.

The guilt she would live with every single day

of her life, but at least she would accept the punishment meted out to her, and maybe it would give her—and the families of her victims—some measure of peace.

She checked on Sparky out the back window. Living at Dad's agreed with him—and, surprisingly, it seemed to agree with Dad, too. If she'd known what a fast friendship Dad and that dog would form, she would have brought Sparky here from the very beginning. Of course, then she might not have met Garrett.

The thought stopped her in her tracks. From the vantage point she had now, that would have been a blessing.

She drew the café curtains against the bright afternoon sun and went to get her purse. She'd put off the trip into the Falls as long as she could if she was going to be back in time to make supper for Dad. But she'd never dreaded anything quite like she dreaded this trip. Even more than turning herself in to the police—which seemed crazy. But it was true. How could she face people after what she'd done?

For a minute she considered going to Springfield for groceries instead, but she needed to check on her apartment and pick up some more of her things. Besides, she couldn't hide out here at Dad's forever. Eventually she would have to go out in public. She may as well get it over with.

She prayed all the way in to town. Selfish

prayers—that she wouldn't have to see anyone she knew.

She drove to her place first, grateful that the garage would allow her to sneak in and sneak out. A blast of stale air lashed her when she opened the door between the garage and the kitchen. Yet, the familiar smells sent a wave of homesickness rolling over her. Brushing off the temptation to feel sorry for herself, she hurriedly gathered up a few clothes and her favorite vanilla shampoo from the shower. She took the things to her car and went back for the computer. She hoped she could figure out how to connect everything again when she got back to Dad's.

Locking up the house, she wondered if it would be for the final time. She needed to make a decision about selling the townhome. She didn't want to impose on Dad—though she suspected he'd rather enjoyed having her around. But she was in no position financially to keep the townhome. And if she was sentenced to prison, she didn't want Dad to have to deal with putting her house on the market.

She drove to Hanson's Market, a smaller grocery store on the west end of town. It was a little more expensive, but she was less likely to run into someone she knew here. What she didn't count on was the fact that while she knew only a few people in the Falls, since the fire—and especially recently, with her photo plastered all over the news—everyone seemed to recognize her.

Almost the minute she rolled her cart into the store, the whispering started. She passed a middle-aged couple poring over a grocery list, but they looked up when she passed, and the woman's friendly expression turned to one of recognition. Bryn didn't miss the words the woman almost hissed at her husband once her back was to Bryn. "That's her! The one who started that fire!"

Bryn knew if she whirled around she would see them staring after her. A minute later, the same thing happened with two young mothers shopping with babies in tow. The expression of recognition, the furtive glances, and a hushed conversation behind open palms. She didn't blame them. She wouldn't have done anything differently had she been in their shoes.

She hurried to the next aisle, but hearing the murmurs that followed in her wake, she quickly abandoned her list, grabbed a few things from the produce section, and pushed her cart toward the nearest checkout stand. Somehow she would cobble up a dinner for Dad with what he had on hand. Next time she would shop in Springfield. And she would figure out a way to disguise herself.

She declined to have the high school kid who bagged her groceries carry them to her car. In the parking lot, she transferred the bags to the backseat of the Accord. She was returning the cart to the rack at the market's entrance when she looked up to see Jenna Morgan coming out of the store, a plastic grocery bag looped over one arm.

Spying her, Jenna gave a little gasp. "Bryn . . ." Her eyes, devoid of makeup, welled with tears. Jenna was several years younger than Bryn, but she had aged ten years since Bryn had last seen her.

Jenna's jaw tensed and she looked away, put up a hand as if asking Bryn to keep her distance. "I'm sorry. I . . . I don't understand how you could . . . Why didn't you tell someone? How could you let this go on for so long?"

"Jenna, I didn't *know*. I promise you, I didn't know. I blocked it out. Or maybe . . . maybe I just fooled myself into thinking I didn't remember. I'm so very sorry. I don't know what else to say."

Two patrons with full grocery carts came out of the store and sidestepped them on their way to the parking lot. Jenna ignored them, took a deep breath, and reached for an abandoned grocery cart as if her legs wouldn't hold her another minute.

Bryn risked a step toward her. "I hope you got my letter . . ."

But Jenna backpedaled as far as the stack of shopping carts allowed, and Bryn backed off.

Jenna's stare bored a hole through her. "I forgive you. Bryn, I forgive you because I know it's

269

the right thing to do. But that's all I can say right now. I . . . I need to go." She made a sound that was a cross between a sob and a groan and brushed past Bryn.

Bryn turned and watched her walk away. Of all those she'd written to, Jenna was the one she thought might understand. Zach and Adam had trained for the firefighter job at the same time. They had the same rank and had been friends. She and Jenna had so much in common. They'd laughed together, griped about their husbands' long hours, shopped together, and helped each other decorate their homes. But if Jenna had turned this cool toward her, how could she dare to hope the others might somehow forgive?

She knew she'd done the right thing in asking for each person's forgiveness. The day after she'd finished the letters, she'd opened her Bible to read—a new habit in which she'd found much comfort—and the pages had fallen open to the fifth chapter of Numbers, where it spoke of the law commanding that if one person wronged another, he should confess his guilt and make restitution.

Of course, there was no way she could ever make restitution for the human lives lost because of her carelessness. Still, she had done what was within her power to do. She had confessed, both to the families and to the law, and she would make whatever restitution the judge decided was fair. God knew that she would give anything—her very life—if that would change what had happened. But it wouldn't. Nothing could ever change the consequences of her carelessness. It was too late for that.

She couldn't control how the people she'd wronged would respond, but she'd at least opened the door, let them know of her remorse, and given them an opportunity to forgive.

She had accepted God's forgiveness and found deep comfort in it. But if Jenna, Susan Marlowe and her sons, Emily Vermontez and Lucas—and Garrett, *oh, Garrett*—if they all chose not to forgive her, to hold her accountable for the lives of their loved ones, how could she ever forgive herself?

28

Garrett looked both ways, pulled out from the school parking lot, and turned the opposite way from home. He'd avoided shopping as long as he could, but now his cupboards were bare. Three nights a week he played pickup basketball with the guys, then made excuses to stay at school until the janitors came in to clean his classroom.

He graded papers before he went home, had lesson plans lined out through spring break, and his room sported a new bulletin board every couple of weeks. He'd cleaned out his desk and the storage closet, even washed the bank of windows that covered the southern wall of the classroom. Anything to keep busy, to not think about what had happened to him.

But he couldn't live on school lunches alone, and drive-through was getting expensive, so tonight he'd decided to brave the grocery store long enough to pick up some cans of soup, cold cereal, and milk. Maybe a frozen pizza or two, though none of the staples he'd grown accustomed to whetted his appetite.

The parking lot at Hanson's was crowded. *Great.* Unless he shopped late at night, he rarely managed to get through the store without running into a parent of one of his students or friends from church—one of the foibles of small-town life that could be good or bad, depending on his mood. Today he just wanted to get in and out—and home.

He cruised through the tiny parking lot waiting for a spot to open up near the entrance. When that didn't happen, he took the nearest space and took off at a jog toward the front door, weaving between vehicles. He zagged around a fifteen-passenger van bearing a logo for the Falls' Senior Center. On the opposite side, he almost collided with an open car door. "Whoa! Sorry about that." He stopped short, waiting for the driver to slide behind the wheel. He recognized the white Accord before his mind registered that it was Bryn getting in the car.

She whirled to face him. Horror painted her features as recognition lit her eyes. "Garrett . . ." His name came out in a whisper. She stared at the asphalt, shaking her head.

He waited for her to meet his gaze, to say something. When she didn't, he glared at her bowed figure. "What are you doing here?"

Her head jerked up. "I—I just came for groceries. For my dad." She pointed to her car. "I wouldn't have come if I'd known . . . you would be here. I'm not that cruel."

"What?" He stared at her. "Why would you say that?"

She shrugged and bowed her head again. She looked awful, her face pale, her clothes hanging on her thin frame.

"Why didn't you answer my calls?" The question was out before he had time to think about whether he wanted her answer or not.

"Surely you don't have to ask that. You . . . you did get my letter, didn't you?"

"I got it." He kicked at a hard clump of asphalt that had broken off of the pavement. It skittered beneath her car. "You couldn't talk to me in person?"

No response.

"You took the coward's way out, Bryn. I think I

at least deserved to hear what you had to say in person."

"Garrett . . ." She rubbed the space between her eyes. "I didn't think you would want to see my face after what I've done."

"Well, you could let *me* decide that."

"You didn't answer my letter. I took that as your answer."

"What's that supposed to mean?"

"That you couldn't—*can't* forgive what I did."

He turned his head away. He wasn't sure he could forgive. Why did he have to come here tonight, of all nights? "So what will happen?"

Confusion clouded her eyes.

"The paper said you turned yourself in . . ."

She nodded. "The arraignment isn't until next month."

"Arraignment?" She'd said it so matter-of-factly. And for the first time, he realized she might go to jail over this. The thought gave him no pleasure.

"Yes," she said simply.

"So it will go to trial?"

"No. I'm pleading guilty. There . . . won't be a trial. I'm living with my dad until . . . until I find out what will . . . happen."

"I'm sorry, Bryn." She seemed so broken. Defeated. He hadn't expected to feel sympathy for her. "I don't know what else to say."

In spite of the gleam of unshed tears, her eyes

went dull. "You don't need to say anything." She reached for her car door. "I'm sorry. I truly didn't mean for you to have to . . . run into me."

He could tell she was close to tears and, for one awful moment, he could only remember that she was his friend, that she was the one who'd made his grief bearable because she was the only one who truly seemed to understand what it was like to lose the one who completed you.

He forced himself to look at her for who—for what—she was. He had to make himself remember what she'd done. Remember Molly. And more than that, to remember Bryn's betrayal. He had grown to love her heart. But now that he knew hers was a heart of deceit—even if it was mostly herself she'd deceived—he couldn't allow himself to be captivated again.

He took a step backward, planned his route back to his truck. He couldn't face anyone after this encounter. Besides, his appetite was gone. He couldn't leave her without a word. So he said the kindest thing he could muster. "I'm truly sorry for you, Bryn. I wish none of this had ever happened."

Let her interpret it how she would. What he really meant was, "I wish I'd never met you."

He wanted the last three months of his life back. He wanted Molly back.

Forcing himself to turn away, he strode back through the parking lot the way he'd come.

29

Tuesday, February 19

"*T*hanks, Daddy."

Bryn forced a smile as her father held the door of the courthouse for her. Judson Meyer had called early this morning, requesting that they come an hour before the arraignment was scheduled. Bryn worried that Meyer's "emergency meeting" was just another attempt by her attorney to get her to make a lesser plea. Didn't he get it? There *was* no lesser plea for what she'd done. It was time to get this over with. She was eager to be sentenced so her father could stop worrying, and so the families of the dead could move on with their lives, knowing that some sort of atonement had been made.

She turned to watch Dad as he came through the door behind her. His color wasn't good today, and his voice seemed feeble. Twice this week she'd seen him pop a nitroglycerin tablet when he thought she wasn't looking. *Please don't let this kill him, Lord.*

Still, in spite of his health challenges, Dad had been the strong one through all this. Yesterday he'd helped her list her townhome with a realtor, and he'd handled most of the communication with Judson Meyer.

She probably would have dismissed the attorney if it weren't for the fact that Dad was so proud of landing Meyer to represent her. She was grateful, yet she had to wonder if things might have moved more quickly if she'd refused an attorney altogether. Why did justice take so long when she wasn't even on trial? When she'd admitted to the crime? It made no sense.

More than three weeks had gone by since her encounter with Garrett in the grocery store parking lot. She hadn't seen him or heard from him since—not that she'd expected to, but she'd found herself thinking about the days of their brief friendship even more since their chance meeting. It grieved her to realize that not only had she lost the gift of Garrett's companionship, but now she dreaded the prospect of accidentally bumping into him again—something that was bound to happen in a town the size of Hanover Falls.

Of course if she wound up going to jail—which she fully expected—bumping into Garrett would be the least of her worries.

"This way, honey." Dad pointed to a sign bearing arrows indicating the various meeting rooms. They found the room where Meyer had said to meet them. The door was ajar and when they entered, he rose from his chair at the folding table and greeted them with an odd grin. What was going on?

After she and Dad were seated, Meyer's smile bloomed. "Seems there's been an interesting and fortuitous twist in your case, Ms. Hennesey."

Fortuitous? That meant something good, didn't it? What had happened?

She looked at her father, who mirrored her puzzled expression and queried the attorney. "What's happened?"

Meyer leaned back in his chair and clasped his hands behind his head. "A resident of the homeless shelter has stepped forward and admitted to starting the fire."

Bryn gasped. "You're kidding? Who? Zeke Downing?"

Meyer shook his head and leaned forward. "It's not Downing. But they are questioning another man as we speak. That's all I know right now, but if this guy actually confessed to the crime, today will go down on your calendar—and mine—as one happy day."

Bryn was speechless. After all that had happened, she might actually go free?

As if he'd read her mind, Meyer beamed at her. Then his smile faded and he shook his head. "I don't get it . . . two people both insisting on claiming guilt for one crime? I tell you, this is one for the books."

Dad reached to put a hand on her back. "Does this mean Bryn . . . is free?" His voice wavered with emotion. "How soon will we know something?"

"Hard to say, but I would think—unless the guy changes his story—we could know something yet today. And yes, if this guy did it, you're home free. There's no way they can prove that you didn't blow that candle out. I always thought your story was shaky."

"But—" Words failed her. *Had* she been wrong about the candle? Had her mind conjured up something so real that it had convinced her, convicted her falsely?

Meyer sobered and held up a hand. "There's always a chance this guy will plead not guilty and then it could go to trial. His attorney would try to point the blame back to you. But given that he turned himself in, that's an unlikely scenario."

"You hear that, honey?" Dad pulled her close. "Maybe this whole mess is finally over."

She nodded. But instead of slipping loose, the knot in her stomach cinched and tightened. She remembered how hard Meyer had tried to persuade her not to plead guilty.

Yet, for the briefest moment she let herself imagine what it would feel like to be free of the guilt and shame she'd lived with all these weeks. Was it possible God had rescued her in a way she'd never dreamed? Her pulse stuttered.

She dared to consider the possibility that her friendship with Garrett might be restored. But she quickly pushed away the thought, afraid to entertain such an impossible dream for even an instant.

Meyer said a man had confessed to *starting* the fire. Maybe she *had* lit the candle, but it was a coincidence that it happened at the same time as an act of arson. Maybe someone else had started the fire, and when they saw that she was getting the blame, they felt guilty.

Who would have done such a thing? And why? *Oh, please, God. Let this be the end of it. I just want it to be over.*

She tried to enjoy the moment, allow relief to wash over her. But the release wouldn't come. This was too easy. Something wasn't right.

"Mr. Edmonds?"

Garrett looked up from the stack of geography tests he was grading. Kathy Beckwith stood in the open doorway to his classroom, beckoning.

"Keep reading, class, I'll be right out in the hallway." He slipped from behind the desk and went out into the hall, where Kathy waited.

"Garrett," she whispered, glancing back toward his open door. She wore an expression of eager expectation.

He gave her a questioning look. Something had happened.

"You haven't by chance been watching the news, have you?"

He shook his head. "No, what's going on?"

According to last night's paper, Bryn's arraignment was today, and though he'd tried to put the date out of his mind, he'd thought of nothing else all morning. Kathy must have heard something. "Is this about . . . the fire?" He'd started to say, "Is this about Bryn?" But that would have given Kathy the wrong idea.

She was nodding. "Someone else confessed to starting the fire. Some homeless guy who was at the shelter that night. Jim was watching Channel 3, and the local news broke in with the report."

Kathy's husband was home on disability leave, and she'd bemoaned the fact that all he did was sit around and watch TV. She didn't look upset now, though. She was absolutely beaming. "They're not giving many details, but Jim said they're saying Bryn might be off the hook."

"How could that be? She turned herself in."

"I don't know." She glanced at her watch. "There will probably be more on the noon news. Do you want me to take lunch duty so you can watch?"

He bent his head, studied the pattern in the gleaming waxed tile. The only television was in the teacher's lounge, and he wasn't about to watch the news with an audience.

He looked up at Kathy. Why did she seem so pleased about the news? Kathy had guessed at his relationship with Bryn, but he'd told her that it was over between him and Bryn. She'd deceived him. There wasn't anything else to say. They'd respected his desire not to discuss it, but Kathy and Mary Brigmann had both defended Bryn to him the day after the news broke that she'd turned herself in.

"Believe me, Garrett," Mary had said, "if it had been me, I would have done everything in my power to convince myself it wasn't true. That's a heavy load to live with."

Kathy had shaken her head and winced. "When I think about how many times I've come home from the grocery store to discover I've left a candle burning . . ." Her voice trailed off, but Mary clucked her agreement, and Garrett had remembered a time when Molly had done the same thing. And she was a firefighter. An argument he'd thrown in her face. She of all people should have known better. What was it with women and candles? Not that he didn't like the effect a little candlelight and the warm scent of vanilla had on his wife . . .

He ran a hand over his face, shook himself from the tender memories. "I'll catch it on tonight's news. I need to get back to my kids."

He turned away, but Kathy put a hand on his arm, forcing him to face her again. "Garrett, if she's innocent, you've got to forgive her. This is eating you up."

He clenched his jaw and held up a hand. He was not going to stand in the hallway outside his classroom and have this discussion.

Kathy's face crumpled. "I'm sorry. I just thought . . . you'd want to know."

He nodded, tried to apologize without words. Her expression told him he'd failed. Well, she'd get over it.

He left her standing there and went back into his classroom. But he had a million questions. Why—knowing that someone else had already taken the blame for the crime—would a homeless guy confess to the same crime? He remembered conversations he and Bryn had had about her work at the shelter. She'd told him that sometimes people were so desperate for a "home"— any place to "belong"—they would commit a crime for the security of jail. Maybe that's what this guy wanted.

That had to be it. Otherwise, Bryn had admitted to something she didn't do. What if she was innocent? Hope tugged at his heart. What if this was all some huge misunderstanding?

But that made no sense. According to the papers, Bryn's confession fit with what the fire investigators found. She had told him herself—in the letter she'd written. But what if she'd been lying? He couldn't guess at what motive she'd possibly have, yet neither did it make sense that she couldn't remember what she'd done until months after—after the fire. After he'd fallen in love with her.

"Mr. Edmonds? . . . Mr. Edmonds?"

He looked up, half surprised to find himself in his classroom. "Yes, Jillian?"

He had to find a way to end his obsession with this mess. With Bryn. He'd been able to think of nothing else. It had utterly consumed his life, and his students were suffering for it.

30

Bryn glanced at her watch. It was almost noon. Her arraignment had originally been scheduled for ten a.m. She'd thought she would know her final fate by now. Instead, they'd been waiting for over two hours for Judson Meyer to come back with news about this new wrinkle in her case.

Dad dozed upright in the chair across from her, his breaths coming in soft snores. Bryn had mentally run through the list of residents who'd passed through the shelter while she was there, trying to think who could conceivably have a reason to set the place on fire. Zeke Downing was the likely suspect. But Meyer had said that it *wasn't* Zeke.

How the attorney knew that, Bryn couldn't guess, but now she wondered if it might be James Friar, the man who'd attacked the teenage resident back when Bryn had first started working at the shelter. Friar was the reason she'd been sneaking around behind Adam's back in the first place.

Like many of the shelter's residents, Friar was

mentally ill and had struggled with addiction to drugs and alcohol. That alone made it unsurprising that he might have sought revenge for being kicked out. If he had indeed set the fire, Bryn's relief would know no bounds.

She'd lived under this cloud of guilt for so long she could hardly imagine what it would feel like to be exonerated. Yet she knew that nothing could change the fact that her acts of negligence had carried the potential to snuff out the lives of Adam and the other heroes.

Even if, by some fluke, the fire had started some other way, she could never truly be absolved of her guilt. But oh, it would be a far lighter burden to shoulder if the fire had been intentionally set. A dim spark of hope kindled inside her, and she breathed in, hoping to ignite it.

The door opened and Judson Meyer stepped through, briefcase in hand. Dad jerked to attention, and he and Bryn both leaned forward.

The attorney placed the briefcase in front of him and heaved out a breath. "Okay, here's what we've got." He eyed Bryn. "The man they have in custody is named Charles Branson. Do you know him?"

"Charlie? Yes. I know him." What did any of this have to do with Charlie?

"He was there that night, right?"

Bryn nodded, thoroughly confused.

Meyer shifted the papers in front of him.

"Branson has apparently been staying at a shelter in Springfield."

"Is that the man you got Sparky from?" Dad asked.

"Yes, but I don't get it. Charlie told them he started the fire? On purpose?"

Meyer nodded. "Said he went up to the office and set a fire in the trash can there. Said he didn't mean to burn the place down, just wanted to create a little excitement."

"No . . ." Bryn shook her head. That didn't sound like Charlie at all. "Why would he do that?" Her mind reeled, trying to figure out how Charlie could have done such a thing. And *when?* It didn't make sense.

"Who did Charlie talk to? Perlson?"

"Yes. He apparently called the Hanover Falls police from the Springfield shelter and made his confession over the phone. Springfield police brought him in last night. He *was* there the night of the fire? You're sure about that?"

Bryn nodded slowly, chewing a corner of her lip. Something was fishy. "Charlie didn't start that fire. Why would he say that?"

Meyer pinned her with a glare. "Exactly. There's no reason for him to lie about something like this."

"I don't know why he would tell anyone that, but there's no way it was Charlie." She recounted the events of the evening again. "I was with

Charlie practically the whole night. I had the key to the office around my neck. Susan had the other key. There's no way he could have gotten into the office without one of us knowing. He's lying."

Meyer's eyes narrowed. "Why would a guy lie about something like that?"

"Bryn . . ." Dad gripped her arm, his voice wavering. "Why are you so determined to be guilty about this? The man confessed—"

"Because I *am* guilty! Why are you—" she leveled her gaze at the attorney, then back at her father—"both of you, so determined to try to get me out of it?"

Dad fumbled for her hand, knitting his fingers with hers. "Because what happened was an accident. It could have happened to anyone. There's been enough tragedy, Bryn. It will serve no purpose for you to sit in *jail*." His voice rose on the word, and he dropped his head, tightened his grip on her hand. "Haven't you lost enough?"

Bryn stared at her father, an awful suspicion niggling at her. "Did *you* talk to Charlie, Dad? Did you try to get him to—"

"Of course not. I don't even know the man, except what you've told me about him . . . being Sparky's owner, I mean."

The confusion in his eyes made Bryn weak with relief. Dad was as clueless as she was about Charlie's motives.

"Didn't you take Sparky to see him a while

back?" Dad let loose of her hand and straightened in his chair. "In Springfield? What did you tell him then?"

Bryn didn't miss Meyer's questioning gaze. She addressed her reply to the attorney. "Yes. A few weeks ago. I drove to Springfield and visited him at the shelter there."

The attorney stared at her. "Did you talk about anything that would have made him come forward?"

She thought for a moment, but shook her head. "I—that was before my . . . dream. We didn't talk about the fire at all. He knew Susan was trying to get the shelter back up and running. That's when he asked me to take Sparky—his dog. We still have Sparky . . . out at Dad's place," she explained to Meyer.

Meyer shrugged. "Maybe the guy just thinks jail would be better accommodations than what he has at the shelter. The place he's in is only a day shelter as I understand it. It's been a cold winter—tough on someone like him."

"Charlie's in a wheelchair. He's a Vietnam vet," she explained to her father, wondering how Meyer knew that. "But it's a decent shelter. And they gave him a job there and let him stay full-time. He was happy there . . . proud of landing the job." She thought about how Charlie had sacrificed Sparky to stay in Springfield. Things weren't adding up.

Meyer rested his elbows on the table in front of him, steepled his index fingers, and rested his chin on the spire. "Well, I can't explain why he'd confess to something he didn't do, but you can't both have done it."

Bryn stared past the attorney. Why would Charlie have told them he started the fire? Besides the fact that he had no motive, he wouldn't have had access to the office unless she or Susan was present, too. Susan would have mentioned something like that to the investigators. And though her memories of that night were hazy, she was almost certain that—except for the three or four minutes it had taken her to go out and check on Sparky that night—Charlie had been with her every minute from the time they came down the elevator from the office.

Meyer's cell phone chirped. He held up a hand and pulled the phone from his belt. "Meyer here." He listened for several minutes, his face growing dark. "You're sure?"

He flipped the phone shut without saying goodbye. Pounding his fist on the table, he blew a curse through clenched teeth.

Bryn waited, thinking the attorney had gotten bad news about another case. But he quickly composed himself and looked hard at Bryn. "So much for that . . ."

"What happened?"

Meyer dropped his head, silent. His hands

formed clenched fists on his knees. Finally he looked up. "I'm sorry, Bryn. That was Perlson. You were right. Branson didn't do it."

Dad jumped up. "How can you know that? Why did he confess, then?" Bryn watched the hope drain from her father's face.

"Branson told the police he used lighter fluid to start the fire. But the investigators' reports said they found no trace of any accelerant."

A chilling thought sluiced down her spine. *Had Judson Meyer somehow talked Charlie into taking the rap for her? Surely he wouldn't stoop that low. Or be that stupid.*

"So what happens now?" her father asked.

Bryn didn't like the hope in his voice. Especially when she knew Charlie was innocent. Charlie's confession didn't change anything. The glimmer of hope that had bloomed, fizzled. And yet she felt relieved for Charlie. "Where is he now? Charlie?"

"They're still holding him for further questioning," Meyer said. "But they'll likely let him go."

"I can assure you he didn't do anything. If they need me to testify—or whatever . . . I know he didn't do it." It broke her heart to think of Charlie locked up. "Can I talk to him?"

Meyer shook his head. "I would strongly advise against it."

"Why?"

"Because Mr. Branson may end up testifying against you."

Bryn closed her eyes. This was getting messy.

"I'm going to ask the judge to delay your arraignment until we can get this figured out. I'm not convinced Branson doesn't know something he's not telling." Meyer narrowed his eyes at Bryn. "And frankly, I'm not sure *my* client is telling me the truth. The whole truth."

31

Wednesday, February 20

*W*alking into the Hanover Falls Police Station was like going back in time. The same uniformed woman who'd been there the day Bryn turned herself in was behind the desk. Bryn told her what she wanted and the woman picked up the phone and called Rudy Perlson.

Through the plate-glass window, Bryn watched the police chief hang up the phone and thread his way through the maze of desks and come to greet her. "You want to talk to Branson?"

"Yes, please."

"I hate to disappoint you, but there's no way he could have done it."

Did they think she *wanted* to pin the blame on Charlie?

"I know he didn't do it. I told my lawyer that. That's why I want to talk to him. I think— Maybe Charlie was trying . . . to take the blame for me."

Perlson absorbed that for a minute. "Then you're a very lucky lady to have someone think that much of you."

"He'll get to go back to Springfield, won't he? To the shelter there?"

Perlson nodded. "As soon as someone can come and get him."

"I can take him back, if that's all he's waiting for." She looked at her watch. "I'd have time."

The chief shook his head. "I don't think that would be wise. You've already got your lawyer and the judge a little befuddled."

Though everyone seemed convinced that Charlie's confession was groundless, they'd rescheduled her arraignment for this afternoon. Meyer had told her the judge would sentence her as soon as she entered a guilty plea. He seemed to have finally given up on trying to convince her to enter a different plea.

"I think you'd better stick around until after the arraign—" Perlson seemed to catch himself and looked at the floor.

She didn't miss the significance. She might not be free to go after the arraignment. "Mr. Branson is free to go anytime," the police chief said, recovering. "We've called the shelter and they're trying to find someone to take him back."

"Maybe my dad could take him." Bryn pointed toward the street. "He's waiting in the car."

"We'll see." Perlson leaned against an empty desk. "I just want you to know that Judge Clyne is a good man. I think he'll be . . . fair with you."

She looked up, surprised at his words, yet at the same time wondering exactly what Perlson thought was fair. "Thank you."

*T*he silence of the courtroom was disturbed by a whispered commotion. Sitting at the table beside Judson Meyer, Bryn couldn't bring herself to turn and face the gallery.

From the media's interest in this story, especially with the complication of Charlie's "confession," Bryn assumed there would be reporters present for her sentencing. Judging by the scraping of chairs and the hushed muttering, the media must be arriving now. She only prayed the judge wouldn't allow cameras inside the courtroom.

Judson Meyer had arranged for her to have a moment with her father after the sentencing, and to leave the building by a side door, regardless of the outcome.

She closed her eyes, suddenly more nervous than she'd been since that day she'd walked into the police station to confess. Would she be leaving in a police car, or would she, by some miracle, be able to go home with Dad?

Oh, Father, whatever happens, please be with Daddy. Comfort him and let him know that You have everything under control.

She believed that. But Dad's disappointment in realizing that Charlie would not be a scapegoat for her had been deep. Once again, she feared for his health.

She felt Dad's hand on her shoulder, as if he somehow knew she was praying for him. Without turning around, she reached her hand up to cover his.

But he leaned to whisper in her ear. "You need to turn around."

She didn't want to show her face to the reporters, who were no doubt just waiting for a chance to catch a glimpse of her so they could describe how pale and gaunt and distressed she looked—or perhaps they would describe her as aloof and cold? She didn't know how the media had spun the story since the whole thing with Charlie was leaked to the press.

Dad's persistent squeeze of her shoulder forced her to turn and look out over the gallery.

What she saw lit fear inside her chest. Seated on three rows of benches behind her, looking somber, were Susan Marlowe and Fire Captain Peter Brennan. Emily Vermontez sat at the end of the row, Lucas beside her in the aisle in his wheelchair and in the row behind them, Jenna Morgan.

Myrna Eckland, from the library, sat at the

opposite end of the bench, head down as if she were praying.

On the opposite side of the gallery, a row of reporters scribbled on notepads and muttered to each other behind cupped hands. And, behind them, Rudy Perlson sat with his arms folded.

Why were they all here? Judson Meyer had made it sound as if the arraignment would be short and sweet. That she simply would enter her plea and then wait to find out what sentence the judge would impose. He hadn't said anything about the families of her "victims"—those whose lives her negligence had snuffed out—getting a chance to testify against her.

Her mouth went dry. Looking over Dad's shoulder, she panned the courtroom again. Overwhelmed, she leaned across the table to Meyer and whispered in a shaky voice, "Are they all going to testify against me?"

He touched her hand briefly and shot her an *Are-you-serious?* look. Shaking his head, he slipped a ballpoint pen from the pocket of his suit coat and jotted a note on his legal pad. He slid the pad to her side of the table.

It read: *No! They are here in support of you.* He underlined the word *support* twice.

Her knees went weak. It seemed unbelievable that the very people she'd harmed—*stolen* loved ones from—could be here to support her. She swallowed past a lump of new grief.

But scanning the room one more time, she realized the one person who mattered most to her—the one person whose forgiveness she most needed—was conspicuously absent. *Garrett.*

32

"Mr. Meyer, your client is still prepared to plead guilty today as we previously discussed?"

"Yes, Your Honor."

"Ms. Hennesey, if you would stand, please, and the clerk will administer the oath."

Bryn rose, thankful for the table in front of her. She placed a trembling hand on the Bible the clerk held, praying her voice would remain steady as she repeated the oath.

"Ms. Hennesey, you are now under oath, and answering any questions falsely may be considered perjury. Do you understand?"

"Yes, Your Honor."

The judge looked at her over reading glasses. "Do you understand the charges against you?"

"Yes, Your Honor."

"And how do you plead to those charges?"

"I plead guilty, Your Honor."

"And do you make this plea of your own volition, without inducements or threats against you?"

"Yes. This is my decision alone."

Beside her, Judson Meyer stepped to the side of the table and cleared his throat. "Your Honor, I would like it noted that Ms. Hennesey makes this plea against her counsel's advice."

The judge studied her. "Ms. Hennesey, is this so?"

"Yes, Your Honor."

"Have you had full opportunity to discuss your case with Mr. Meyer and to be apprised of the possible consequences of a guilty plea?"

"Yes, Your Honor, I have."

The judge slipped his glasses up on his nose, picked up his pen, and scratched out something. "Ms. Hennesey, are you satisfied with Mr. Meyer's representation of you, and absolutely certain of the plea you've entered? Can you verify that you wish to plead guilty because you are guilty, and that you understand all possible consequences of this plea?"

"Yes, Your Honor."

"Has Mr. Meyer explained to you that you have certain rights under the law and if you plead guilty, you will be forfeiting these rights?"

"He has, Your Honor."

The judge read the same list of rights Judson Meyer had asked her to read at their first meeting. Only somehow they seemed more grave coming from the judge's lips. But nothing had changed what she knew to be true. She *was* guilty of the charges against her, and nothing in the judge's questioning changed that.

"Ms. Hennesey, do you understand each of the rights I have just described?"

"Yes, sir . . ." She corrected herself. "Yes, Your Honor."

"You understand that by pleading guilty you waive these rights and that you will not have a trial."

"I do."

"And you do not wish to change your plea?"

It seemed he had given her a dozen chances to back out. And with each time he questioned her, she felt a bit less certain. As if he were asking her a trick question and making sure she fell for it, hook, line, and sinker.

She glanced at Meyer, but his expression was inscrutable.

She cleared her throat. "I don't want to change my plea, Your Honor. I plead guilty."

The judge took off his glasses and hung them from the neckband of his robe. He clasped his hands in front of him and waited, as if for some signal.

After a minute of deafening silence, he looked at Bryn, kindly, she thought. She held her breath.

"Before sentence is imposed, Ms. Hennesey, you have the right to address the courtroom. It is not a requirement, but should you so desire, the law does afford you that opportunity and that right. Do you wish to make a statement?"

Meyer had told her she would have this opportunity, and she'd written out a brief statement. She unfolded the page and stared at the words swimming before her. They seemed utterly inadequate and futile. But she could not remain silent. The people who had come—she still couldn't quite fathom that they'd come in support of her—deserved to hear her apology in her own words, from her own lips.

From her heart.

She folded the paper in half, then in fourths and laid it on the table. She was thankful no one expected her to look anywhere except at the judge. "Your Honor . . ." She hadn't choked out two words, and emotion clogged her throat.

She closed her eyes and prayed she wouldn't break down. "Your Honor," she started again. "I only want to say again how terribly sorry I am for the tragedy my negligence caused. There are no words that can take away the pain I've caused, and there is no way to bring back any of our loved ones . . ."

She paused. Meyer had warned her not to let her statement be about herself in any way—her own pain, or her fate at the hands of the court. She hadn't intended to garner sympathy with her implied reference to Adam. But she did share in their sorrow. Like them, she had lost someone she loved. *Two someones.* "I only hope that when this day is over, those who lost loved ones in the fire will feel that justice has been served. And I pray that they will someday find a way to forgive me for what happened. I would give anything—my very life—if I could go back and make things right." She bowed her head. There was nothing more she could say.

The judge didn't speak for a few seconds. From the corner of her eye, Bryn saw Meyer nod at the bench, acknowledging that his client was finished speaking.

The next minutes were a blur of vaguely familiar legal terms as the judge restated the charges against her, the penalties and demands of the law.

"Ms. Hennesey has demonstrated that she is a law-abiding, conscientious citizen who has volunteered many hours of service to this community. In light of her own loss—the death of her husband—it is the opinion of this court that Ms. Hennesey can make restitution far more effectively by giving of herself through community service than by being incarcerated. And in fact, she has already demonstrated her giving nature with the volunteer work she's performed in the past. Further, it is the opinion of this court that no useful purpose would be served by incarcerating her. Ms. Hennesey poses no threat to society, her actions were not intentional, and she is obviously remorseful over her negligence. Therefore . . ."

The judge's voice droned on in a soothing monotone, but the only words Bryn heard clearly, the only words that had meaning for her were *proba-tion* and *community service*. And those words sent gratitude coursing through her.

Judson Meyer covered her trembling hand with his on the table, and she thought he looked pleased with the outcome. She trusted he would explain everything in detail once they left the courtroom.

After more formalities that passed in a haze of relief, the judge dismissed the courtroom. Bryn didn't turn to face the gallery until the soft hum of people leaving the room had died down. But she did allow herself to lean back into her father's waiting embrace.

She couldn't remember when his arms had felt so strong.

33

Garrett sat hunkered on the floor in front of the sofa, stroking Boss's head, waiting for the news to come on. It seemed all he did when he was home anymore was wait in front of the TV.

Tonight his heart was heavier than usual. Bryn's sentencing was today.

He had a bad feeling about it. What she'd done was classified a felony. He fully expected to hear that she'd been given a prison sentence. And if she was headed to prison, he would carry at least some of the blame.

His eyes gravitated to the crumpled letter on the coffee table: Susan Marlowe's plea with the surviving spouses to attend the arraignment in a show of support for Bryn. He picked up the letter and read it for at least the dozenth time:

In case you're not aware, the penalties for involuntary manslaughter in Missouri are serious. Surely none of us—no matter what we think about Bryn's negligence—believe that she deserves time in prison. Bryn was one of the best volunteers to ever work at the shelter.

You've probably heard by now about Charlie Branson, one of the shelter's residents who thought so much of Bryn that he confessed (falsely) to the crime himself. I think that speaks loudly of Bryn's character.

Those of you who talked to her, or received a letter from her, know how devastated she is over what happened. And please don't forget that she lost her own husband in the tragedy. Please think how you would feel if you were in her shoes. What happened to Bryn could have happened to any one of us. We've all done foolish, thoughtless things that could have resulted in harm or death to another human being. The only difference is that we weren't "caught."

I beg you not to let the tragedy of your own loss end in more tragedy—the useless act of a good woman being sent to prison, possibly for the best years of her life, for what was clearly an accident.

Susan had asked them all to meet at the front of the courthouse so they could walk in together, in a show of solidarity.

He'd considered going. He truly had. But in the end, he simply couldn't make himself do it. The media would be swarming afterward, looking for interviews. They no doubt knew about his and Bryn's friendship—*former* friendship. He would be the first one they'd swoop down on, hoping for a sensational story.

And what could he say? That he'd forgiven Bryn? He wasn't sure he had. That he was there in support of her? Could he have said that honestly?

He didn't know the answer to those questions. There was a part of him that wanted her locked away. Far away. Not as punishment for what she'd done, but so he could forget about her. Put her out of his mind. So he could somehow go on with his life. Or what was left of it.

He wondered how many of the others had shown up. Was he the only one who'd disappointed Susan? Disappointed *Bryn*? Had Bryn even noticed that he wasn't there? Did she still think about him?

So many questions. He'd never had questions

about life—about anything—before Molly died. Everything had made sense before. Everything had been so easy.

The pulsating theme music for the evening news jangled his thoughts, and he pushed Susan Marlowe's letter aside and punched the volume on the remote.

The sentencing was the top story. A young male reporter posed in front of the courthouse and delivered the news in exaggerated tones.

"A Hanover Falls woman who admitted to causing the fire that destroyed the Grove Street Homeless Shelter in Hanover Falls and killed five firefighters entered a plea of guilty this afternoon. Judge Anthony Clyne placed Bryn Hennesey on five years' probation, suspending imposition of a sentence, meaning Hennesey will have no conviction if she completes probation. Judge Clyne set several probation conditions, including two hundred hours of community service to be performed over the next two years.

"We talked to Hennesey's attorney, Judson Meyer, following the arraignment and sentencing earlier today."

The camera cut to the attorney. "I thought Judge Clyne's sentencing was fair. My client insisted on pleading guilty despite the possibility of a harsh sentence. It's rare for someone to refuse to pursue a lesser sentence, and I think Ms. Hennesey is to be commended. By comparison, two hundred hours is a significant proviso, but Judge Clyne feels my client can make restitution and be a far better example by performing community service. I'm glad the community seemed to agree." Meyer put his head down and walked away from the camera.

The reporter continued, "About twenty citizens were present at the sentencing, including Hennesey's father and several spouses of the deceased firefighters, most of whom appeared to be there in support of Hennesey."

A clip of Susan Marlowe played, her voice faint and wavering, her hair blowing in front of her face. "I believe today's decision is best for everyone involved. It is obvious Bryn is devastated by what happened. I think she's suffered enough, and I hope today was a day of forgiveness, a day of moving forward."

"That was Susan Marlowe," the reporter explained. "Marlowe's husband, Lieutenant David Marlowe, died in the blaze. Marlowe was also the director at the Grove Street Homeless Shelter at the time of the tragedy." The reporter's tone changed to a more somber note. "Not everyone present, however, spoke in support of Ms. Hennesey."

A handsome middle-aged couple appeared on the screen to the voice-over of the reporter. "The parents of Engineer Zachary Morgan, the first fireman to die in the blaze, spoke out against what they saw as a much too lenient sentence."

"Justice was not served today," the man said through clenched jaws as his wife wept openly beside him. "The sentence that woman received was a joke. Five heroic people lost their lives in that fire. Our *son* lost his life in that fire, and this woman basically walked away scot-free."

Garrett pressed his back hard against the sofa, feeling his defenses rise. Beside him, Boss whimpered and looked up at him, obviously sensing his anger.

Garrett stroked the dog's bristled coat. The news anchor moved on to a new story. Garrett clicked the volume on the remote, and the news became a mumbled drone. Could these people not see how shattered Bryn was over what she'd done? What purpose did they think it would serve for her to rot in jail? For the first time, he let himself imagine what jail would have been like for Bryn. The relief that pumped through his veins, knowing that she'd been spared that fate, left him feeling physically drained.

But you weren't there for her.

The accusation hit him hard. Why could all the others forgive so easily? She had been his dear friend. More than a friend. Why had he written her off so easily?

Two sides of himself warred with each other.

She deceived you.

She said she didn't know.

But how could she not? She should have told

306

someone right away. Think of all the times you talked about the fire—about Molly's death and Adam's. Why didn't she say anything?

She was scared. Maybe she wanted to believe she really hadn't left that candle burning.

That's what she told you. Why couldn't you believe it?

And the two voices went on arguing until Garrett finally hauled himself off the floor and went to the kitchen for a bowl of cereal. Boss padded after him. He'd grown to love the homely mutt. He wondered how Sparky was doing out at Bryn's dad's. He'd heard that Bryn was staying out there permanently now, trying to sell her townhouse.

What would she have to do to fulfill her community service? An image of Bryn in an orange prison-issued jumpsuit, picking up trash along the side of the Interstate, formed in his head. He shook it off. She'd been granted probation. She wouldn't have to spend even a night in prison. Again, relief flooded him.

He thought he'd quit caring about her after she admitted to him what she'd done. Why couldn't he get her off his mind now? This ordeal was over. He was supposed to be able to go on from here. Put everything out of his mind, chalk it up to a learning experience, and move forward.

But the more he tried not to think about Bryn Hennesey, the more she crowded his thoughts.

307

34

*T*he sun spread its warmth across the country road, and winter-bare branches cast a tracery of shadows on the gravel surface. Bryn's breaths came rapidly as she tried to keep up with Sparky on their morning walk.

More than a week had passed since she had stood before the judge and declared herself guilty. In many ways, it seemed like a lifetime ago.

In the days since, she'd established a pleasant routine at Dad's, no doubt made more pleasant when she compared it to the life she might well have been sentenced to. She filled her lungs with the brisk February air and reveled in her freedom.

She felt as if she'd been given a brand-new life. A little like the way she'd felt the night she gave her life to Jesus in seventh grade. A clean slate. No one had to remind her that what she enjoyed wasn't because she deserved it, but because a judge had mercy on her. She intended to do everything in her power to make Judge Clyne look back on his decision as one of the best he'd ever made. And maybe in the process, she could sway those who weren't convinced his decision had served justice.

Dad tried to protect her from the contro-versy—hiding the newspaper whenever there was something negative in the editorials or a blurb about her role in the fire, or about the fire itself. She'd played by his unspoken rule that the TV didn't go on until after the evening news and was turned off before the ten o'clock news began.

But more than once, she'd allowed herself to google the news stories. It hurt to know that there were at least a few who thought Judge Clyne had been far too lenient with her sentence.

Approaching the intersection, she persuaded Sparky to turn around and start back home. In spite of the clear skies and warm sun, the winter breeze was chilly, and she pulled up her collar and quickened her pace.

She was taking Sparky to Springfield later this morning for another visit with Charlie. She hadn't talked with him since he'd tried to take the blame for her, but she had some things she wanted to say to the man.

The minute Charlie rolled his chair into view—half-cringing, eyeing Bryn as if he were in trouble—she knew he was expecting a good scolding from her. She wouldn't disappoint him, but first things first.

She hurried forward and bent to wrap her arms around him. Charlie let loose of the wheel grips on his chair and returned her embrace with an anemic pat on the back.

She didn't care if it made him uncomfortable, she had to hug the man. She swallowed her tears and stepped back to look him in the eye. "Thank you, Charlie."

He cleared his throat. "I don't know what you're talking about."

She tucked her tongue in her cheek and gave him a *don't-even-start-with-that* glare.

He chuckled and waved her off. "Okay, maybe I sort of know what you're talking about." He wheeled his chair toward the cramped seating area near the entrance to the shelter. "Come and sit with me for a while."

"I brought Sparky again."

"You did?"

She nodded. "He's out in the car. It's pretty cold outside. Do you think they'd let me bring him in for a few minutes?"

He rocked his chair back, then forward, then turned 90 degrees. "Hang on. Let me ask Timothy."

He disappeared down the hall and was back in a few minutes with the director, whom Bryn remembered as "Red."

Bryn rose and they shook hands.

"We're really not supposed to allow animals in, but I'll make an exception today . . . since it's so cold out."

Bryn started to thank him, but something stopped her. A thoughtless "exception" to a rule had caused untold grief. Even now, its ripples affected her life, Charlie's . . . so many others.

As if he'd read her mind, Charlie reached out and put a hand on her arm. "It's okay, sis. You've got permission. Timothy makes the rules here. He can bend 'em if he wants to."

She swallowed hard, but nodded. "Okay. I'll go get him. Be right back." She mouthed a thank-you to the director. "I won't stay long."

Tim waved her off. "No . . . take your time. It's okay. We'll consider it therapy for this guy . . . right, Charlie?" He squeezed Charlie's beefy shoulder.

She hurried to the car and was back in two minutes with a wound-up Sparky. Charlie met them at the door.

Again, Sparky seemed to remember his old friend and greeted him with a slobbery kiss. The smile on Charlie's face made it all worthwhile. When Sparky finally settled down, parking with his big, soft head on Charlie's lap, Bryn put a hand on the veteran's arm.

"Thank you, Charlie."

He just looked at her, waiting.

"What you did, Charlie, it wasn't right. But . . ." She blew out a breath. "I can't tell you how much it means to me. That you would be willing to take the fall for me like that."

"I was afraid you were going to go to jail, sis. What did it matter if I went? But you . . ."

"It still wasn't right. You didn't deserve jail. I did."

He looked around the shelter. "Jail, homeless shelter, what's the difference?"

"Charlie . . . you don't mean that."

"Listen, I did what I thought I had to do. I'm sorry if it complicated things. But I wasn't going to sit here and let you go to prison for a mistake anybody could have made. For all I know I distracted you that night, coming up, bugging you to play cards."

She wagged her head. "No, Charlie. It wasn't your fault in any way."

"Still, I couldn't have lived with myself if you went to the slammer over this."

"Well, thank you. Believe me, I'm very happy to be free. And I don't want to encourage your little shenanigans, but"—she flashed a grin—"my attorney thinks it may have helped my case to have you . . . do what you did."

"Well, I don't know nothin' about that . . . I'm just glad you got off."

She nodded. "It reminds me of Someone else who did the same thing for me. And for you, too." She winked.

His eyes held a quizzical glint.

"It was a long time ago." Bryn grinned. "About two thousand years ago, when a certain Someone took all the blame for all the bad things I've ever done or will ever do. You, too, Charlie."

Charlie shook his head, looking disgusted, and backed his wheelchair up a few feet. "Now, don't go trying to make me out to be as nice as that Jesus of yours, sis."

She laughed and leaned forward, clapping him on the shoulder. "Don't worry. You've got a ways to go." Her throat grew thick. "But that was a good start. A really good start. Thanks, Charlie."

He shrugged. "So I hear you have to do community service, is that right?"

She nodded. "Two hundred hours . . . over two years," she added quickly.

He gave a low whistle. "So you'll be picking up trash in the ditches or something? That's a shame. What a waste."

"Actually . . . I thought I'd ask Susan if she needs help getting the new shelter up and running. Maybe you can come back to the Falls, Charlie. Sparky would like that." Even as she said it, she thought about Dad and how attached he'd grown to the dog.

"You're sweet to mention it, sis, but I think"—he glanced up at the ceiling—"the man upstairs seems to have me here in Springfield for a reason. I'll probably stay."

Bryn wanted to cry. She hugged Charlie so he wouldn't see the tears welling behind her eyelids. "It won't be the same without you."

He made a *pffttttt* sound. "Nah, sis, you'll take some other worthless geezer under your wings, and you'll forget all about me."

Now she didn't care if he saw her tears. She rose and took a step back from his chair. "Never, Charlie. I'll never forget you."

He plucked at a nonexistent thread on his sleeve. "Enough of this kind of talk." He rubbed at rheumy eyes. "Now look what you did. I've got somethin' in my eye."

Through her own tears, Bryn laughed. "Those are called tears, Charlie. They're good for you."

"Yeah, yeah. So they say . . . so they say."

35

Monday, March 4

The hay bales and pumpkins on the porch had been replaced with pots of purple kale and pansies, but otherwise Susan Marlowe's house looked the way Bryn remembered it from the night Susan had called them all together to talk about reopening the homeless shelter as a living memorial for the firefighters who'd died.

So much had happened since that night. Memories of that first evening at the coffee shop with Garrett swirled through her mind, and she brushed them away like a pesky cobweb. She'd thought of Garrett so often in the days since her sentencing. She missed him. Missed the sweet friendship they'd shared. Missed having someone who understood how hard it was to be single again, how hard it was to have lost Adam so tragically.

She'd thanked God a hundred times for the leniency of her sentence, but sometimes she wondered if prison might have been easier than losing the man who'd become her closest friend. But she couldn't blame that loss on anyone but herself.

She shook her head, trying to banish the thoughts. She had too much to be grateful for to worry about what might have been.

She reached for the doorbell and stood waiting, admiring the tidy country home in an effort to keep her mind off the nerves that prickled.

The door opened and Susan squinted through the glare of the storm door. "Bryn." Susan didn't quite smile, but she opened the inner door. "Come on in. How are you?"

Bryn hesitated. "I'm sorry I didn't call first. I wasn't sure—Well, I should have called first." The truth was, she hadn't been sure Susan would take her call. She'd decided to take a chance that Susan wouldn't kick her off of the property.

But Susan opened the door wider and drew her inside. "Nonsense, please come in."

"Your flowers are pretty," Bryn said, pointing at the perky yellow and violet pansies as she stepped over the threshold.

"Well, it's a little early. I took a risk that we won't have another freeze. I may have to haul them inside for a few nights, but . . . I needed a touch of spring."

Bryn nodded, understanding, realizing that she'd been longing for the promise of a new season as well. She followed Susan into the kitchen.

"I made a pot of coffee. It's decaf, but it's still hot. Can I pour you a cup?"

"That would be nice. Thank you."

She slipped onto a chair at the table Susan indicated in the sunny breakfast alcove and watched while Susan fixed a tray with coffee and cream.

"Your house is beautiful. You really have a knack for decorating."

"Thank you. It's something I enjoy, though I haven't done much since—" She stopped abruptly.

But Bryn nodded, not wanting to make her feel uncomfortable. "I understand. I've kind of lost the heart for the things I used to love, too."

Susan didn't reply, but worked in silence, pouring coffee and carrying the tray over to the table. She placed a brimming cup on a saucer in front of Bryn and took a seat adjacent to her at the small table.

"Bryn, I—"

"Susan—"

They both spoke at once and laughed nervously as their words collided.

Bryn took the lead. She was the uninvited guest, and she hadn't meant to make Susan feel uncomfortable. "I came to ask you a favor, Susan, but first, I just wanted to say again how sorry I am. I know that sounds so incredibly . . . lame . . . but I am so very sorry."

Susan reached across the table and placed a hand on her arm. "Oh, Bryn. I should have replied to your letter. It was awful of me to ignore it the way I did, and I—"

"You don't need to apolo—"

"No, Bryn . . . Let me finish." Susan pressed her lips in a firm line and bowed her head. When she looked up, there were tears in her eyes. "I feel terrible for letting you carry the blame. I'm—I'm so grateful you don't have to go to—" She stopped, chewed the corner of her lower lip. "I'm not sure I can ever forgive myself for not speaking out in your defense."

"What do you mean?" She wasn't sure what Susan was getting at.

"It was as much my fault as yours, Bryn. I'm the one who bought those candles, brought them to the shelter. I knew you and the others lit them sometimes, and I never said anything."

"But you did. We knew we weren't supposed to light them."

"Yes, but I didn't enforce my words. I turned a blind eye. I should have been more strict—not just about that. About a lot of things. The guys smoking in the entryway. Getting those mattresses out of there. It's just . . . it took every minute, every ounce of energy I had to take care of what absolutely had to be done. I let things go that shouldn't have been let go."

"It wasn't your fault, Susan."

"I just couldn't— My boys needed me, Bryn. If I'd turned myself in . . . if I'd had to go to jail, it would have killed them. *Killed* them."

Bryn patted Susan's hand, then felt funny acting motherly toward this woman who was probably almost old enough to be her mother. "No one went to jail, Susan. And I don't think anyone would have thought you should be held responsible."

But Judson Meyer's words came back to her: *Even if Ms. Marlowe didn't light the candle herself, it was completely irresponsible for her to allow it on the premises.* If the case had been allowed to go to trial, might Susan have been implicated and asked to share the blame?

Bryn cleared her throat. "The reason I actually came, Susan . . . I need to line up some community service projects to fulfill my sentence. I don't know where you are on getting the shelter back up and running, but is there any way you'd consider letting me help with that—as part of my community service?"

Susan stared at her. A soft smile lit her eyes. "You won't believe this, but I just found out yesterday that we got a building."

"Really?" The timing seemed too much to be a coincidence.

Susan nodded vigorously. "It's those office buildings across the street from the old shelter—the site. We wouldn't even have to change the name. It could still be the Grove Street Homeless Shelter."

"That's wonderful, Susan. You sound happy about it."

Susan sighed and wiped at the corner of her eye. "It's kept me going . . . to have something worthwhile to do. But now that we have a building, I'm feeling overwhelmed. There's so much to do. This building is set up for business offices, not sleeping quarters. We'll have to at least put in showers and a kitchen area before we can open."

"Is the city going to help? Did they approve the request for the memorial money?"

Susan smoothed the paper napkin under her saucer. "Not yet, but I think they will. We could sure use that money. The whole place needs painting and we have to get all the inspections done before the sale can go through, but the owners are giving us the same kind of deal the hospital gave us last time, selling it for a little bit of nothing. The place has been on the market for almost three years, and—" She stopped, and looked at Bryn.

Susan's face was flushed with anticipation and purpose, and Bryn smiled to see her so energized.

She waited, hoping Susan hadn't forgotten her question, yet not wanting to press her.

"Oh! And I'd love to have you back. I didn't mean to leave you hanging." Susan laughed. "Truly, Bryn, it would be an answer to prayer. What did you have in mind?"

"I didn't even know you had a place . . . I was going to offer to help you look for a place, or do fundraising . . . whatever you needed. But hey"— she pushed up her sleeves—"I'm good with a paintbrush, and I can clean, or contact plumbers or . . . just about anything." She gave a nervous laugh. "I didn't want to have to go around to schools and give talks about fire safety." The sudden image of herself standing before Garrett's fifth graders with a fire safety chart started the tears flowing.

"Oh, honey . . ." In one smooth motion, Susan leaned across the table and wrapped her arms around her. For the first time in a long time, Bryn let herself think about her mother and how much she'd missed Mom through the awful ordeal she'd just come through.

Susan patted her back and let her cry for a minute. Then she rose and refilled their coffee cups. When she sat back down, she took a sip of coffee and looked hard at Bryn. "I really have been meaning to call you. About your letter." Susan gave her a crooked smile. "Your letter was precious. And . . . of course, I forgive you."

The simple words affected Bryn in a way she hadn't expected. *I forgive you.*

A groundswell of hope filled her. Was it possible . . . ? Did she dare to hope the others might forgive as easily as Susan had? Could Garrett—who had spoken so often of vindication—find it in himself to speak those healing words to her? *Oh, please, God. Let him forgive me, too. Even if I never get to hear those words from him, don't let him be eaten up with bitterness.*

She turned her focus back to Susan, let herself think about the "yes" answer Susan had given her. How fitting that she would be allowed to be a part of getting the new shelter ready to open. How very like the Redeemer of her soul.

Thank You, Lord.

"Thank you, Susan." Bryn could barely choke out the words.

36

Friday, April 18

Garrett retrieved an out-of-bounds ball and motioned for a sub. Trudging to the sideline, he wiped the sweat from his forehead with the sleeve of his T-shirt. He stood there, breathing hard, watching the other guys play and wondering why they didn't look the least out of breath. But between basketball and walking Boss, at least he was getting back in shape. Slowly. But sometimes basketball made him feel like an old man. At thirty-two. Not good.

Fifteen minutes later, a couple of the guys called it quits and the game disintegrated.

Winded as he was, he wished they'd keep playing. "Come on, guys . . . one more game."

"Sorry, gotta get moving," Jim Benton said, throwing a towel around his neck. "The wife's got plans for me tonight."

"Lucky you," a couple of the guys ribbed.

"Ha! Don't I wish. Not those kind of plans, sadly. She's having a garage sale tomorrow, and I've got to clean out the garage."

Garrett laughed at their good-natured joking, but he ached with envy. Looking around the gym, he realized he was the only man here who wasn't going home to a wife or a girlfriend.

He would have happily cleaned out a garage if he could have shared the chore with Molly.

Or with Bryn?

The thought seemed to come out of nowhere. For some reason, he'd mourned Molly more deeply since the whole thing with Bryn had happened. He hadn't talked about it, even with his teacher friends. But he'd come to realize that Bryn had short-circuited the grieving process for him. Not her fault. His alone. Nevertheless, starting up a relationship with her had kept him from dwelling on his profound loss. And he needed to dwell on it.

A couple of weekends ago he'd pulled out the photo albums Molly had scrapbooked along with their wedding pictures. He'd even sorted through the digital photos on his computer that they'd never gotten into albums.

From Friday to Sunday night, he'd relived the special life—the blessed life—he'd shared with Molly Lynn Granger Edmonds. It had hurt like crazy. But it had helped, too.

The following Monday morning, he'd made a call he'd put off for too long. He'd called Molly's parents and told them what he wanted to put on her gravestone, then had called and ordered the stone. Somehow, with that act, he'd let go of some things that needed letting go. And since then, he felt the way he had at the end of that winter of his sophomore year of college. He'd come down with mono right after Christmas break. The campus health center had sent him home to heal. He'd spent the next two and a half weeks lying on the sofa, head throbbing, barely able to swallow, let alone eat anything solid.

Fearing he'd never be healthy again, one morning he woke up and swallowed without pain. The following morning he went through an entire day without napping. His appetite came back, and he gained back a few of the fifteen pounds he'd lost. Little by little he grew stronger. And, one day, he knew he was truly well.

That's how he felt now. He knew he was gaining strength every day. He hadn't fully recovered yet, but he knew now that he would. Eventually, he would.

Still, he dreaded trying to fill another long weekend. He almost envied Bryn for the community service she had to fulfill. *Nothing says you can't do a little community service of your own volition, Edmonds.*

School would be out in another five weeks, and except for teaching two weeks of summer school, he hadn't lined up work for his off time yet. He'd never worried about it before. His checks were spread out over the year, and any extra money he made was icing. And Molly had liked having him home. "That way I get a vacation, too," she'd always said. And he hadn't minded taking over the cleaning and laundry, and even the cooking, in the summer. They'd grill out on the deck every night Molly was home, and when she wasn't, he'd grab fast food and go hit a couple buckets of balls on the driving range.

But everything had changed, and he knew himself well enough to know he could not sit home even one day this summer. *You'd go stark raving mad, Edmonds.*

Man, shut up already.

He'd been talking to himself way too much

lately. A bad habit. At least he wasn't talking to himself out loud yet.

Give it time . . . that'll come.

"Great." The sound of his voice startled him, and he couldn't help but laugh and roll his eyes.

"What's funny?" Jim asked, toweling the sweat from his hair.

"Nothing . . . have a good weekend." Garrett waved, grabbed his gym bag, and headed for the car. At least Boss would be waiting for him when he got home. The pup didn't mind if Garrett talked to himself.

Maybe he'd treat Boss to a run on the riverwalk tonight. He'd avoided the place lately. Too many memories there—of both Molly and Bryn.

Boss had been content with a daily walk around the maze of parking lots outside Garrett's apartment complex, but he'd be ecstatic at a chance to play by the water.

*T*he idyllic weather had brought people out in droves, and Garrett let Boss set the pace as they walked along the sidewalk on the east bank of the river. He was grateful Boss had chosen a leisurely walk. Garrett had gotten more than his aerobic workout on the court this afternoon.

He said hello to a couple of people from church as they passed and determined that he wouldn't miss services this Sunday like he had the last two weeks—for no good reason, really.

As they came to a place where the river narrowed, Boss stopped abruptly and sniffed the air. He turned to face the opposite bank, planted his stubby legs, and gave a sharp bark.

Garrett knelt on one knee and stroked Boss's neck. "What's the matter, boy? Are the rabbits out? Huh? Did you see a jackrabbit over there?"

He shaded his eyes and looked across the water. A black Labrador trotted alongside a couple heading his way on the walk. The dog reminded him of Sparky, and the many times he and Bryn had walked the dogs together. Maybe Boss thought it was Sparky, too. Did dogs recognize and remember each other the way humans did?

He couldn't hear the voices of the couple, but when they started around the curve, his pulse stuttered. It was Bryn holding the leash. It *was* Sparky. The man she was with looked to be around seventy. Probably her father. They were eating ice cream cones, engrossed in conversation.

Bryn looked beautiful and carefree, smiling as she nibbled on the cone. The transformation from the last time he'd seen her, when he'd run into her at the grocery store, was stark. She'd been pale and gaunt then, barely able to look him in the eye.

The same surge of relief he'd felt when he heard about her lenient sentence came now. And like before, two halves of him battled. If he cared anything about Molly, would he be so glad Bryn had gotten off easy?

And yet, he cared about Bryn. Whatever she'd done, however she'd deceived him, he couldn't seem to help the fact that he still cared.

He watched as Bryn stopped and knelt to untangle Sparky's leash. Her father said something, and she laughed up at him. Her musical laughter floated across the water. That laugh had once been like a tonic for him. The memories flooded back, and he jumped to his feet as if breaking the surface of murky river water.

He quickly calculated the distance between them. If he kept walking, he'd meet Bryn and her father somewhere on the footbridge that connected the two banks of the riverwalk.

Panic shot adrenaline through his veins. What would he say to her? How could he face her father? He didn't want a repeat of that night at Hanson's.

"Come on, Boss." He clicked his tongue and veered off the path onto the grassy knoll that rose up to meet the lot where he'd parked his pickup. "Come on, boy. Let's call it a day."

He jogged up the hill, tugging an unwilling bulldog after him, not daring to look back.

He'd accused Bryn of taking the coward's way out that night at Hanson's. Apparently he was no better.

37

Wednesday, April 23

ℬryn picked flecks of paint out of her hair and pushed the bandanna off her forehead. "Do you want this wall the same color as the rest, or are we using the paler green?"

Susan nudged clear safety glasses down on her nose and studied the room. "Hmm . . . I'm not sure. What do you think?"

"Hey, you're the one with the decorator savvy. I'm just the grunt. But I do like the way the day-room turned out using the two different shades. I think it makes the room look bigger—at least with that yellow shade."

"Okay. Then the paler shade it is. But first, you go take a break. And that's an order." She crossed the room and took the paintbrush out of Bryn's hand. "You've been working since seven this morning."

She'd actually arrived here at the site shortly after six, but she wasn't about to tell Susan that. Susan had given her a key to this office complex that was the future Grove Street Homeless Shelter, and the last few days, she'd awakened before sunrise, driven in to the Falls, and put in an hour of work before anyone else came in.

The city had finally approved their request, and donations for the firefighters' memorial had allowed them to hire some of the work out, but they were trying to do as much as possible themselves. She stretched and rubbed the small of her back. Her muscles ached from the hours of work she'd put in over the last month. One hundred and three hours, to be exact. She'd turned last week's tally in to her probation officer, and he'd teased her about trying to squeeze two years of work into two months.

Sometimes she felt a twinge of guilt that she was enjoying her "punishment" so much. And yet, in so many ways, what she was doing seemed the most fitting restitution she could possibly make.

She picked the ladder up and carried it to the unpainted wall.

"Is this what you do on breaks, Bryn? Haul ladders?" Susan stood with arms akimbo.

"Let me finish this wall, and then I promise I'll go home and eat something. Maybe even take a nap."

Susan rolled her eyes. "And come back and work till dark, if I know you. By home, do you mean your dad's?"

"No, my house here."

"Have you moved back in to town?"

She shook her head. "I'm still out at Dad's. But I'm thinking about moving back into the townhouse. Let my dad have his life back."

"Getting a little tense out there, is it?"

"I'm more worried that the longer I stay, the harder it will be for Dad when I leave."

"You might be surprised how willing he is to let you go."

Bryn stared at Susan, not sure what she was getting at. She was pretty sure Dad would try to talk her out of moving back into town, but now that she was so involved in the work at the shelter, she was eating up a lot of gas getting back and forth every day—sometimes twice a day.

Living at Dad's had helped her stretch Adam's insurance and pension payments, and if she could find a decent job at all, she'd decided to try to hang on to the townhome. She was ready to have her own life again. Maybe Dad was, too.

Susan touched her arm. "I didn't mean to imply you'd overstayed your welcome. That's none of my business. I just know with Davy—as much as I enjoy having him around, I don't want him there forever. For his own sake as much as mine."

Susan's son had ended up quitting college in the middle of the semester and was living at home. He'd helped with the shelter on occasion. It had been hard for Bryn to face him. Like most of the people she'd written letters of apology to, she'd never heard back from Susan's sons. Susan claimed they'd forgiven her, but Davy was pretty messed up, and she didn't think he had been before he'd lost his dad.

Susan brightened. "Hey, you knock yourself out and get that wall done. But I'm going home for lunch, and you'd better not be here when I get back."

Bryn laughed, but a lump formed in her throat—one of gratitude for Susan's undeserved friendship. Every day there were reminders of the tragedy her carelessness had caused. Sometimes she thought it would be easier to move far away where no one knew her story. But the thought of having to confess what she'd done all over again, having to reveal her secret every time she applied for a job, every time she made a new friend—if she ever fell in love again—quickly made her realize that it was a blessing to live right here where everyone knew what she'd done and—for the most part—accepted her and had forgiven her.

She frowned, though, remembering her conversation with Myrna Eckland last week. She'd gone to talk to Myrna about getting back her job at the library. It was obvious from the minute she walked into the library director's office that Myrna was not happy to see her. She told Bryn they weren't looking for anyone and that she didn't "foresee needing additional help anytime in the future." She'd coolly dismissed Bryn and closed her office door behind her.

That hurt, but Bryn could take a hint. She'd shed a few tears when she got back to her car. The incident had hammered home the fact that there might always be struggles because of the black mark on her life. But even as she wept, she'd felt God's loving arms around her. This was her life now, but God would be with her. It was a promise she embraced anew every single morning when she opened her eyes and remembered the terrible thing that had happened.

She hadn't told Dad yet, but she had a job interview at Hanson's Market tomorrow. She'd heard checkers made pretty decent money, and though the thought of meeting the public like that every day scared her witless, she felt like it was the direction God was leading her.

She couldn't keep sponging off of Dad. Maybe Susan was right, and even if Dad balked at Bryn's plan to move back into town, if he was ever going to be able to retire, he needed to be putting away the money he was spending to feed her. She couldn't live with her daddy forever. Not if she wanted to move on.

Sparky would stay with Dad. She smiled, realizing that was probably one point of her leaving that Dad would declare nonnegotiable. She'd miss him, but the change in Dad since he and Sparky had bonded did her heart good. For that matter, the changes in Sparky were nothing short of a miracle. Maybe he'd just grown out of puppyhood, but Dad had the dog trained to sit, stay, roll over, play dead . . . she'd lost track of their repertoire, but it was impressive. It would be a small sacrifice to leave the dog with the man who'd become his true master.

She pictured herself moving back into the apartment and felt an equal mix of excitement and apprehension. It would be hard to come out of hiding, as she'd essentially been at Dad's. But it was time. With God's forgiveness, with Judge Clyne's sentence, and now the opportunity to help get the shelter rebuilt, she'd been given a new chance at life.

This time, she would take it.

38

Friday, June 20

"Okay, guys, come on now . . . quiet down. Does everybody have their goggles?"

Garrett looked around the table at the eager, suntanned faces eyeing him through the oversized safety goggles he'd borrowed from the high school science lab. They were finishing up the first full week of summer school, and already he'd grown to enjoy the little ragtag group of third, fourth, and fifth graders who'd been assigned to his class. He was determined to make summer school a positive experience for them, and this week's science experiments had proved just the ticket.

He smiled to himself, thinking about the reactions he was bound to get with today's little display of pyrotechnics. "Okay. I think we've got everything we need . . ." He loosened the lid from a jar of elemental sodium, the magic ingredient in today's demonstration.

"We've been talking about chemical reactions. Remember how the baking soda—sodium bicarbonate—reacted to the vinegar? What happened?"

Matthew, a wide-eyed third-grader with an ear-to-ear smile raised his hand. "It fizzed up all over the place. Like a volcano!"

"Yeah, it was awesome!" Brittney Lane, another of the third graders, propped her elbows on the table and leaned in for a better look at the materials Garrett had assembled.

He winked at her. "If you think that was awesome, wait till you see what happens today. We've saved the best for last." He cleared his throat and tried to look menacing. "Brittney, you might want to move back a little."

The students laughed, and choruses of "Cool!" went up from the fifth-grade boys.

"Who remembers the chemical name for plain old water?"

Hands shot up. "H_2O."

"That's right. Today we're going to find out what happens when you mix plain old H_2O with elemental sodium." He took the lid from a gallon jug of water. "Mark, would you pour some water into the beaker? About half full."

For once, Garrett's biggest troublemaker did as he was told. The other kids looked on.

Garrett lifted a chunk of the soft metal out of the jar with tweezers and used a scalpel to cut off a small piece. "Did you notice that the sodium is stored in oil in the jar? Can anyone guess why that might be?"

Blank stares all around.

"Well, you're about to find out why it can't be stored in water. Think about what we're studying. Chemical reactions."

A dozen heads leaned in close.

Garrett looked around the table, checking that everyone still had their goggles on. "Okay, stand back a little."

He placed the beaker inside an aquarium and carefully plunked the lump of elemental sodium into the water. The beaker sparked and burst into flame. For several seconds, the little ball of fire hopped across the water, producing *oohs* and *aahs* from the budding scientists. Garrett had observed the chemical reaction often enough to know that the kids' faces were more fun to watch even than the miniature fireworks display.

When the hunk of sodium had been consumed and the flame extinguished, Matthew looked up at him with that trademark smile. "Can we do it again, Mr. Edmonds? Please?"

The other kids took up the chorus. Garrett smiled and reached for the tweezers.

"Get a bigger piece this time!" Mark shouted. "We can blow up the whole school, man!"

Garrett laughed. "Not gonna happen. This isn't something to mess with. But I'll tell you what, you go home tonight and ask your parents to help you Google 'elemental sodium and water,' and you'll see what a big hunk of this stuff can do."

He repeated the demonstration and had their undivided attention as he explained how the chemicals reacted with each other. Looking up at the clock a few minutes later, he was surprised to find it was almost ten o'clock. "Hey, guys, we need to wrap this up. Put your glasses away and take your seats, please."

When they were all settled in working on individual projects, Garrett's growling stomach reminded him that he hadn't taken time for breakfast this morning. Kathy had brought some of her famous Snickerdoodle cookies to the teacher's lounge, and he decided to make a quick run for a cup of coffee and a cookie.

He backed toward the door. "You guys keep working. I'll be back in a few minutes." He slipped out the door and waited outside for a second, listening to be sure they stayed quiet.

He went to the door of Lucy Brighton's classroom next to his to ask her to keep an eye on his class for a minute, but it sounded like she was in the middle of a lesson. No problem. He'd pour a quick cup of coffee and wolf down the cookies on his way back to the classroom. If he hadn't mentioned he was stepping out for a minute, the kids wouldn't even have missed him.

The cookies were as good as he'd imagined, and he licked the last crumbs off his lips and headed back to the room, trying not to spill his coffee. Kathy Beckwith stopped him in the hall, and they talked for a minute about a field trip they were planning for the last day of summer school.

He glanced at his watch and was startled to realize he'd been gone almost five minutes. "I've got to run," he told Kathy.

He took another sip of coffee, then took off as fast as his full coffee cup would allow.

He was twenty yards from his door when a blast like a gunshot echoed through the halls. It sounded like it had come from his classroom.

His heart pounded in his ears, and hot coffee sloshed out on his hand. When he heard the screams, he was certain they came from his classroom.

In a single motion, he deposited his coffee cup on the floor by the janitor's closet and took off at a sprint down the hall.

Throwing open the door, he was met by a haze of smoke. The girls and the third- and fourth-grade boys were huddled behind Garrett's desk whimpering or crying. The two fifth-grade boys stood with their hands over their mouths, looking down at Mark Lohan, who lay in a heap on the floor.

In a split second, Garrett knew exactly what had happened. The open jar of elemental sodium and a beaker roiling with smoke told the story.

"Jillian, go get Mrs. Brighton. Now!" Garrett rushed to Mark's side, knelt beside him, and put a hand on his neck. *Oh, please, God. Please, let him be breathing.*

Mark moaned and stirred, and to Garrett's immense relief, he rolled over onto his back. Before Garrett could stop him, he struggled to his feet.

"Are you okay?" Garrett put his hands on the boy's shoulder and looked him in the eye. "Did you get burned?"

Mark shook his head, shamefaced.

"He put a whole big hunk of that stuff in the beaker!" Matthew tattled.

"Shhh." Garrett hushed them all and turned back to Mark. "You're sure you're not hurt?"

"I'm okay. I didn't know it would do that. I swear. I didn't know."

Thank God he's all right! Garrett's knees went weak with relief.

By now the hallway outside his room was filled with curious students and teachers.

"What happened?" Lucy Brighton hustled in, her face white as chalk, voice quavering.

Garrett held up a hand and motioned his students to take their seats. Turning to Lucy, he forced his voice steady. "A little extracurricular experiment, apparently. It looks like everybody is okay."

Lucy shooed her students back to her room next door, and within a few minutes the hallway outside Garrett's room was quiet again, his students' heads bent over their work.

But Garrett was deeply shaken. It was bad enough that he'd left his classroom unsupervised for almost five minutes, but he'd been utterly careless to leave that jar of sodium where the students could get to it. Every year some kid wanted to try a bigger chunk. He knew the temptation that stuff was, once the kids saw its magic. To make matters worse, he'd left the beaker of water sitting where he'd left it, intending to clean up while the kids were at recess.

He watched Mark carefully until lunch. He seemed to be fine, though it was a subdued version of Mark Lohan—no doubt thinking he was headed for the principal's office the minute the recess bell rang.

Garrett debated sending him to the school nurse's office. But if he did that, he'd have to file an accident report. He was lucky—

No. Trembling, he realized the truth: he was

blessed beyond expression. When he thought about how much worse it could have been . . . if one of the kids had been badly injured—or God forbid, killed . . . He shuddered at the thought.

And suddenly, his thoughts took him where he hadn't been willing to go before. If Mark had died, if five of his students had been killed or maimed by the explosion, how could he ever have lived with that guilt?

Might he have been tempted to somehow exonerate himself by slipping into denial?

Of course he might have. What normal person *wouldn't* want so badly for what happened not to be true, that he would somehow make himself believe he wasn't guilty?

Knowing himself the way he did, he might have tried to shift the blame onto someone else. Blame Kathy for distracting him in the hall, or blame Mark for doing what any curious fifth grader might have done.

What he'd done today was no less negligent or careless than what Bryn had done. If anything, his negligence was worse because the safety and lives of *children* had been entrusted to him.

The *only* reason Bryn Hennesey had sat before a judge, and Garrett Edmonds would not, was the outcome of their mistakes.

He'd been "fortunate" no one was hurt. Blessed with an outcome he could live with, blessed beyond what he deserved. For some unfathomable reason, God had spared him a tragedy that made him physically ill to even consider.

Why hadn't God extended the same grace to Bryn? Garrett would never understand that as long as he lived. It certainly proved that in this fallen world, life wasn't fair.

He let himself dwell on what had happened, and carried the comparison further. What if one of those kids had been Bryn's child? Could she have ever forgiven him?

He thought of her sweet spirit, the compassion she'd shown to Charlie and to her father, to the homeless people at the shelter—even to the dogs, taking Sparky in on such short notice for Charlie's sake.

He let himself remember the days he and Bryn had spent together, and he was pretty sure he had his answer. She *would* have forgiven him. Difficult as it would be, he didn't think she would have allowed anger and bitterness and unforgiveness to fester the way he had.

He sank into a chair, suddenly drained of energy. He owed her an apology. He'd treated her as if she'd acted purposely and maliciously. She'd been neither. She'd made a mistake. A terrible, consequence-filled mistake. But a mistake nonetheless.

Part of him wanted to get in his truck and go talk to her this very minute. But he felt a gentle prompting in his soul. There was Someone else he needed to make things right with first.

39

Garrett wiped his palms on his khakis and picked up the phone, every bit as nervous as he'd been as a gangly teenager the night he'd called to ask Melissa McGuire to the prom.

Where had that thought come from? The comparison bothered him. He wasn't asking Bryn on a date. But for a week now, he'd known that he needed to call her and apologize.

As of this afternoon, summer school was over, and he didn't want to face next week—and the rest of the summer—without at least attempting to make things right with Bryn. He didn't deserve an easy pardon, but he hoped she'd at least hear him out. He had to at least try.

He tried her cell phone and got a message that it was no longer in service. He was tempted to give up, but he'd heard that Bryn had moved in with her father shortly after she'd turned herself in. He called Information for Hugh Terrigan's number and had the operator dial it for him.

The phone rang three times before the answering machine picked up. A male voice instructed him to leave a message, but midway through the recording, the answering machine clicked off and the same male voice came on the line. "Hello? This is Hugh . . ."

"Mr. Terrigan, this is Garrett Edmonds. Does Bryn happen to be there?"

An overlong pause. Bryn's father must know who he was. "Bryn isn't here."

"Do you know where I could reach her?"

"May I ask why you're calling?"

He closed his eyes. He wouldn't blame Bryn's father if he refused to tell him anything. "I owe her an apology. It's . . . kind of a long story, but I'd like to talk to her, if she's willing."

"Bryn moved back to the Falls a few weeks ago. She's careful about her phone . . . the media kind of stalked her for a while. I don't feel comfortable giving out her number, but I can tell her you called."

"I'd appreciate that."

Another pause. "I think Bryn would like to talk to you. She's doing her community serv—" He stopped, as if he'd said too much, but then seemed to change his mind. "She's helping Susan Marlowe get the homeless shelter ready to open again. She spends most of her time down there lately. I don't think she'd mind me telling you that. You know where it is?"

"Right across from the old one, right?"

"That's right. She's probably there now."

"Thank you, Mr. Terrigan. I appreciate it. If

you're sure she wouldn't mind, I might try to catch her there yet this afternoon."

"You go with a paintbrush and some elbow grease, I guarantee she won't mind."

Garrett chuckled and thanked him again. He replaced the phone in its cradle, an idea beginning to form. But entertaining it, he laughed out loud when he realized it wasn't his idea at all, but one Hugh Terrigan had planted as deliberately as if he'd had a shovel and a load of dirt.

The realization gave him courage, and he headed to the bedroom to change clothes.

*P*aintbrush in hand, Bryn stood back to admire her handiwork. The new woodwork in the room that would serve as one of the shelter's family quarters gleamed under the fluorescent lights. Everything looked pristine. Bryn inhaled. The sharp scent of paint added to the effect of "fresh and clean." A few touchups to the paint job, and a couple of days to let everything dry, and the room would be ready to furnish.

They'd had quite a few donations of furniture— beds and mattresses, some old sofas for the day-room. But Susan had invited her to go scavenging at garage sales on Friday. They needed end tables and lamps and other items that would make the place feel homey.

Susan had poured herself into getting the shelter reopened, and though she often expressed frustration at how long it was taking to get things ready for the opening, Bryn was amazed at the progress they'd made even since she'd come on board.

She fell into bed exhausted every night, but she truly looked forward to returning to the site each day, eager to see what miracles they could accomplish in the next eight or ten hours.

A quiet knock behind her made her do an about-face.

Her breath caught. "Garrett?"

He stood in the doorway wearing ragged jeans and a T-shirt, wielding a paintbrush in one hand and a broom in the other. "I wondered if . . . you needed any help in here?"

She tried to speak and only sputtered. "How did you . . . ? Did you know I . . . ?"

"Your dad told me I'd find you here," he explained. "I hope you don't mind."

She shook her head, a little in shock, and a lot curious about why he'd come. She nodded toward the broom and paintbrush he held. "Did you talk to Susan"—she pointed down the hall—"about where she wants you . . . working?"

He leaned the broom against the wall in the hallway and stepped into the room. "I told Susan I wanted to talk to you." He looked as if he thought she might ask him to leave.

Bryn waited, not knowing what to say, but not inclined in the least to ask him to leave.

"She said I should try to talk you into taking a break. She suggested coffee and maybe some dinner—" He hesitated, looking at the dust-streaked floor. "It was her idea, but . . . I like it. Would you want to go get something to eat? With me? Just for a little while? I—I'd like to talk to you, Bryn."

Something about his demeanor made her want to cry. He was different. Something had changed. "I had a sandwich earlier," she said, "but coffee sounds good." She looked pointedly at his clothes. "You look like you came prepared to work. Don't feel like . . . just because Susan said—"

"I did come to work, but I mostly came to talk to you. Coffee would be great. You look like you could use a break."

Suddenly aware of how she must look, she tucked a wayward strand into her ponytail and brushed off the seat of her jeans. "Um . . . maybe we could do a drive-through?"

He smiled. "You look great, but . . . yeah, drive-through's a good idea. I didn't exactly dress for the occasion." He flushed and held up the paint-brush in his right hand. "Well, I did, but—" He shrugged. "Different occasion."

Her mind went a million different directions. Why had he come? What did he want? She followed him down the corridor to the entrance area. "Wait here. I need to let Susan know where I'm going."

"Sure." He tucked his fingers in the pockets of his jeans and hooked his thumbs on the belt loops. He looked like a shy little boy. It was a nice look for him.

She found Susan in the kitchenette arguing politely with the guys who were putting in the new cabinets.

"Oh, hey, Bryn, Garrett Edmonds was here looking for you . . ."

"Yeah, he found me. You okay if I take a short break?"

Susan looked at her as if she must have heard the question wrong. "Would you *please* take a break? Good grief, if that man can get you to rest for two seconds, I have half a notion to hire him on for that purpose alone."

Bryn gave her a sheepish smile. "We—I won't be long."

"Take your time. Take the rest of the night off if you want. It's Friday night. You've put in your time this week. More than." She motioned toward the cabinet installers. "I think I'm heading home myself as soon as these guys are done."

"Okay . . . see you next week, if not tonight. Have a nice weekend."

But Bryn knew Susan would be there until ten or later, like she was every night. Funny that Susan worried *she* was the one who needed to take a break. Bryn suspected Susan was using work as an escape. Or, more likely, that she was counting on her work at the shelter to fill the empty place that only David Marlowe could fill.

But she was the pot calling the kettle black on that count. Mandatory or not, her work here wasn't motivated by entirely the right reasons.

She waved and went to find Garrett, her heart lighter than it had been in a very long time.

40

"So, do the hours you're putting in at the shelter fulfill your community service?"

Bryn swallowed the sip of coffee she'd just taken and looked at Garrett. He sat angled behind the steering wheel, one elbow resting on the wheel, the other clutching a tall mocha.

His question took her by surprise, yet she could see in his expression that he hadn't meant to hurt her by bringing up the subject of her sentence.

She took another sip of her latte. "Do you mind if I roll the window down a little?" They'd gone through the drive-through and come around to park in front of the coffee shop.

"Not at all." Garrett turned the key in the ignition and waited for her to lower the window before he turned off the accessory.

The evening sun warmed the right side of her face, but she had a feeling the sun wasn't entirely to blame for the overheated cab. Being here with him brought back memories that were better left buried.

"Hey, how's Sparky?" It was an obvious attempt to change the subject he'd broached, and she was grateful.

"He's out at my dad's in the country. Dad's got him so well trained you wouldn't know him. He's been really good for Dad. How about Boss?" she risked. "Or . . . do you still have him?"

"I have him. He's been really good for me, too. Those two dogs must have been conspiring."

Bryn laughed at the thought.

A brief silence fell between them, but it wasn't uncomfortable.

"So tell me about the shelter," Garrett said after a minute. "The place looks good. You seem to like it there."

"I do. Sometimes I feel a little guilty that—well, it doesn't feel like punishment. It feels like a reward."

He picked an invisible piece of lint off the upholstery. "The paintbrush and broom weren't just props, Bryn. I'd like to help."

"That would be great. We could use your help, we really could." Why had he suddenly decided to be a part of the shelter project?

"I've got the rest of the summer off. If there's a place for me. If you don't mind me . . . horning in, I'll be there whenever I can."

"There's plenty of work to go around. And

Susan will be thrilled to have an extra set of hands. She's shooting to reopen by September 1. A couple of the shelters in Springfield have people they'd like to send us by then—to get them closer to their families and support systems. There's still so much to do before we open." She hesitated, then plunged in. "But . . . *why*, Garrett? I don't understand why you're—" She shrugged.

He nodded, as if he'd expected her question. "A lot of reasons. I . . . I need to explain some things, Bryn. I need to ask your forgiveness."

She didn't know how to respond. So she waited.

He closed his eyes and pressed his lips together. For a minute she thought he might be praying. When he looked at her again, there was pain in his eyes. "I'm not even sure where to start. I've been . . . so wrong about so many things."

She felt on the verge of tears. She shook her head, willing her voice to steady. "I don't understand. Garrett, I'm the one who should be asking for forgiveness. What . . . what are you doing?"

"But you did ask forgiveness. In every way possible. Your letter . . . what you said in court that day. I just wasn't . . . I wasn't willing to give it. But I am now. I'm sorry . . . I should have started by saying that. I forgive you, Bryn. You can't even imagine how much I understand, how much I empathize with you now."

"Garrett, you don't need to—"

"No. Please, Bryn." He held up a hand. "Let me say what I came to say. I *need* to apologize. And"—he gestured toward her coffee cup and gave a self-deprecating smile—"you might want to sip slow. The list is long."

She tried to muster a smile but was shaken deeply by his drastic change of heart.

His expression turned serious again. "First of all, Bryn, I'm so sorry I wasn't there that day at the courthouse."

"Garrett . . ." She waved him off.

But he shook his head. "No. I should have been there. Susan sent us all a letter and asked us to come and support you, but . . . I just couldn't face you yet. Or maybe it was myself I couldn't face. I was . . . confused. I didn't know what to think about the whole thing. But . . . I know God wanted me there, and I flat out ignored Him."

"Garrett, it's okay. I understand. I do. I would have had the same questions if the tables had been turned."

He shook his head. "No . . . I'm not sure you would have. I think you have"—he shrugged—"I don't know . . . a little more faith in people than I do. I could never have worked at the shelter like you did. I mean, sure, I can paint and clean, but when it comes to the people . . ." He shrugged. "It takes a special gift to treat those people with dignity, the way you treated Charlie. I don't have that gift."

She smiled. "And I could never teach a class of fifth graders. Ever."

He laughed at that but quickly sobered. "I need to tell you something. Something happened about a week ago that . . . changed everything for me."

Bryn sat, enrapt, as he told her about a science experiment he'd conducted during summer school. She was no scientist, and she wasn't sure where he was going with this story. Was he trying to make some sort of analogy to the chemical reaction? Her face must have told him she didn't get it.

He smiled at her confused expression. "Hang with me . . . You'll understand why I'm telling you all this in a minute."

She didn't think the waver in his voice was from humor, and as his story went on, she grew concerned.

The sun dropped quickly behind the building, and the neon lights flickered on along the little strip of shops beside the coffee shop. Garrett set his coffee cup in the holder on the console, reached across the cab, and touched her arm briefly. "I left the room—just to go get coffee." He dropped his head.

She clapped her hands over her mouth. "Oh, Garrett . . ." She could guess what was coming, and her heart broke for him.

"I should have known. Every year some kid wants to toss in a bigger chunk of sodium. It was foolish to not put things away, lock stuff up where the kids couldn't get to it. And beyond foolish to leave the kids alone with that stuff."

Darkness fell as he continued his story, telling her how he'd come back down the hall a few minutes later to hear what sounded like a gunshot.

A rush of emotion rolled over her, and her hands began to tremble. *Please, God. Oh, please, no . . . Don't let this story end the way I'm afraid it's going to end.*

But Garrett must have read her mind, for he hurried to reassure her. "No, no . . . it's okay. Everything's okay. Nobody even got hurt. It all turned out fine."

The relief she felt for him drained every ounce of energy from her. To her horror, everything she'd been through came back in a tidal wave of memory. She put her face in her hands and wept.

Garrett scooted across the seat, and, as if no time at all had passed since that day they'd skated at Ferris Park, he took her in his arms. She didn't resist and leaned her forehead against his chest, grateful for his presence.

He stroked her hair and whispered, "I'm so sorry. I'm such an idiot. I didn't think how it might affect you, to hear that."

She looked up at him. "I'm glad everything turned out okay. I . . . I don't know why I'm blubbering . . ."

He loosened his embrace on her, as if he'd just

realized he was holding her, as if giving her a chance to "escape." But she didn't want to escape, and when she didn't move away, he put his arms around her again.

"My point is, Bryn, the only difference between what happened to you and what happened to me is that no one died on account of my carelessness. But they could have! I'm not one ounce less guilty. Maybe more! Those were *children* in my care. Their parents trust me to keep them safe." His breathing quickened as if he were reliving the incident in his mind. "When I think about what could have happened . . ."

She felt him shudder, and she wanted to somehow erase the memory for him. Neither of them could ever do that. Yet she knew now that God could somehow take those awful memories and harness them for good. He'd already begun to do so in her life. And she suspected the fact that Garrett was here with her now demonstrated that God was working in his life as well.

"I just wish I'd been more understanding of what happened to you. I'm ashamed of the way I handled it. I'm sorry for so many things."

She pulled away now, leaned against the passenger door so she could look into his eyes. "We're all different, Garrett. None of us knows how we'll handle something until we're in the thick of it."

"That might be true, but I think our faith—or

lack of it—comes out when we're . . . tested. I'm not very proud of what came out of me. The way I treated you—" He hung his head for a minute before he met her eyes again. "I'm ashamed," he said again. "And I'm sorry. Do you think you could forgive me?"

"Of course I forgive you, Garrett. I don't think there's anyone in the world who wouldn't understand why you felt the way you did about what happened . . . about what I did."

"I'd like another chance . . . to make things right. I don't think it was my imagination that we had something special between us. At least something . . . promising." He drew back and looked at her, as if he might see the answer in her eyes. "Do you think we could be friends again?"

She thought about the way it had felt to be in his arms, and she wanted to say *yes, a thousand times yes.* But something niggled at her. She closed her eyes and tried to think how to voice her fears. "I keep thinking . . . if we're friends—if we someday become . . . more than that—how many times in our lives will we be asked to tell the story of how we met?"

"Oh." He shook his head slowly and gave a humorless smile. "I guess I hadn't thought about that."

"I don't mean to borrow trouble. But will we—will *you* feel bitter every time we're reminded? To have to relive it all over again? It makes me shudder to think of having to tell the whole story to casual strangers. Or to always have to tiptoe around the truth—because it will make people uncomfortable."

His smile turned genuine, and he pulled her into his arms again. "I guess we'll have to make the ending to our story so great that it makes them forget all about the beginning. Are you willing, Bryn? To let God write a new ending to our story?"

She smiled up at him. "I think maybe He already has."

You will know the truth,
and the truth will set you free.
JOHN 8:32

*D*ear Reader,
The research for this book took me far out of my comfort zone, especially when it led me to volunteer in our local homeless shelter. I began my stint as a volunteer for completely self-centered reasons: seeking accurate information and details for my novel. But God—as I suspected He would—is using my ongoing experience to build character in me, sometimes painfully. Not only have I been forced to recognize a judgmental spirit, and a tendency to store up my treasures here on earth rather than in heaven, but through this experience, I hope I have grown in faith and compassion for others.

This novel explores a tragedy that devastates a small town, and the life of one woman in particular. When tragedy strikes, it's hard to imagine where God could possibly be. How could a loving God allow the kinds of tragedy and pain that we all eventually experience if we live long enough? And yet, the Bible tells us, "In this world you will have trouble." Even more difficult to understand is that this trouble serves to make us stronger in our faith and more compassionate toward others.

We shouldn't be surprised when trouble strikes.

Since that fateful day in the Garden of Eden, we have lived in a world of tragedy, sorrow, and pain. Some of it is present simply because we live in a fallen world, and some of it is the result of our own sin, or sin in the lives of those we love.

None of us are immune, but the difference Christ makes in our lives means we don't have to walk through trials and tragedy alone. God has promised to be with us every step of the way, comforting, healing, listening to our cries. And redeeming not only those tragedies that strike us when we've done nothing to deserve them, but redeeming even the sins and mistakes we've committed that have brought well-deserved pain.

1 Peter 1 tells us:

In his great mercy he has given us new birth into a living hope through the resurrection of Jesus Christ from the dead, and into an inheritance that can never perish . . . In this you greatly rejoice, though now for a little while you may have had to suffer grief in all kinds of trials. These have come so that your faith— of greater worth than gold, which perishes even though refined by fire—may be proved genuine and may result in praise, glory and honor when Jesus Christ is revealed. Though you have not seen him, you love him; and even though you do not see him now, you believe in him and are filled with an inex-

pressible and glorious joy, for you are receiving the goal of your faith, the salvation of your souls.

As my husband and I have gone through a time of difficulty recently, these words from the Bible give us great comfort and help us realize that the most agonizing things we might suffer here on earth are nothing compared to the joy we will experience when we see Jesus face to face. This is a truth that can set us free. Until that day, as I face the trials of this world, I hope my faith may be proved genuine. That when people look at my face, instead of the stress lines, pinched forehead, and eyes red from crying that I see in the mirror, others will simply see the joy of Christ shining through me.

Deborah Raney
July 28, 2009

Discussion Questions

1. In *Almost Forever*, Bryn Hennesey foregoes sleep to stay up and play cards with Charlie, a homeless man, because "she knew the real truth—he was lonely. Just needed someone to sit with him." When have you felt lonely and needed someone to simply sit with you? Was that wish fulfilled in a surprising way? If so, how? How can you see past surly behavior to what someone is really thinking and feeling? How can such knowledge put others' behavior toward you in perspective?

2. When Adam's firefighting team shows up at the shelter, Bryn is caught. She knows he doesn't like her working there, and she's worried about her husband finding out. Have you and a loved one ever disagreed strongly about something one of you wished to do—even if that something was a good thing (such as Bryn's volunteering at the shelter)? How did you work it out? What lesson(s) did you learn?

3. Bryn "felt numb, unwilling to let her mind function, for fear it would reveal a truth she could not bear." If you were Bryn, standing there watching the homeless shelter burn into a charred skeleton, knowing there were people inside, and

wondering if you were responsible, what would you be thinking? Feeling? How would you respond outwardly?

4. In the beginning of *Almost Forever*, Bryn is annoyed and frustrated by her husband's control of her. "Since the day they'd started thinking seriously about having a baby, Adam had gone overboard worrying about her. If the sidewalks were slick, he walked her to the car. If she got out a ladder to change a lightbulb, he jumped in and did it for her. He'd about come unhinged when she got a speeding ticket a couple of months ago . . ." How does Bryn's thinking about Adam's treatment of her change throughout the story?

5. When Garrett is at the funeral, he realizes "he would just have to find some way to go on without the woman he'd loved for as long as he could remember." Have you loved—and lost (whether physically or emotionally)—someone dear to you? If so, how have you handled that loss? What, if anything, has changed from the initial time of your loss to now? How can thinking long-term help in times of loss? Share a story, if you have one.

6. Have you ever left a candle burning without meaning to? Disabled a smoke alarm? Left a child unsupervised for a minute too long, like

Garrett, or perhaps, like Jenna, maxed out your credit cards? How does the story of *Almost Forever* put even such small acts of irresponsibility into a different light? How can small decisions influence all of life?

7. "We just have to trust God even when we can't understand why things happen the way they do. God loves us and is with us, even—maybe especially—in the hardest times," Bryn tells her friend Jenna.

Jenna's response? "I don't know how you can say that, Bryn. After everything that happened. You say God's with us, but where was He when Zach and Adam were trapped in that building? If He's so all-powerful, why didn't He stop that fire from starting in the first place? Why did He let that homeless guy get away? You can't have it both ways. Can you?"

Do you tend to agree more with Bryn or Jenna? Why? How does your view of God influence your thoughts and actions—and entire lifestyle?

8. Bryn continues to rack her brain for that "elusive memory. Blowing out a candle was like turning out a light or unplugging the curling iron before you left for work. You did those things without even thinking . . . That had to be why she couldn't seem to come up with a lucid memory." Have you ever lost a moment? Not been able to

remember doing something—like locking your door before you left for work or whether or not you mailed a bill? What were the consequences, if any?

9. When at last Bryn knows that she is the one responsible for the fire, she says she is ready to pay for her crime. But her father insists that she hire an attorney. If you knew you were guilty of a crime, would you hire an attorney? Why or why not? Do you think it would have been acceptable for Bryn to try to avoid the penalty for what she'd done, knowing it was an accident?

10. "There wasn't a prison dark enough or a sentence long enough for Zeke Downing as far as he [Garrett] was concerned." Yet, when he finds out that the person has been caught, he feels no joy—only a numbness. How is revenge "sweet"? How is it not like you thought it would be? (Explain, using a story from your own experience.)

11. Bryn writes each of the victims' family members an apology note. If you were her, would you have done that? Turned yourself in and written apology notes to the families? Why or why not?
Have you ever been asked to forgive something of the magnitude of Bryn's mistake? If you were one of the victims' family members, how would

you respond to receiving such a letter? Would you be able to forgive? Why or why not? And if so, what would that forgiveness look like?

12. Bryn's biggest worry is disappointing her father (and also causing him to have a heart attack with the stress). Whom might you have disappointed by the way you've lived your life? By the decisions you've made? Are there ways in which you could still make restitution?

13. Did you expect Bryn and Garrett's relationship to move forward so quickly? Why or why not? Do you think this was good for their grieving of their spouses in the long run, or not? Do you think their youth played a factor in the length of their grieving? What about the fact that their spouses died under identical circumstances? Can one person "replace" another, in your experience? Explain.

14. Have you ever felt betrayed by someone you loved and/or trusted? What happened? Was that the whole story or only part of the story? How can you lay the matter to rest—either in your own mind, or between you and that person?

15. Do you think it's possible to write a new ending to *your* story, as Bryn and Garrett are in the process of doing by the end of the book? Why or why not?

16. "It's sad that in a town this small we would need a shelter," Bryn says.

"And that's just it. I think the people who are opposed to reopening the shelter have the idea that if we don't open a shelter, the homeless will just go away. But it doesn't work that way. 'The poor you will always have with you . . . ,'" Garrett replies, quoting John, chapter 2, in the Bible.

Susan Marlowe gathers together the grieving families and puts a new challenge in front of them—to *do* something with their pain. To help the city see that their town needs a homeless shelter for people like Charlie . . . and, yes, even for people like Zeke Downing.

How do you view the homeless? If you saw a homeless person on a street, what would you do? say? think? Has meeting Charlie Branson through this story made a difference? If so, how will you, like Susan and Bryn and Garrett, act on that difference?

About the Author

DEBORAH RANEY dreamed of writing a book since the summer she read all of Laura Ingalls Wilder's *Little House* books and discovered that a little Kansas farm girl could, indeed, grow up to be a writer. After a happy twenty-year detour as a stay-at-home wife and mom, Deb began her writing career. Her first novel, *A Vow to Cherish*, was awarded a Silver Angel from Excellence in Media and inspired the acclaimed World Wide Pictures film of the same title. Since then her books have won the RITA Award, the HOLT Medallion, and the National Readers' Choice Award, and she is a two-time Christy Award finalist. Deb enjoys speaking and teaching at writers' conferences across the country. She and her husband, artist Ken Raney, make their home in their native Kansas and love the small-town life that is the setting for many of Deb's novels. The Raneys enjoy gardening, antiquing, art museums, movies, and traveling to visit four grown children and small grandchildren who live much too far away.

Deborah loves hearing from her readers. To email her or to learn more about her books, please visit www.deborahraney.com or write to Deborah in care of Howard Books, 216 Centerview Dr., Suite 303, Brentwood, TN, 37027.

Center Point Publishing
600 Brooks Road ● PO Box 1
Thorndike ME 04986-0001 USA

(207) 568-3717

US & Canada:
1 800 929-9108
www.centerpointlargeprint.com